Liam

The Cosantóir (Protectors) MC | Book 3

Michael Geraghty

Hold Fast Publishing

Chapter 1

T he din from the mole boring its way through the earth echoed across the chamber. Liam O'Farrell stood by, watching the motion with his Sensear headset firmly in place. The noise was blocked out, and all he could hear was the chatter in his ears coming from other Sandhogs working in the tunnel with him. Once he recognized the rapid spin of the mole slowing down, he slipped his headgear off, hearing the last rotations and whirs. Not long after, the job site whistle blew to indicate the end of another long day beneath the surface for his crew.

Liam gathered his gear and joked his way toward the elevator shaft. He watched as the last crew went up, leaving himself alone to ride up. Before him, his father and grandfather always reminded him that if Liam were ever a project leader, it was always his job to be the last man out to ensure the team was safe. Nearly twenty years after, he always heeded those words. Liam grabbed his worn flannel shirt, gave a loud whistle to get the attention of anyone who might be nearby and shouted, "Last trip up!" before pressing the elevator button to begin the slow ascent.

Even after his time as a Sandhog, Liam hated the drastic temperature change once he reached the surface. It didn't matter what season it was up top or if you had been sweating all day down below. That initial rush of the atmosphere above felt like getting hit with a steam blast, so much so that he routinely began opening his jumpsuit before he reached the top of the elevator shaft.

Liam's judgment proved correct, and the heat enveloped his body. Early October meant faster darkness at the job site in Sloatsburg. The nighttime lighting was already in place to brighten the area for the crew coming for the night shift. He opened his jumpsuit further, letting the sleeves dangle around his waist. The taut muscles in his arms, shoulders, and torso, covered with tattoos, made him a more intimidating presence if that were even possible. The only man on-site who could rival his size was Demon, a former professional wrestler who worked the tunnels alongside him on many projects.

Sandhogs, both longtime veterans and new workers on the site, acquiesced when Liam made his presence in the worksite trailers known as a Hog House. They stepped aside so he could get to his locker and strip down before stepping over to the shower to wash off the day's work. Liam's size made showering awkward since his height nearly reached the showerhead. The tepid, trickling water barely made a dent in the dust and debris in his hair and on his body. Liam knew he would get a much better cleansing in his own bathroom at the Hog House of the Cosantóir, the motorcycle club he and many other Sandhogs were part of.

Liam wrapped a towel around his waist and made his way back to his locker. He slipped into a plain black T-shirt and made sure to pull his long black hair out the back, sending it down to his shoulders. Before he had the chance to slip into his boxer briefs and jeans, Kearney, the attendant of the Hog House, appeared from around the corner.

"Liam!" he shouted.

Liam abruptly turned, water from his hair drizzling onto one of the newbies changing across from Liam.

"Fuck, man, watch it!" The young man scowled, wiping drops from the back of his neck and face. "Asshole."

The men in the row of lockers went silent and cast a glance toward Liam to see how he would react.

"I don't think I've had the pleasure," Liam said with a forced smile, extending his hand to the younger, much smaller man. The worker looked up at Liam and his muscular form.

"Roger," the man said shakily.

"Sorry, Roger," Liam said. "I was coming off a twelve-hour shift and was covered in mud and shit from the tunnels. I didn't mean to taint you with clean water."

Liam stepped close to Roger, pinning the young man against the lockers.

"Is it okay if I put my pants on now?" Liam asked. "I'm not fond of just swinging in the wind like this, you know."

"Yeah, sure, no worries," Roger stammered. Liam squinted down at the newbie.

"Who's shift you on tonight, Roger?" Liam asked.

"I'm not sure. It's my first day."

"I'd make sure you know so you don't piss the wrong person off," Liam said. He swiftly brought his right hand up and slammed it into the metal next to Roger's head, making the young man jump and close his eyes.

"Liam, quit fuckin' with the new guy," Kearney barked from the end of the aisle. "Put your dick away and come to the front. Your da is on the phone."

"Maybe I'll see you tomorrow, Raj." Liam chuckled.

He finished dressing and pulled his gear from his locker. Liam glanced at his cell phone and saw several missed phone calls from his father. Conor's injuries as a result of his accident months ago had kept the old man away not just from the job sites but the club activities as well, leaving more responsibility to Liam. Liam enjoyed the taste of the power he received, relishing giving orders and making more decisions for the Cosantóir.

Liam reached for the cordless phone he saw on the counter next to where Kearney was traditionally stationed. He plucked the phone, cleared his throat, and brought it up to his ear.

"What are you wearing tonight?" he asked softly.

"Doesn't that ever get old for you?" his father complained. "Christ, Liam, you're thirty-five."

Liam laughed heartily.

"Relax, Da," he answered. "You're gettin' cranky sittin' around in that chair all day."

"Damn right I am," Conor grumbled. "It gives me more time to look at the small details of all we have going on, too. I need to meet with you tonight at my house."

"Cripes, Da, I just finished work." Liam sighed. "I just want to go back to Hog House, get a pint, maybe a smoke, and see what girls are around for—"

Conor cut off his son before he could finish that thought.

"I don't need to hear about it. I'm sure whoever you are planning to grace your presence with can wait. I'm telling you, not as your father but as the Ceannaire, that you will be here within the hour. Understand?"

The seriousness in Conor's tone got Liam's attention.

"I'll be there," he groused as he hung up the phone.

"Everything all right?" Kearney asked as he put the phone back in its charger.

"Yeah... the old man has a bug up his arse, is all," Liam lamented.

"Well, I miss him around the site," Kearney replied. "He's one of the few old guys still working the job back when I was."

"Yeah, nothing like hearin' the two of you tell your Stone Age stories about how much tougher the work was back in the day." Liam laughed.

"Ahh, get out, you eejit," Kearney said, waving his hand in disgust.

"K," Liam said to get the old man to look back at him. "Who's running the work tonight?"

Kearney stepped over to the computer and checked the lineup for the evening.

"Brody Callahan."

Liam nodded.

"Ask Mud to buzz me at some point, will ya? I want to see how the new guy does."

"Got it. You're not gonna hassle the rookie more, are ya? We have a hard enough time keeping workers the way you vets scare guys off."

"Nah, I'm just curious." Liam chuckled before taking a twenty out of his wallet and putting it into Kearney's tip jar.

Kearney smiled, revealing a few missing teeth in his grizzled grin.

"Thank ya kindly." Kearney nodded. "The young guys rarely give me squat. They think I'm just a broken-down errand boy."

Liam turned away from the counter and looked about. Few veterans worked the weekend night shift these days, so the room hosted mainly new faces.

"Listen up, ya scrubs!" Liam barked. "Kearney busts his ass while you guys are lounging around or working the tunnels all night long to make sure you have what you need. You get food, drinks, a TV, a place to sleep, and more, all with no questions asked. Show him some feckin' respect and put somethin' in the jar for him. I expect to hear he made good money this weekend when I come back in on Monday. I hear anything else, and there'll be hell to pay, especially if you ever end up workin' for me. Got it?"

Liam watched as the new faces looked shaken. Several nodded in agreement as they sat up while others hustled up to the counter, wallets open and bearing gifts.

"That should help." Liam smiled.

"My best to your da," Kearney answered.

Liam made his way out of the makeshift home and into the dusk toward his motorcycle. He pulled his emerald green helmet on, letting his hair drift out the back of the protective hat before he started up his bike. The engine roared, startling more than a few workers moving across the lot from their cars toward the work area.

Liam sped north on 17M, stopping at a red light in Tuxedo before reaching Tuxedo Park, a historic luxury community. He glanced at the car to his left to see three women seated in a BMW convertible. Each were dressed for clubbing on a Friday night.

"Evening, ladies," he shouted, turning up his Irish brogue. Liam knew his traditional accent helped him win over a woman, young or old, more than once. The woman in the car's passenger seat, a blonde in a short skirt and belly shirt, smiled immediately.

"Nice bike," she shouted back to him. "You're able to handle it?"

"I can handle many things." Liam grinned. "Why don't you hop over here and find out?"

"Arianna, quit messing around," the girl in the back seat interjected. Liam noticed that girl looked a bit fearful of him on his bike and in his club regalia. "The boys are waiting for us."

"Arianna, if you ever decide you're tired of playing with the boys and want a man instead, come see me at the Hog House," Liam told her as he revved his bike.

"Where's the Hog House?" Arianna inquired.

"You must be a virgin... to the area." Liam smiled as he looked at her. "Ask around, darlin'. You'll find me if you want to."

A honk from behind Liam caused him to glance up at the light, which had long switched to green. Liam turned, raised his middle finger to the driver behind him, and tore off down the road, ignoring the posted speed limit of 55.

Liam closed in on the location of the Hog House, just south of the Harriman train station. The temptation to turn up the hill and head home or turn back and find out where the young ladies and their 'boys' were going so he could lure Arianna away was great. However, Liam knew what his father had asked of him, and he drove on into Harriman and toward his father's house.

He turned left when he reached the home's driveway and went to the front of the house. Liam saw a couple of bikes from other Cosantóir present and a few cars, causing him to wonder what Conor had going on. He knew his father struggled with health issues right now, but Conor had sounded like his crotchety self on the phone just moments ago. He dismounted and went up the front steps, letting himself into the house.

Liam barely got inside before Jameson, Conor's faithful pit bull, bounded into the room to greet the visitor. As soon as he saw Liam, the dog barked happily and rolled onto his belly. Liam laughed and squatted down to pat Jameson's stomach a few times before they engaged in some playful wrestling on the floor. Jameson, as usual, got the better of Liam and was on top of him in seconds.

"Don't get him all riled up," a female voice chided. Liam glanced up to see Maeve, Conor's live-in girlfriend, with her hands on her hips.

"Ahh, he's fine," Liam said as he scrambled off the floor. "He would be disappointed if I didn't do that with him when I came in."

Liam glanced over as he saw Siobhan, his brother's girlfriend, turn the corner from the hall.

"Hey there, Ginger," Liam said to the redhead. "What are ya doing here? I figured you and my brother would be shacked at your place."

"Nice greeting, Liam," Siobhan answered playfully. "He's in with your da."

"They're in there waiting for you," Maeve told Liam. "I'll bring you a pint if you want."

Liam nodded and walked down the hall before knocking on Conor's office door. The door unlocked and slowly opened. Liam saw his brother Finn sitting in one of the leather chairs in front of his father's desk. Cillian, Conor's best friend and a Cosantóir member for many years, had opened the door and led Liam inside.

"Finally," Conor said with exasperation as he saw Liam enter. "What took you so long?"

"Da, I was leaving work. How fast did you feckin' think I could get here?"

"Right, right," Connor offered, shaking his head. "I just didn't want to get too far into things without you being here."

"Too far into what? What's going on?"

"We have an issue to handle," Conor stated.

"Something up with the club?" Liam asked. "We've enough shit rolling on us the last few months as it is. What else can happen?"

"It's not the club... not directly, anyway," Conor told him. "We need to make a run, and it has to be soon."

"You're gonna have to explain things clearly to me, Da," Liam answered. "I worked twelve hours, I'm parched, and don't feel much like thinking right now."

"A run," Conor insisted. "Someone's in trouble. We need to get her out of town."

"You talkin' about your little side project?" Liam asked. "I thought that was between you, the youngster, and Ginger out there. She's the expert in helping women in danger. I don't know anything about it."

"Well, you're about to learn," Conor said, bidding his son to sit down. Another knock occurred on the door, and Cillian pulled the door open. Siobhan appeared with a pint of Guinness and handed it to Liam. She turned to leave before Conor stopped her.

"Vonnie, stay," he asked.

"What?" Liam reacted with surprise. "Women don't come to meetings in here or talk about club info. Those are your rules, Da."

"She knows more about this case than the rest of us," Finn told his brother. Finn got out of his chair so Siobhan could sit down.

"I've been helping a young woman for a few weeks now," Siobhan began. "She's in some serious trouble. Her boyfriend is the father of their four-year-old. He doesn't do anything to the little girl, but he's vicious to the mother—physically, verbally, and emotionally. She needs out. I've set up a plan to help her get to her parents in Peru, but it's going to take some steps. First, I need her to disappear, and it has to be tomorrow. I've talked to her, and she's scared, but she's ready to go. I have everything in place."

"Then what do you need us for?" Liam asked. "If you're all set, just do it."

"It doesn't work that way," Conor said. "We have to give them the protection they need to get from A Safe Place to their next safe destination. Normally, I just do it myself or bring some extra muscle along with me. I'm in no condition to do anything like this now. That's where you come in."

Liam looked at his father, then at Siobhan.

"No, Da," Liam insisted. "I appreciate that you help these women, but you don't need me to be a part of that. Besides, to be frank, I don't want to do it. Have the choir boy do it," he said, nodding toward his brother.

"He's already helping out from here," Conor replied. "He's taking care of the legally blurred lines, shall we say, and he's footing the bill for this."

"What about Preacher?" Liam said quickly, looking at Cillian. "He's the guy with the good heart, faith, and all that."

Conor wheeled his chair from behind his desk, so it was in front of where Liam sat.

"Listen," Conor said, looking into Liam's dark eyes. "Let's be honest for a moment here, boy. At some point, I'm not going to be able to run the show anymore. I don't know how long it's going to take me to recover from these injuries. It's time for you to step up and start being the leader you have been groomed to be. It goes beyond barking out orders at the job site or with the Cosantóir. This is part of who our club is, Liam. If it's ever going to be yours to run, you have to become part of that, no questions asked."

Liam sat back, the leather of the chair making the only noise in the room. He glanced at the participants around him and then at the cold pint in his hand. He drained the Guinness, put the glass down on the edge of his father's desk, and stood up, taking three steps toward the door. Liam jiggled the door handle and looked to make sure the door remained bolted shut.

"What do I have to do?" He sighed.

Chapter 2

The cracks of the sunrise peeked through the front window of Quick Chek, giving Olivia Guerrero the only sunlight she experienced over the last several days. A hectic work schedule at the restaurant at Millie Malone's and catering gigs kept the days and nights blending together without any outdoor time at all. Having someone quit her part-time job at Quick Chek meant her manager asking her to take more overnight hours as well, pushing Olivia to the limit. Sleep seemed like a far-off fantasy that happened only during whatever downtime daylight hours she had.

Olivia completed cleaning the floor between the few early-risers out on a Saturday morning, getting gas and coffee when the morning crew rolled in for their shift. Olivia smiled and sighed before moving the bucket filled with dirty water back to the utility room so she could empty it before punching out. She moved behind the counter to grab her bag and go over what she had accomplished during the night with Amy Miller, the morning shift leader.

"Damn, you got a lot done being by yourself," Amy said with awe.

"I had to do something to keep myself awake," Olivia yawned. "It gets pretty dull here overnight if you don't. I just changed out some of the coffee, so you should be good for a while. And tell Stuart if he leaves his soda bottle caps all over behind the counter again, I'm going to smack him. I hate that shit."

"Ugh, and the way he pulls those little rings off and flings them around?" Amy asked.

"YES!" Olivia yelled, causing a customer to turn and look as he plucked two energy drinks from the refrigerator.

"Are you on again tonight?"

"No, thank God." Olivia smiled. "It's my first day off in weeks. I haven't had a break lately between the restaurant, catering, here, and then watching Daniela. So I might just sleep the day away."

"Too bad," Amy replied as she rang up the young man with the energy drinks. She gave the man a quick smile, and she watched him adjust his glasses. "I think it's going to be one of the last hot days we get around here before fall really kicks in. My friend Barb is having a barbecue tonight if you want to come with me. She says she has a few single guy friends coming."

"Tempting, but I don't have time for parties, let alone guys right now," Olivia bemoaned.

"Have you even done anything since you turned twenty-one?"

"I had a drink at the restaurant with Erin and Anna after work the day after my birthday," Olivia said. "That's been pretty much it."

"Liv, you need to get out and live a little," Amy advised.

Olivia took her hair out of the ponytail she typically wore while at work and let her long brown hair cascade down well past her shoulders. She ran her hand through the lightly-tangled locks and shook her head.

"Eventually." Olivia smiled. "I'll text you later about the party. If I'm feeling up to it, I'll meet you there."

"Yeah, I know what that means," Amy answered with disappointment.

"No, I really will, I promise." Olivia crossed her finger over her heart for emphasis before walking toward the door.

"Get some sleep!" Amy yelled as Olivia blindly waved to her.

Olivia crept to her car, parked on the far side of the parking lot. She got into the front seat of her Ford Focus and started it up, listening to the muffler rattle loudly as she did. The car needed work—a lot of work in her mechanic's mind—but Olivia had other needs and plans for the money she had scrimped and saved for years now.

The ride home was just a minute or two down the street toward the Lexington Hill development where Olivia resided. In a perfect world, she would walk to work and save herself the extra use of her car, but working the night shift made it less than ideal for walking along the side of the road with no sidewalks and little shoulder. She gave the car extra gas, so it chugged up the hill that led to the building she resided in with her sister and niece.

Olivia pulled into one of the guest parking spots across the street from her condo since their assigned condo spot already had a vehicle in it. Unfortunately, it was not a car she wanted to see in their slot. Instead, it was a black motorcycle. Olivia stopped as she reached the bike, knowing full well it meant that Benny was inside. The thought of pushing the bike over ran through her mind, but she knew it just meant Benny would take it out on Beatriz like he did everything else.

Olivia went down the short wooden steps to the front door, took a deep breath, and flung the door open. The blaring TV shot out immediately, and a quick glance to the living room allowed her to see Benny sprawled out on the couch, a bottle of beer in his hand and a cigarette burning down in the ashtray on the table in front of him. Olivia also spied Daniela playing with her Legos on the floor near the sofa.

"*Tia!*" the little girl shouted as she raced over and hugged Olivia around the legs.

"Hey, sweetie." Olivia grinned, patting the little girl's head before lifting her to give Daniela a kiss on the cheek.

"Mama's making pancakes if you want some," Daniela said proudly.

"Sounds yummy," Olivia agreed as she put Daniela down.

"Don't forget about my fucking eggs," Benny yelled from his position on the couch as he looked up at Olivia.

Olivia moved around to the front of the sofa, blocking the prone Benny's view of the wrestling he watched on TV.

"You can't smoke in here," Olivia said, putting out the cigarette. "You're going to get us kicked out, and we'll never get our deposit back. The landlord smells it every time he shows up, and the burns in the carpet don't help either."

Benny shot up to a sitting position, glaring at Olivia.

"Who cares?" Benny said as he took another draw on his beer. "This place is a dump anyway."

"This 'dump' is what we can afford," Olivia spat back. "Maybe if you actually paid some child support for your daughter instead of spending it on booze, cigarettes, drugs, and who knows what else, we could get a better place."

Benny stood up, forming an imposing presence in front of Olivia, but she refused to back down.

"Bea!" Benny shouted. "Get your sister out of my fucking face before I knock her out!"

"Just take that first swing, *cabrón*. After that, I'll be more than happy to return the favor."

Beatriz stepped out of the kitchen, holding a plate of golden pancakes, and placed them on the small folding table in the dining room. She rushed over and stood in front of Olivia, facing her.

"Liv, please," she said quietly. "Not in front of Danni."

Olivia glanced to her left and saw the toddler staring at the adults. Olivia turned her gaze back to her sister, noticing the bruise marks on Beatriz's upper arm and the scratches on her neck.

Benny smiled over Beatriz's shoulder and then rested his chin on her back and laughed. Next, he draped his hand around Beatriz's neck before squeezing it.

"My eggs done yet, or are you burning them while we chat with your sister?"

Beatriz rushed off to the kitchen to catch the scrambled eggs just in time before they overcooked.

"They're good!" she yelled shakily.

"Don't forget the bacon either," Benny shouted.

He bent down, grasping his beer and finishing it off before tossing the empty bottle back on the couch.

"Can you get that, *coño*?" He laughed at Olivia.

Olivia glared at Benny before bending over and plucking the bottle off the sofa. She felt Benny's hand graze across the backside of her jeans, and she stood up abruptly, turning to face him.

"You've filled out nicely," Benny said in a low voice. His right hand drifted to Olivia's hip and made its way up just short of her breast. "If you ever decide you want to..."

Olivia smiled and placed her palm on Benny's face as his hand crept higher. Then, she reared back and cracked her flat palm across his face as hard as she could, knocking Benny off balance. He recovered enough to stand back up and move toward Olivia. Still, she quickly moved her left hand down to Benny's crotch, squeezing his balls as tightly as she could until he yelped in pain.

"Doesn't feel like you're worth the trouble, *imbécil*," she said as she twisted more to the right, causing Benny to collapse to the floor, groaning.

Beatriz appeared holding a plate of bacon and looked on, stunned as Benny lay on the floor.

"What did you do?" Beatriz said fearfully.

"What needed to be done," Olivia answered. She walked over to Daniela and picked her up, taking her down the hall as fast as she could move. Olivia entered her room, turned the lock on the door, and then turned the bolt Olivia had put on a long time ago to help keep Benny out. She lay on the bed with Daniela beside her. The muffled cries of Benny echoed before loud footsteps came down the hall, and fists pounded on her bedroom door. The initial noise startled Daniela, and she hugged her aunt tightly.

"Why is Daddy mad now?" Daniela asked as she closed her eyes.

"Who knows, sweetie?" Olivia lied as she tried to soothe her niece. First, she saw the door handle jiggle several times. Then, she heard what sounded like Benny throwing himself against the door to no avail before the yelling commenced and moved back toward the living room and dining room. Of course, it mainly was Benny doing all the screaming in a mixture of English and Spanish, but Olivia heard enough of it to know things would not end well. The sound of shattering glass and plates rang out before the clear and distinct slaps and then sobs of her sister. Shortly after, Olivia recognized the slam of the front door. A fist pounding on the glass of her bedroom window caused Olivia to jump and hug Danni tighter.

"I'm coming back for you later, bitch," Benny growled. "I'll be teaching you a lesson you have needed to learn for a long time."

Olivia heard the roar of the motorcycle engine before it faded away as Benny left. Moments later, a soft knock on the door came from Beatriz.

"Liv, open up," Beatriz cried.

Olivia opened the door to see the swelling under her sister's left cheek. Olivia led Beatriz into the room, and Beatriz sat on the bed and hugged Danni.

"He's gone... but he'll be back later. I've never seen him this angry," Beatriz sobbed.

Olivia sat next to her sister and lightly rubbed her back.

"It's going to be okay." Olivia tried to reassure her, though she was unsure if that was true. "You know what we need to do, and it has to be now. Do you have everything ready?"

"I wanted to bring a few more things," Beatriz pleaded. "I... I think I need more time."

"No!" Olivia shouted before reining in her voice. "Bea, no more delays. It's going to get much worse... for all of us. Besides, they told us not to bring much, so it looks like we might be back. Just take what you absolutely need. We need to be ready to go in an hour, tops."

Olivia walked over to her closet and pulled out the backpack she had packed days ago.

"Do you have Danni's bag ready?"

Beatriz nodded.

"It's in my closet—the pink one with Peppa Pig on it."

"Okay, go get it and get your stuff ready," Olivia said, helping her sister off the bed.

"Where are we going?" Daniela asked.

"We're going to take a little trip," Olivia said sweetly.

"But I wanted pancakes," Daniela pouted.

Olivia bent down, so she was face to face with her niece.

"I promise we'll get some pancakes when we are out, okay? Now, come with me so we can clean up a little bit out there so Mommy can finish getting ready."

Olivia took Daniela's hand, and the two walked down the hall to the mess that scattered over the floor in the dining room and kitchen. Olivia turned off the stove and began picking up the pieces of shattered glass plates. She heard Beatriz rummaging through the closet on the opposite side of the wall to the kitchen.

Once the shards had been swept up, Olivia pulled out her cell phone. She typed out a group text message to Erin and Anna first.

We're leaving this afternoon. I'm not sure when I'll be back. I'll keep you posted. I'm sorry.

Olivia then went to her purse, pulling out the slip of paper with a phone number on it. She entered the number in her phone and sent a separate text to it.

We're in danger. We're coming now.

Nervous energy coursed through her body after sending the message. Moments later, her phone buzzed with a return message.

We're ready.

Chapter 3

Liam groaned when he recognized that the constant ringing sound of the phone was not part of his dream but his cell phone. He peered with his left eye to spot the screen of his phone lit up before he reached over and grabbed it. The call was from Finn, and it was barely 8:00 a.m.

"Feck," he mumbled as he sat up in his bed.

After considering declining the call or flinging the phone across the room, Liam sullenly answered instead.

"This better be because someone is dead, little brother," Liam growled.

"I know it's early," Finn began.

"Early? Cripes, man, it's not even eight on a Saturday... my day off. Besides that, I was up late last night doing"—Liam glanced over and saw the blond head on the pillow next to him, snoring lightly—"things."

"Trust me, I wouldn't call if it wasn't important," Finn stated. "We have to be ready to move earlier today, if necessary. Something happened this morning. She's here with Siobhan at A Safe Place. What time can you get here?"

"Jaysus, brother, I don't know," Liam said as he rubbed his eyes and then his temple. "I'm not packed or nothing yet. How long is this going to take? What if I need to ask for time off work? This is a big hassle for me, man. I've still got someone here with me, too, and by the looks of her, I'd hate to kick her out early."

Liam's eyes scanned the curve of the bare back lying next to him, and he let out a chuckle.

"Stop thinking about yourself for five minutes, will you?" Finn scolded. "You committed to this; we're counting on you. We just have to move the timetable up a few hours, is all. Conor and Preacher will take care of anything you need with work. Hurry up and pack and get over here as soon as you can, okay?"

"Right," Liam grumbled before hanging up.

He leaned back against his headboard and glanced down at the girl next to him. It had taken little effort to lure Arianna away from her friends and back to Hog House to spend the night with him. He had quickly tracked down the trendy restaurant location they went to nearby and sat at the bar, waiting for the moment she got up and walked by. Five minutes of talking had her saying good night to her table and getting on the back of Liam's bike. Liam knew she went with him to get back at her wealthy family or tell the story to her friends that she went to a biker's house, but he didn't care at all. He got to spend the night with a lithe beauty that he could brag about as well.

Liam pulled the blanket back that Arianna had wrapped around her so he could get a better look. He saw the bright pinkness on her backside and recalled with a smile the spanking session he had treated her to before they had sex. He reached down and cupped one of her cheeks in his large palm, and Arianna wriggled before waking.

"What time is it?" she asked groggily before rolling over to look at Liam, baring her pert breasts.

"Time for you to get going, darlin'," Liam said.

"What?" she asked as she sat up.

"I've got things to do and places to go. Sorry. If you were expecting breakfast in bed, you were with the wrong fella."

"How am I supposed to get home?" she squeaked. "You brought me here."

"True," Liam said as he rose from the bed and walked toward his private bathroom on the opposite side of the room. He left the door open while he urinated.

"Call one of your friends to get you," he said callously.

"Seriously?" she said, aghast at both the remark and the sound of Liam peeing.

"What did you expect, poetry and roses? Look at me, darlin'," Liam said as he flushed and then moved to the doorway so Arianna could see his naked form. "You wanted to be able to tell everyone you fucked a biker. Congrats. Now you have a few choices. You can call your friends, call a ride service, or hop in the shower with me. Any of those is good with me."

"Bastard," Arianna grunted as she grabbed her panties off a chair. "Should I look for the cash on the dresser by the door too?"

Liam stood silently for a moment.

"Darlin', you don't look like you need the extra cash. I'm sure Daddy takes real good care of you. But if you want me to throw you a hundred, you were worth it."

"You're an unbelievable pig," Arianna shouted as she put her skirt on. She grabbed her shirt, pulled it into place, and gathered her things to storm out of the room.

"What, no goodbye kiss?" Liam chortled.

"Go to Hell," she spat, attempting to slap his face. Liam grasped her wrist and held it.

"I'm the one who does the spanking, remember?" Liam smiled. He watched as Arianna blushed at the memory before she jerked her hand from him and fled the room.

Liam laughed heartily as he stepped back into the bathroom and turned the shower on, washing away yesterday.

Liam took his time preparing for the trip, packing a leather duffle bag with a few days' worth of clothes and essentials. Next, he went into the small safe he kept hidden in the floor of his closet and grabbed cash and his gun, stuffing both into the bag as well. Liam also ensured he had his knife, pulling it from its sheath to test the blade. Finally, he grabbed his leather jacket off the hook on the back of his bedroom door, locked the door, and walked out to move downstairs.

The entertainment room was light, with most of the Cosantóir already out for the day for a weekend ride. Rory, the house bartender and handyman, stood polishing the bar when Liam entered.

"Anyone around?" Liam asked from across the room. He saw a member sprawled out on the couch, snoring.

"Get your arse up," Liam yelled as he kicked the couch. "Take a room if you need to sleep. Don't do it in here."

"Sorry," the member mumbled before scrambling off the sofa and toward the stairwell to go upstairs.

Rory laughed before answering Liam.

"I tried getting him up hours ago. He wouldn't budge. No one's around. Most went out riding today. I think it was a day trip up to Albany or Troy. Preacher left earlier than them. He said he had somewhere to go."

"I'm heading out." Liam signaled. "I might be gone a few days. Preacher and Finn know."

Rory nodded.

"Have fun," he said, turning back to the bar.

"I doubt it." Liam huffed as he went out the front and then walked around the garage in the back, where officers of the MC were allowed to park. He stowed his gear in his saddlebags, put on his helmet, and headed out to get to A Safe Place.

He pulled into the gravel parking lot, swinging his bike in front of the building. As he dismounted, he caught a glimpse of two bikers parked across the street, watching him. Liam locked his helmet onto his bike and, instead of moving to the front steps of the building, made his way across the street to get a better view of who looked on.

As he neared, he saw the biker to his right get off his bike and stand up. He wore a brown leather jacket, but Liam couldn't distinguish the colors or emblem on it until he got closer. It was then that he saw they were Caimans. Liam caught a view of the reptile logo, blood dripping from its jaws. He also noticed that the biker still seated was Benny Moreno, leader of the Caimans.

The younger biker stepped in front of Liam as he got close to Benny's bike.

"Stand down, Junior," Liam said with a smile, seeing the significant size advantage he had over the young man.

"Easy, Chato," Benny said to his mate. Chato obediently stepped aside.

"Weird seeing you out here, Liam," Benny said as he lit a cigarette before offering one to Liam.

"I was about to say the same to you, Benny," Liam admitted as he refused the smoke. "No cigarettes for me. Didn't you hear those are bad for you?"

Benny laughed as he took a puff.

"What isn't today, huh?"

"Why are you here, Benny? This isn't your territory. If you're coming down here to start problems…"

"No problems, friend," Benny answered. "My woman lives here in Harriman. A little bird told me she might be over there." He pointed toward A Safe Place with his cigarette.

"Only reason she would be in there is if you made her run there," Liam said directly. "You know they have cameras every which way over there to see you."

"That's why we're sitting here." Benny smiled. "Out of view. I just want to see her and talk to her. We had a bit of a misunderstanding this morning. So now, I ask again… what are you doing here, Liam? They just gonna let you waltz in there?"

"They are," Liam told him. "My brother's lady runs the place. He's in there and asked me to stop by."

"Rumor has it that the Cosantóir gives a hand to funneling women out of the area. Of course, you wouldn't be here to do that with my woman, would you?"

"I don't know anything about that, Benny. You know me. You think I have the time to do that shite? I'd rather be riding, drinking, or doing anything else," Liam confessed.

"Good to hear." Benny nodded before tossing the butt of his cigarette on the ground.

"Careful, Benny," Liam warned. "If they spot you, they'll have cops here in a flash to roust you. I'm sure you and Shorty here don't want any trouble."

"I hear you," Benny said. "Vamos, Chato," he barked to his mate. "Maybe I'll see you later, Liam."

"Probably not," Liam told him. "Go grab some lunch or something. Rhodes has a great burger and biker parking."

Liam turned and walked back across the road to the front steps of A Safe Place. He climbed the steps, looked into the camera, and waved, waiting for the door to open. He turned back and saw Benny and the other biker pulling away.

A large man pulled open the door and stood in front of Liam.

"Wow, you're a big fella, aren't you?" Liam laughed.

"The name is J.J., and yes, I'm a big guy. Don't give me trouble, and we'll be cool," J.J. retorted. "Follow me."

J.J. led Liam down the hall until they reached the door with Siobhan McCarthy's name on it. J.J. knocked sharply and swung the door open.

"He's here," J.J. said as he let Liam into the office.

"It's about time," Finn complained. "Christ, Liam, I called you hours ago. This was as fast as you could get here?"

"I told you I wasn't ready," Liam answered. "You asked me about tonight, not eight a.m. You're lucky you got me at all. So what's going on?"

"We need to move faster," Siobhan answered. "There was a problem this morning with the boyfriend."

"That boyfriend wouldn't happen to be Benny Moreno, would it?" Liam asked.

"How did you know that?" Siobhan asked.

"Because he and one of his lackeys were perched across the street watching the place. I went over to him, and he said he heard she was here."

"Are they still out there?" Siobhan said, grabbing her phone. "I'll call the police."

"They left, but I'm sure they'll be back. Benny knows about what goes on here; he told me as much. If you're mixed up with them, nothing good is going to happen. People think our club is bad. The Caimans make us look like choir boys," Liam answered.

"Then we need to move now," Siobhan said. "Cillian, can you go get them from down the hall?"

"You bet," Cillian agreed and quickly left the room.

"You have everything you need?" Finn asked.

"I think so," Liam offered. "It's just a day or two, right?"

"Hopefully," Siobhan said. "Get them to the safe house in Lancaster, South Carolina. From there, we have people getting her to the airport so she can get to Peru."

A knock at the door had Cillian reentering with not just a woman with bruises on her face but with a younger woman and a toddler in tow as well.

"What the hell?" Liam said. "You told me it was just the woman. I'm not some feckin' babysitter service, too."

"The toddler is her daughter, Daniela," Siobhan told Liam. "Of course she is going with her. The other woman is her sister, Olivia."

Liam looked closely at the younger woman, taking in her long brown hair, dark eyes, and form.

"You're the girl from Quick Chek, right?" Liam asked. "You were there when everything was going down with Preacher and his woman."

"If by woman you mean Anna, then yes," Olivia told him.

"Why does she need to go too?" Liam barked. "It's just one more person to slow things down."

"Beatriz doesn't know how to drive," Olivia explained. "I thought I could split the driving with you and make sure they get there safely. Siobhan said this was all worked out."

"It is, Olivia," Siobhan assured. "Liam, Olivia can assist you with the drive down in the van."

"Van?" Liam inquired.

"We got a used minivan brought up today," Finn told him, handing him a set of keys. "It's all gassed up and packed. It's in the back of the building."

"I'm not driving some feckin' soccer mom car," Liam growled. "I'm riding my bike, or I'm not going."

"That's not how it works," Siobhan said.

"It does if you want me there," Liam replied. He tossed the keys toward Siobhan, but Olivia snatched them out of the air.

"If this asshat doesn't want to go, it's fine. We'll go without him. I'll drive the whole way and then fly back like we planned. We don't need him. Go home."

"That's all I need to hear," Liam said and turned toward the door before Preacher stopped him.

"Liam, we went over this," Preacher started. "They can't do this alone; it's too dangerous, especially now that we know the Caimans are aware of what's happening. You want to leave them at Benny's mercy? You know what will happen. It's the right thing to do it, and you know it."

"I'm still not driving the van," Liam bargained. "I'll ride my bike and follow them. I can keep a better eye out if I'm not in the car and distracted by all this nonsense anyway. They can patch into my Bluetooth in my helmet. Take it or leave it."

Siobhan and Finn looked at each other before turning to Beatriz and Olivia.

"*Nosotras necesitamos la protección*," Beatriz said quietly to her sister.

"*No, nosotras no*," Olivia said sternly. "*El es un gran patán.*"

Beatriz tried to stifle a laugh as Liam glanced at her.

"*Por favor. Estoy asustada.*"

Olivia nodded to her sister.

"Fine." Olivia resigned herself. "Let's just get going. Don't fuck this up," she warned Liam before turning and leaving the room.

"What was all that?" Liam asked, shocked that this woman would stand up to him.

"Someone who won't take shit from you." Finn laughed. "Let me give you all the final details while they get their stuff together."

Liam tried to pay attention to his brother, Siobhan, and Preacher telling him about the trip, the plans, and the expectations, but he only half-paid attention. Instead, his mind was more on why he had tolerated the tongue lashing and arguing from Olivia.

Chapter 4

A bright orange sunset settled in over Harriman just as Liam pulled out to follow the tan, non-descript Kia Sedona out of the parking lot. He and others had checked the area before departing, ensuring none of the Caimans were within sight when they left. With the coast clear, Liam gave the nod, and Siobhan signaled to Olivia to leave the rear of the building.

The plates and registration of the van were such that they could not be traced back to A Safe Place, making it more challenging for anyone to track where they might go. Liam ensured that the Bluetooth in his bike helmet could connect to one of the burner phones given to Olivia and Beatriz by Siobhan before hitting the road. Between the work of A Safe Place and the Cosantóir, they would make sure it was like Beatriz and Daniela disappeared without a trace. Liam knew Benny would never go to the police to report Beatriz missing. Doing so would just turn tighter scrutiny back on him and the Caimans, something Benny never wanted. However, Liam also figured Benny would use any means necessary to get to the woman who escaped him.

Liam remained vigilant in following the van and doing all he could so neither his bike nor the car would draw any attention as they drove onto I-78 and headed into Pennsylvania. As soon as their vehicles were comfortably on I-78 and headed toward I-81 to move farther south, Liam noticed the speed of the van uptick quite a bit. A quick glance at his own speedometer let him know he was approaching eighty and was working to keep up.

"Hey, girly," Liam roared into his microphone. "You need to slow down."

Liam heard distinct chatter in Spanish before he got a response.

"The faster we get there, the faster we are done, and then you can go home," Olivia answered.

"The more you speed, the more likely it is that you get the attention of cops or anyone else. If you get pulled over and ticketed, it won't be long before the Caimans know about it. You really have no clue who you are dealing with, do you? Slow the feck down!"

More muttering in Spanish crackled over the headset.

"I don't care if you want to curse me out," Liam stated, "but at least do it in English, so I know what you're callin' me."

A small laugh could be heard, and Liam managed to crack a smile.

Night settled in as the van crossed Maryland and West Virginia before reaching the Virginia state line. Communication with Olivia had been sparse, leaving Liam to his own thoughts for much of the ride. His focus stayed on getting there and back so he could return to what he knew best instead of getting treated like a glorified errand boy and bodyguard.

Not long after crossing the border, Liam saw the van signal to get off the highway. The move grabbed his attention immediately.

"Everything okay?" Liam asked.

"I need to stop for gas," Olivia said. "I'm surprised we made it this far. The gas light has been on for miles."

"Jaysus, girl, you can't do that," Liam warned. He followed close behind as the van turned to the exit ramp and stopped at a nearby Mobil station that opened all night.

The car rolled to a stop in front of the gas pumps, and Olivia hopped out. Liam parked right behind them and dismounted his bike. He saw Olivia walking toward the pump with a credit card and reached out and snatched her arm.

"What the hell are you doing?" Liam barked.

"Paying for the gas," Olivia yelled, pulling her hand away. "What's the matter with you?"

"No credit cards," Liam told her. "Credit cards can be tracked. Cash only. I'll go in and pay."

Liam marched off toward the convenience store to pay when Beatriz came running up to him.

"Excuse me," she said softly. "I need to use the restroom. May I?"

"You don't need my permission," Liam said as he kept moving forward.

He grabbed the store's glass door and pulled it open as Beatriz snuck in ahead of him with Daniela trailing behind her. Liam watched as Beatriz scurried toward the bathrooms before she stopped and turned toward Liam.

"Can you watch her, please?" Beatriz asked, moving from side to side.

"Seriously?" Liam said with surprise.

"I'll just be a minute," Beatriz answered before darting into the bathroom, leaving Daniela standing there next to Liam.

Liam glanced down at the diminutive girl by his side now. Daniela looked up at him like he was a giant.

"You're big," she said in awe.

"Well, you're small," Liam replied before turning to the cashier.

"Fill it on number three," he told the young man, handing him fifty dollars. Liam then reached over and grabbed a Snickers bar and tore the wrapper open before taking a bite.

"This too," he said, holding up the candy.

Within just one bite of the chocolate, Liam felt a tug on his jeans. He glanced down and saw Daniela standing there, holding up a package of Reese's Peanut Butter Cups to him.

Liam let out a deep sigh.

"And this," he told the man, shaking his head. He took the peanut butter confection so the man could scan it before handing it back to Daniela. She beamed up at him and hugged the candy tightly to her chest.

After paying, Liam looked back to see Beatriz still in the restroom. He began walking to the front door of the store to go outside. Daniela ran up alongside him as the door opened and took his right hand as Liam walked. Liam stopped when he felt the little girl's hand become engulfed by his. He shook his head once again and kept moving, with Daniela hustling along and taking five steps to every giant one he took.

Liam gazed at Olivia as she stood stretching as she waited for the gas tank to fill. He watched as she yawned and reached up high, causing the pale blue T-shirt she wore to ride up and expose her flat belly. Liam's eyes narrowed as he stared too long, catching the look of Olivia as she noticed and put her arms down quickly. A smile had crept across her face, but not because Liam stared.

"What are you doing?" She laughed as she talked to Daniela, holding tightly to her new friend.

"*El gigante me compró caramelos*," Daniela said happily.

Olivia burst out in laughter.

"What did she say?" Liam asked.

"She said the giant bought me candy." Olivia laughed again.

Liam looked down at Daniela, who had opened the wrapper and was already munching on the first peanut butter cup.

"Don't forget that I'm a giant," Liam growled. "We eat what we want... even kids."

Daniela stopped chewing and then laughed.

The gas pump clicked to indicate the tank was full. Liam reached over and grabbed the hose, brushing by Olivia so he could return it to its rightful place.

"Do you need the bathroom... or want something from inside?" Liam asked as he looked down at Olivia.

"I'm good, thanks," she replied. "Just tired. I haven't slept in about thirty-six hours."

"Christ, woman. You can't do that and drive safely," Liam chided.

He looked around the location and saw a motel sign just up the road on the right.

"We can crash there for the night and leave early in the morning. You need to get some rest. Where the feck is your sister?"

Liam looked over at the store and saw Beatriz hustling through the door and back toward the van.

"I'm sorry," she apologized. "My stomach is a little upset from the ride... and everything else."

"We're going to get rooms over there for the night," Olivia said to her sister. "I need rest."

"But... shouldn't we keep going? To get there faster?" Beatriz shook nervously.

"It's not safe for me to drive, Bea," Olivia added.

Liam watched as Beatriz nodded.

"Why do you have my purse?" Olivia asked her sister, pointing at the brown bag in her hands.

"I must have grabbed yours by accident when I got out," she said, handing the bag back to Olivia. "It was dark, and I was in a hurry."

"Can we end the chit-chat now and get going?" Liam asked.

Liam got back on his bike and started it up, turning toward the exit of the lot. He idled, waiting for Olivia to follow behind him. Once he saw her there, he made the short trip up the street to the Endless Motel. Liam immediately saw the irony in the name since the place was small, with perhaps just eight or nine rooms indicated as they drove into the lot. He parked his bike out front of the office and signaled for Olivia to stay in the van for now.

Liam approached the office with a bell jingling as he walked through the door. His first thought was that the place eerily reminded him of *Vacancy* with Kate Beckinsale. The motel owners made snuff movies with the unaware guests as stars. But his suspicions grew more extensive when the gentleman crept out from behind the gaudy curtain separating the back room from the front desk.

The clerk seemed to be a cross of Steve Buscemi and Gollum, baring bad teeth in his nearly bald head as he smiled at Liam.

"Well, howdy," the man said to Liam. "How can I help you?"

"I need a couple of rooms," Liam stated. "Two next to each other."

"You got a reservation?" the man questioned.

"You serious?" Liam said, tilting his head. "Your parking lot is empty. Have you had a guest this month?"

The clerk cackled a laugh before he broke out into an obvious smoker's cough.

"That's a good one," the man said, regaining his composure. "I got plenty of room for you."

The man craned his neck outside to see through the van's front window where Olivia and Beatriz sat, playing with Daniela.

"They all with you?"

"Yep," Liam said, taking out his wallet.

"You're not gonna be loud all right, are you? We like it quiet around here."

"Fella, don't worry about it," Liam said with a scowl. "How much?"

"One night, two rooms... seventy-five dollars," the man said, turning the guest book to Liam. "I need a credit card."

"No, you don't," Liam said, handing the man two one-hundred-dollar bills before turning the guest book back to the clerk.

"I don't want any trouble from you. The last thing I need is the cops out here again."

Liam peeled off another hundred and handed it to the man.

"No trouble, and we were never here," Liam said. "Keys, please."

The clerk smiled again and handed Liam the keys to rooms eight and nine.

"Eight's got the shower with the best flow and hot water," the man said proudly. He then handed Liam a stack of clean towels and some toiletries clearly pilfered from another hotel.

"Thanks," Liam replied before exiting.

He walked over to the van, and Beatriz rolled down the window to greet him. He handed her the key to their room.

"Room eight," he said, pointing toward the end of the row of rooms. "I'm in nine, right next door."

Liam rode his bike the short distance to in front of his room while Olivia pulled the van next to him. Olivia, Beatriz, and Daniela hopped out, all with small bags in tow. Olivia unlocked the door and flipped the light on, but Liam entered the room first. He did a quick check of the sparse place, checking the surprisingly clean bathroom and under the beds for any potential surprises. He also glanced behind the picture of the local mountains hanging in the room and the air vents, looking for cameras that Gollum may have set up for a peep show.

"Looks okay," Liam said. "I know it ain't the Ritz, but it's just for tonight. The guys said the shower in here is good, at least."

Daniela jumped on the nearest bed and clicked the TV on.

"Is Dora on?" she asked her mother.

"I'll check," Beatriz said as she flipped channels.

"I'm going to run to the restaurant down the street and see if I can get us some food," Liam told Olivia. "Lock the door and stay put. I'll bellow for you when I get back."

"Cheeseburger, please!" Daniela yelled to Liam with a smile.

"Yeah, yeah," Liam answered as he walked out the door. Olivia shut the door, but Liam didn't hear her lock it.

"Lock the feckin' door!" Liam shouted. He finally heard the lock turn before he went to his room to stow his gear.

After bringing his bags into the less-than-stellar accommodations, Liam got back on his bike. He went to the Evergreen Bar and Grill positioned just down from the motel and the convenience store. Liam pulled the door open and saw the place partially filled with patrons. He garnered looks from everyone as he stepped toward the bar and grabbed a stool right at the corner. The bartender, who looked like he could be Gollum's brother, sauntered over.

"What can I get you?" the bartender asked in a raspy voice.

"I was hoping to order some food to go," Liam told him.

"I'll have to see if Eddy still feels like cooking tonight," the man huffed.

Liam shook his head in disbelief. He reached back into his wallet and pulled a twenty out.

"Tell Eddy I would sure appreciate if I could get four cheeseburgers with fries," he said as he handed the man the bill.

The bartender smiled and nodded and made his way through the swinging doors that led to the kitchen.

The bribery alone on this trip is gonna bankrupt me, Liam thought.

The bartender reappeared with a grin on his face.

"You're in luck," he beamed. "Eddy's working on them right now. Can I get you a drink while you wait?"

"Got any Guinness?" Liam asked hopefully.

"What's that?" the man spat.

"It's beer... never mind. Just give me two fingers of good whiskey," Liam said, pointing to the dust-covered bottles on the top shelf behind the bar.

The bartender blew the dust off the bottle before pulling out the cork of the barely-used Laphroaig to pour the drink. Liam watched as the golden nectar went into the glass he hoped was clean before it was slid in front of him. Liam took a sip and the warm liquid soothed him. He nodded gratefully at the bartender, who then went to cater to other customers.

Liam scanned the room, recognizing that this was clearly a local haunt. That reassured him that the food was probably good and the pours fair, even if this was a place the average traveler wouldn't find rated on Yelp.

A blond woman appeared from the swinging doors holding two bags when he was almost done with his drink.

"These must be for you," she said sweetly with Southern charm.

"Yes, ma'am," Liam answered politely, taking the bags.

"Ooh, a big boy with an accent," she observed. "You've got my attention now."

"Tell Eddy I said thanks for keeping the kitchen open," Liam said, taking the last drop of whiskey from his glass.

"You can tell her yourself," she smiled. "That'll be thirty dollars."

Liam took another fifty from his wallet and handed it to Eddy.

"That should cover the food and my drink and a little something for you," Liam told her.

"I only get a little somethin'?" she asked. "That's disappointing. Where are you staying around here?"

"The Endless Inn down the street," Liam told her as he stood up.

"Ahh... Georgie's brother Clem runs the place," Eddy confirmed for Liam. "Place is kind of a dump. I might have a better place for you to go," she flirted.

"Any other night would get a yes from me, darlin'," Liam admitted with a grin. "I'm on the road early tomorrow. Maybe another time."

"Your call, stranger." She smiled.

Liam nodded toward Eddy and made his way out to his bike. The temptation to turn back and take Eddy up on her offer loomed largely. Surely the devil on Liam's shoulder would convince him to return, but the angel grew stronger this time, and he turned toward the motel.

Before getting back, Liam returned to the convenience store. He picked up a random array of sodas and juice for the girls and a four-pack of Guinness he knew he was overpaying for. He laid his items on the counter and then reached down and grabbed two packs of peanut butter cups.

He returned to the motel, brought his food and drinks to his room, and then went over to deliver the rest next door. He knocked loudly, announcing, "It's me!"

The door unlatched and creaked open enough for an eye to look out while the chain still held the top portion locked. Beatriz peered out and then opened the door the rest of the way so Liam could enter.

"Dinner," he announced, placing the bag on the small, rickety table in the room. Daniela ran over to the table and sat down.

"Cheeseburgers?" she asked.

"Indeed," Liam told her, pulling one of the wrapped burgers out of the bag. "And fries."

"Thank you, thank you," the toddler said gleefully as she munched a French fry.

"Olivia, *comida*!" Beatriz shouted as she sat down and grabbed a burger for herself.

Olivia appeared from the bathroom wrapped solely in one of the towels Liam got when they checked in. Liam watched as she approached the table, the towel held tightly under her arms but barely coming down to her mid-thighs. Her hair still dripped lightly onto her shoulders. Liam surged from within at the sight of her, but he took a deep breath and stepped aside as she moved past him to sit at the table.

"You didn't get anything for yourself?" Olivia asked as she opened her cheeseburger.

"No... I mean, my food is in my room," Liam said as he pulled himself together. "I got you some sodas too. I didn't know what kind of diet stuff you liked, so there's a bit of everything and some juice for the rugrat."

Olivia reached into the plastic bag, pulled out the apple juice bottle, twisted the cap, and passed it to Daniela. She then grabbed the one regular bottle of Coke in the bag and took it for herself.

"I don't like that diet junk." She grinned as she took a gulp of soda.

Liam leered as Olivia wiped some soda from her lips with the back of her hand.

"Okay, if you need me, I'm next door," Liam said as he moved to the door.

"Why don't you come in and eat with us?" Beatriz asked.

"Nah, do your girly stuff. Enjoy. Lock the door," he demanded.

Liam shuffled back to his room, diving into his meal. The fries were surprisingly crisp and delicious, and the burger was cooked to perfection.

"Kudos to Eddy," Liam said to himself as he polished off the burger.

Liam heard laughter coming through the thin motel walls. He checked his cell phone and noted a message from Finn, asking how things were going. He let Finn know they stopped for the night but gave no hint of where they were, as per their protocols.

Liam shed his leather jacket, grabbed one of the cold cans of Guinness, and made his way out of the room to the front porch outside his room. He sat in the rusted chair positioned under the eave, put his feet up on the plastic table, and opened the nitro can so he heard the familiar hiss before he began to drink.

Few, if any, cars drove by their location, and the night was quiet. Sipping his stout, Liam calculated how much farther they still had to go before they reached Lancaster. His calculations still put them about six hours or so away, meaning he likely would have to spend a night in Lancaster before he could head back home and be finished with his quest.

The door to room eight creaked open, and there stood Olivia, wearing a black tank top and black sleep shorts. She looked over at Liam as she quietly closed the door.

"They are both asleep in there," she said quietly. "Mind if I hang with you?"

"Free world," Liam said, taking another sip of his beer.

Olivia pulled up a similar-looking rust-riddled chair next to Liam's and sat. She glanced at the Guinness can Liam held.

"Do you have another of those?" she asked.

"How old are you?" Liam inquired. "I'm not corrupting a minor or anything."

"I'm twenty-one, smart guy," Olivia shot back. "I turned legal a few weeks ago. Besides, from what I hear about you, corruption is kind of your thing, isn't it?"

"The cans are inside," Liam told her. He watched as she sauntered into his room and heard the can pop open. Olivia came out of the room, taking a swing of the beer, her tank top riding up to expose that flat stomach again that Liam couldn't help but stare at until she sat back down.

The two sat quietly for a few minutes, with Liam shuffling his boots on the old wood of the porch.

"I know I was kind of rough on you when we left Harriman," Olivia began. "It's only because it's important to me that Bea and Daniela get away and are safe. Everything needs to go well so they can go home, and it's my job to make sure that happens."

"I've been treated worse," Liam replied. "That's a lot to take on, you know."

"I owe her that much," Olivia admitted. "When our parents sent us here, I was only twelve. Bea took care of me, made sure I went to school and did everything. She worked three jobs before she got pregnant. After that, Benny kind of took advantage of her. If she didn't get away from him, at some point he would kill her."

"More than likely," Liam said straightforwardly.

He looked over at Olivia and saw the shock on her face.

"What? It's true. Benny Moreno and the Caimans are killers. They are involved in nasty shit. Do you know how many of them are already in prison? Guns, drugs, prostitution, porn—you name it, they are in it. Your sister is lucky she made it this long. Have you thought about yourself at all?"

"What do you mean?" Olivia asked.

"When you go back to Harriman, Benny will know it was you who helped your sister disappear," Liam explained. "You think he's just going to let that pass? You may want to do your own disappearing act."

"I'm not leaving," Olivia said adamantly. "That's my home. I have a plan, and I'm not afraid of Benny Moreno."

"Darlin', you should be afraid of him," Liam instructed. "Not many guys scare me, but Benny will go to great lengths to get what he wants, and he doesn't care who is in the way. I hope your plan involves living in a cave somewhere."

"Thanks for your reassurance," Olivia said sarcastically. "Don't worry about me; I'll take care of myself."

Liam laughed out loud.

"What's so funny?" Olivia asked angrily.

"*Chomh ceanndána le miúil*," Liam scoffed.

"What the hell does that mean?"

"Ah, you and your sister aren't the only ones who can speak another language. It's Gaelic. My ma used to say it about my father all the time. It means stubborn as a mule."

"Seems to me we both have that trait," Olivia shot back.

"Fair enough." Liam held up what was left in his can of Guinness.

"*Sláinte*," Liam offered.

"I know that one from Millie's." Olivia laughed. She clinked her can to Liam's. "*Salud*."

Liam finished off his drink and crushed the can in his hand. Olivia did the same and went to hand the squashed aluminum to him.

"I'm going to bed," she said as she got out of the chair, dropping the can in front of her.

Liam watched as she bent to pick it up, spying every movement Olivia made until the moment she turned to him and handed him the trash.

"Thanks for the drink," she said, looking into Liam's dark eyes. He stared back into hers, her body so close to him he could pick up the faint scent of the lavender motel soap she used in the shower. "And thank you for helping us."

"No problem," Liam said as he tried to gather himself. "Lock the damn door when you get in there. You never know who might try to get in."

Olivia gave Liam a soft smile.

"See you in the morning," she said as she crossed into her motel room and locked the door.

Liam released a large exhale before standing up and going to his room.

"There better be cold water in that feckin' shower," he grumbled.

Chapter 5

Tossing and turning most of the night on a lumpy bed six inches shorter than his body meant horrid sleeping conditions for Liam. So when he spied the sun rising through the tissue paper-thin curtain on the front window, he happily rose and showered to prepare to get on the road as early as possible.

The frigid shower water emulated what he experienced the night before when he needed to cool off after his talk with Olivia. Typically Liam could handle an experience with any woman and come out on top—literally and figuratively. However, Olivia presented something much different than what he was accustomed to. She seemed immune to his usual path of charm and had no problem putting him in his place. An attitude like this in a woman usually made Liam more determined to get what he wanted. Still, Olivia threw him off his game, and he was unsure how to deal with it. The cold shower helped for sure, and now he hoped to just put it out of his mind, tackle the project at hand, and get back to Harriman and the life he loved as fast as possible.

Liam stepped onto the front porch, bag in hand, and loaded up his bike. He paced over to knock on the door to the room next to his to wake the ladies, but when he heard quiet, he opted to give them a few more minutes and seek out coffee instead. He pulled his leather jacket on to take the fall chill out of the morning air before climbing on his bike and heading out.

The only place that looked open was the famous gas station/convenience store, so Liam took that option. He walked into the shop to see things bustling with customers. So many men dressed in fatigues carrying hunting gear were about getting snacks, sandwiches, and beverages for their outings. Liam sighed and moved toward the coffee machines. He wrangled three cups into a tray, grabbing cream and sugar packets in case that was the drink of choice, though he took his black. He also remembered to take an apple juice for Daniela.

Liam stood patiently in a line before the register, grabbing an impulse buy of a box of Krispy Kreme glazed donuts as he waited. Then, when he was just one person away, there was a tap on his shoulder. He spun around to notice Eddy standing there with a smile and a coffee in her hand.

"You're up early." She smiled at him as she sipped her beverage.

"So are you," he said with surprise.

"Actually, I haven't been to bed yet," Eddy yawned. "The place closes at four, and then I had some clean-up to do, so I'm heading home now. Looks like you got enough coffee for a crowd there."

"Yeah... I'm just grabbing stuff for friends before we hit the road," Liam said.

"Too bad you're leavin'," Eddy added. "It's nice seeing a new handsome face around here."

Liam chuckled as it was his turn at the register. He placed his tray down to grab his wallet and paid for his items.

"I'll get hers too," Liam said, pointing to Eddy's coffee.

"Wow, good-looking and a gentleman too." Eddy grinned. "Not what I expected at all. Now I really wish you were stayin'. I owe you something."

"Nah, just good karma," Liam told her as they walked toward the door. Once they got outside, Liam noticed an orange Dodge Challenger parked near his bike. He also noticed that the car had New York plates on it, and there were two men in brown leather jackets standing around the vehicle.

Liam halted before turning the corner and swiveled to Eddy.

"If you really owe me something, you could do me a favor right now," Liam said in a hushed tone.

"I think I like the way that sounds," Eddy purred.

"This is going to sound weird, but I think those two guys over there are looking for my friends, and not in a good way. Do you think you could distract them away from their car for a few minutes so I could get out of here? I know it's a lot to ask, but..."

"Say no more, honey." Eddy smiled. "Southern hospitality coming up."

Eddy took off the full zip sweatshirt she had on, tied it around her waist, and undid two buttons on her blouse to show off her assets more. She then grabbed Liam's tray of coffee and put hers in the tray as well before sauntering toward the two men.

Eddy turned the corner, stumbled, and spilled the coffees in full view of the two men.

"Shit!" she yelled, causing the men to turn and look at her.

She glanced up and smiled at them, waving them over to her. Eddy had made sure to get enough liquid on her white shirt that it became sheer, showing herself off even more.

"Do you think you fellas could give a lady a hand?" Eddy asked coyly.

The men began their slow walk over as Liam had made his way around the building from the other side so he came up behind them. He watched as the men stood leering and fawning over Eddy's flirting. She made sure to put her hand on one of their arms to keep the man turned toward her and away from spying Liam.

Liam quickly removed his knife from its sheath on his right hip and made two rapid stabs into each tire on the driver's side of the car. He then climbed onto his bike, starting it up with a roar and pulling out of the lot just as the men were turning to look at him and race back to their car. The guys clearly wore Caiman jackets, and Liam sped back to the motel.

He jumped off his bike and leaped onto the patio to pound on the room eight door firmly enough that he rattled the front window of the room.

"Get up!" he yelled.

Olivia pried open the door and stared at Liam groggily.

"What's going on?" she asked.

"We need to leave... now! The Caimans are here looking for you. So grab your shit and get in the van."

Olivia's eyes widened. She turned and yelled something in Spanish to her sister.

"We'll be out in two minutes," she rushed.

Liam stood guard outside the room, and within moments Olivia and Beatriz were leaving the room with their bags. Beatriz held a still sleeping Daniela in her arms as she hurriedly got the toddler into her car seat.

Olivia shut the driver's side door and started the van. She rolled down the window to look at Liam.

"How did they find us?"

"I don't know, and I'm not staying around to ask. I slowed them down for a bit to give us a head start. Let's hope it's enough to get us to Lancaster without any problems. Just be cool about it. Watch your speed and don't draw attention to yourself. They saw me, but I don't know if they are aware of what you're driving. I'll stay a couple of cars behind you. It might help keep them off you a bit. If you need anything, use Bluetooth."

Olivia nodded and backed up the van to leave, and Liam followed behind her on his bike.

Both vehicles drove past the convenience store on the way out of town to get to the highway. Liam glanced and saw the Challenger still parked where it was, with one guy leaning on the passenger door while the other looked to be arguing into his cell phone. Thankfully, it looked like Eddy was long gone from the area.

Traffic on 81 was light on a Sunday morning, allowing the drivers to make good time as they ventured farther south. However, it wasn't long before they turned off 81 to get on 77 south toward North Carolina. They crossed through a foggy, mountainous area before the North Carolina border, prompting Olivia to crackle into Liam's Bluetooth.

"This fog is terrible. I've never driven on a mountain like this," Olivia said.

Liam heard the tension in her voice.

"Just take it slow," Liam told her. "It will get better once we get on the other side. You got this."

Olivia was quiet for a bit, and Liam had trouble figuring out where the van rode in the fog ahead of him.

"Want me to sing to ya?" Liam offered.

"What?" Olivia said, bewildered.

"They say singin' can help calm people down."

"No offense, but I don't think you singing right now will help," Olivia said. Liam heard laughter coming from the van and smiled.

Once the vehicles began their descent on the other side of the mountain, the fog started to thin out and clear. The sign welcoming visitors to North Carolina was visible, along with posts about an upcoming rest stop.

"Let's pull off for a minute," Liam ordered, getting Olivia to go to the rest stop.

Liam parked next to the van, and Beatriz and Daniela raced out so they could go use the restroom. Olivia sat in the driver's seat as Liam walked up to the driver's side window. He saw that Olivia seemed visibly rattled.

"You okay?" Liam asked.

"Yeah, just stressed beyond belief." Olivia sighed. "Between the Caimans and that drive…"

"It's fine if you're scared, you know," Liam told her.

"I never said I was scared," Olivia shot back. "I've got this. Don't worry about me. Worry about yourself."

"Easy, tiger," Liam responded, lifting up his hands. "I'm on your side, remember? Who do you think helped you get out of Hicksville without them spotting you?"

"Well, maybe if you hadn't insisted on us stopping, we would be there already with nothing to worry about," Olivia answered angrily. "Did you ever think of that?"

"Jaysus, you're a piece of work, you know that?" Liam spat back.

Beatriz and Daniela appeared at the van, spying the tail end of the conversation.

"What's wrong?" Beatriz said.

"Nothing," Olivia answered stoically. "Let's get back on the road. We're only two or three hours away."

Liam turned to go before Daniela stepped in front of him.

"Here, Gigante," Daniela said, offering the other half of her peanut butter cup to Liam.

"Thank you, darlin'," Liam answered, taking the candy. "At least one of you is grateful!" he yelled.

Liam munched on the candy as he put his helmet back on and started his bike. He watched as the van left the rest stop lot, and he followed behind.

Most of the trip progressed with radio silence between the two vehicles. It wasn't until hours later that Liam had a call come in when they had just passed Charlotte and were headed toward the South Carolina border. His phone announced that it was his brother, Finn.

"Hey," Liam said curtly.

"How's it going?" Finn inquired.

"Peachy," Liam answered. "The ride has been long, the driver is bitchy, and the Caimans found us in Virginia. But, overall, it's been a shite-ton of fun. How are you? Did you get to sleep late, have breakfast and a warm shower, or did you just tumble with Ginger all morning long? I haven't had any of those things."

"How did the Caimans find you?"

"I have no idea, brother," Liam answered, "but they were waiting for me when I went to get morning coffee. Some quick thinkin' and help got us out of there, but it won't be long until they are onto us again."

"How close are you?" Finn asked.

"Less than an hour, I'd say," Liam replied. "Does the girl know where to go when we get to Lancaster?"

"Yes, we gave Olivia the heads-up about who to contact. I'll ask Siobhan to reach out to them to let them know you guys are close. Do you need me to send some brothers down to help you? You'll only have to be there for a day after you get her to the safe house. After that, they'll make sure she gets on the plane to Peru."

"Nah, I think I'm good," Liam said confidently. "I've got my blade and my gun. I'm covered."

"Christ, Liam," Finn replied angrily. "You can't carry a concealed weapon through those states."

"Right now, I think the illegal carry charge would be pretty low on the list of laws we are breaking, don't you think so, counselor? You want me to get her there safely? Then I'm going to do what I need to do."

"Just keep me updated," Finn told his brother. "And let me know when you're on your way back."

"How's the girl getting back home?" Liam asked about Olivia.

"We're getting her a ticket to fly back to New York when her sister leaves."

"You know you're bringing her back to a shite-storm, right?" Liam said firmly. "Benny will track her down first and do God knows what to find out where her sister is. She'll be dead in a week."

Quiet echoed on the phone line.

"I know," Finn said solemnly. "We tried to convince her to go to Peru and be with her family. She refused. I had the plane ticket purchased, and Da had all the fake IDs made. She said she was coming back no matter what. She's pretty stubborn."

"So I've noticed," Liam grumbled.

"Is she getting to you? She's not falling for the Liam O'Farrell charm?" Finn said sarcastically.

"Feck off, brother." Liam scowled.

"Wow, she is getting to you," Finn replied seriously. "Liam, don't let urges cloud your judgment, okay? You and Da are always saying when feelings get in the way, mistakes are made. Keep your distance."

"Don't start spouting advice off to me," Liam shot back. "You're the little brother and the prospect here, not me. Don't you forget THAT. I'm fine. Go back to your brunch or whatever. I'll talk to you soon."

Liam hung up on the call before Finn had a chance to respond further.

"Feckin' eejit," Liam groused. "No one tells me how to act with a woman. Yeah, she's gorgeous and feisty, but she's a pain in the arse."

"Did you say something?" Olivia's voice answered over Bluetooth.

Liam froze as he had forgotten the mike was open to the van once the call ended.

"Just callin' you a pain in the arse for driving so fast," Liam said, clearing his throat. "Slow the feck down. We're almost there. Don't mess it up now."

"Yeah, yeah," Olivia answered.

Follow your own advice, boy-o, Liam thought. *Don't mess it up now.*

Chapter 6

Late afternoon settled in by the time Olivia drove the van into Lancaster. She asked Beatriz to double-check the address of the safe house they were to go to first. The nearest shelter stood in Rock Hill, not far from Lancaster. Still, Siobhan had arranged a more secret location so they didn't have to take any chances of someone waiting for them to arrive that could cause trouble. So they would go directly to a private home instead and spend the night there. Then Beatriz and Daniela would get transported to Charlotte International Airport for the first flight out. Even the airplane ride was carefully planned, with as short a layover as possible at George Bush Intercontinental Airport in Houston. A Safe Place even managed to get someone willing to escort them to Houston for protection. All the angles seemed planned well, as far as Olivia could tell.

Even though she didn't want to show it, Olivia's one worry was what would happen to her after this. The goal of making sure Beatriz and Daniela escaped was her primary interest. Still, as they got closer to finishing this end of the journey, she had concerns about what might happen afterward. Olivia made arrangements to live with her employer, Erin, temporarily in Harriman while looking for her own place. However, she also knew that Liam had correctly assessed the situation. Benny would realize it was Olivia who assisted Beatriz in getting away. He and the Caimans would try and make her pay for it.

"*Aquí*," Beatriz said as she pointed to a nondescript yellow house set back from the street.

Olivia looked at the rearview mirror and saw that Liam was close behind them. She signaled to turn up the gravel driveway and slowly made her way toward the home. The house appeared small from the outside, and Olivia worried there would be enough space for them.

The van pulled to a stop at the top of the driveway, and Olivia silenced the engine.

"*Espera aquí*," she told Beatriz as Olivia got out of the vehicle. She saw Liam had parked his bike directly behind the van and had taken off his helmet, shaking out his long, black hair.

"I think this is it," Olivia said to Liam quietly. She watched as Liam glanced down at his phone to verify the address.

"Looks right to me," he told her. "Only one way to find out."

Liam strode toward the front porch of the house while Olivia trailed a bit behind. She looked back at the van constantly to ensure that Beatriz and Daniela were safe.

Before Liam knocked, the door swung open. A bearded gentleman appeared and squinted at Liam as he stood.

"Can I help you with something?" the man said warily in a Southern drawl.

Olivia peeked out from behind Liam and came forward.

"I think we're supposed to be here," she said warily. My name is Olivia Guerrero, and—"

"Enough said," the man replied, cutting her off. "Are they in the van?"

"Yes... yes, they are," Olivia replied.

"Okay. I'll open the garage. Pull the van inside so it's out of sight," he said quickly before going back inside and closing the door.

Olivia raced back to the van and got inside, nodding to Beatriz. She waited for the garage to open and slowly moved the vehicle inside. She noticed in the side mirror that Liam ducked into the garage as the car moved in. As soon as the van cleared the opening, the doors began to shut.

The gentleman walked over and opened the passenger door so that Beatriz could exit.

"You must be Beatriz," he said with a smile. "My name's Don. I spoke with Siobhan this morning. We're going to make sure you get home safely, don't worry."

Olivia helped get Daniela out of her car seat before gathering the two bags in the van that belonged to her sister and niece.

"Good." Don nodded. "You packed light, just as we asked. The less time you have to spend waiting around, the better. You'll be able to bring these on the plane with you, so there's no checked luggage. I have your new passports and IDs in the house, along with your tickets. You've probably had a long drive. We can go inside and eat if you would like. My wife, Brandy, has made some excellent barbecue for you."

Don swung the door open so that Beatriz and Daniela could step inside the house. He then turned to Olivia and Liam.

"So, here's the plan," Don began. "It's about a forty-five-minute ride back to the Charlotte airport. They are on the first flight out to Houston at six a.m. Our escort will meet us at the airport at four a.m., so we'll be leaving early. What time is your flight back to New York?" he asked Olivia.

"I think it's at six also," Olivia said, trying to find the ticket information she had. "I don't have my old cell phone. They told me to leave it with them and gave me this burner phone."

"It's okay," Don said, trying to calm Olivia down. "We'll make sure it gets to you. Here's the problem. You two can't stay here tonight."

"Hold on," Liam interrupted, stepping up. "No offense, pal, but I don't know you from Adam. So how do I know they will be safe with you all night?"

"I'm sorry, but that's the way this all works. It's better if we all aren't in the exact location. It's a tight squeeze here as it is with two more people in my home. So I booked a room for you at the Carriage Inn down the road. It's far from fancy, but it's just one night and in the budget for all this."

"One room?" Olivia added with surprise.

"Sorry, that's all I could get," Don apologized. "Besides, you should have your protection with you anyway. From what Siobhan told me on the phone, you already ran into some problems. But, unfortunately, we can't take any chances. Leave the van here. I have someone coming to claim it tomorrow, who will dispose of it."

"How am I supposed to get to the hotel and the airport?" Olivia asked.

Don glanced over at Liam, and Olivia turned to look at him. Liam smiled and shrugged his shoulders.

"I guess I'm the chauffeur now as well as the bodyguard, babysitter, and ATM." Liam huffed.

"He only has a motorcycle," Olivia complained. "Can't I just stay here with Bea and Daniela? They might need me."

"Trust me, they will be fine," Don reassured. "There's no other way that will ensure this all works and everyone is safe."

Olivia rubbed her temples as a stress headache made it hard to think.

"Okay," she said, resigned. "I guess that's it. Let me get my bag out of the van."

"Make sure there's nothing left in there," Don added. "I'll see you two in the morning, bright and early."

Olivia went to the van to retrieve her bag. She heard the garage door close and lock as Don went into the house. Olivia quickly scanned the van to see if anything else remained. She noticed the Winnie the Pooh bear lying on the back seat. It had been Daniela's companion for the last several months. Olivia snatched it up so she could return it to her niece in the morning before slamming the van door shut.

Liam stood by the side door that was the exit from the garage. He opened the door, so Olivia could walk through first. She paced directly to his motorcycle while stuffing the Pooh bear into her backpack.

"So, how do we do this?" Olivia barked.

"Do what?" Liam said. He opened one of the compartments on his bike and removed the spare helmet he had. Liam handed it to her.

"It's easy," Liam told her. "You put the helmet on, and I drive. Just try not to fall off."

Olivia looked on as Liam straddled the bike and waited for her to get on behind him. Olivia went to put the helmet on, adjusting her long brown hair so that she could fit the contraption on her head, but she had trouble with the chin strap. Liam let out an audible, irritated sigh.

"Let me help you," he moaned as he dismounted the bike.

Liam placed his large right hand under Olivia's chin, tilting her head up, so she stared directly into his dark eyes. It was the first time she had gazed at him up close, and she studied the determined look on his face. The smell of his leather jacket permeated the air, and the touch of his rough hands on her chin combined to make the moment more electric to Olivia than she had expected.

"Ready now, Your Highness?" Liam added sarcastically as the helmet adjusted to fit perfectly.

"You're such an ass," Olivia responded.

"I do my best," Liam told her as he sat on the Harley and started it up.

Olivia cautiously climbed behind Liam and positioned herself on the passenger seat. She lightly placed her hands on Liam's hips.

"You're going to have to hold on tighter than that, darlin'," Liam spoke.

Liam reached back and grasped Olivia's hands, pulling them tightly around his waist. She gasped as he forced her body to press against his.

"Make sure to keep your feet up on the pegs," he said into the Bluetooth headset of Olivia's helmet. "I don't want to mess up your fancy pedicure."

"Just drive," Olivia grumbled.

Olivia held firmly to Liam as he maneuvered and traversed the streets of Lancaster to make his way to the Carriage Inn. She kept her grip and closed her eyes often, feeling uneasy throughout the ride. She did find comfort, however, in wrapping her arms around the biker. Olivia found herself resting her head on his back and holding her hands on his muscular body. Even through his leather jacket, she knew there were ripples underneath unlike any she had experienced before.

A hint of disappointment enveloped Olivia when the ride ended at the hotel. She opened her eyes as the engine turned off, and she gazed upon the building. Liam turned off the motorcycle and took off his helmet before dismounting and looking back at Olivia. He shrugged his shoulders and went to speak before Olivia cut him off.

"I know, I know... it's not the Ritz," she said, waving him off.

Liam removed his bag from the bike and walked to the front entrance with Olivia trailing behind him. She noticed she was watching Liam's movements more than before. He had a confident swagger when he walked, no matter what he seemed to be doing at the moment. As soon as he entered the lobby, he put his hand out to stop Olivia from walking farther until he looked around to check for any problems.

"Take a seat," he ordered. "I'll get us checked in. I don't want anyone knowing your name or who you are."

"Why?"

"At this point, I don't think we can trust anyone. Your sister and niece might be fine where they are, but we're out in the open and are easy to spot. We need to be careful. Just sit."

Liam turned to Olivia, gripped her shoulders, and planted her on the nearby cushioned chair in the lobby while he went to the front desk.

Olivia watched the exchange between Liam and the woman working at the desk. While she couldn't hear the conversation going on, she knew by Liam's demeanor and the woman's laugh at the counter that he was putting on his charm. In moments, Liam returned, holding the key card for their room.

"I tried to see if I could charm another room out of her," Liam said as they walked toward the elevator. "No dice. I guess you're stuck with me."

"Great." Olivia sighed.

Olivia trudged behind Liam out of the elevator and down the hall to their room. Liam flung the door open, walking inside and doing a cursory check of the place. He nodded and waved Olivia in, and she entered.

"Well, it's better than that other place in Virginia," Olivia said as she plopped down on one of the double beds, feeling no give on the mattress.

"Trust me, I've stayed in much worse places than both of them." Liam laughed.

"I'll bet you have," Olivia answered. "So, now what?"

"What? We kick back and relax until morning, and then we can both get out of here. We have to get up early to get to the airport if you want to be there to say goodbye to your sister."

Olivia reached into her bag, took out the Winnie the Pooh bear, and gave it a small hug.

"I guess I'm really feeling it now. Bea and Daniela are going to be gone. I might not see them again for years."

Olivia's chest tightened a little, and her eyes began to well up with tears.

"Oh no," Liam said to her. "No crying, okay? You knew this was going to happen and should have been ready for it."

"Are you this much of a callous asshole all the time?" Olivia spat.

"Pretty much," Liam agreed. "It's not callous—it's called being realistic. It's the way it is, darlin'. You could probably still go with them if you want to. I'm sure Finn can arrange it for you. Otherwise, you have to deal with it. Welcome to the adult world."

"God, you're a self-centered prick," Olivia yelled, throwing a pillow at Liam. She watched as he grabbed the pillow out of the air and placed it down on the other bed.

"That's me." Liam chuckled. He lay down on the other bed, tucking the pillows behind his head.

Olivia climbed onto her bed, tucked a pillow under her head, and rolled onto her side to face away from Liam. She gripped the Pooh bear a little bit tighter as she shut her eyes.

A loud series of bangs jolted Olivia up on the bed, gasping for air. She turned and looked at Liam and saw he slept. At the same time, the

TV blared with some military movie sounding explosions and gunfire every ten seconds. She reached over and grabbed the remote from the nightstand between the two beds to turn the TV off. Then, she climbed off the creaking bed and went into the bathroom.

Olivia splashed water on her face and then tied her hair back into a ponytail. Everything was so close to being finished, and the anxiety of it all crept into each thought she had. Once Beatriz and Daniela got on that plane, all their lives would change forever. Olivia breathed deeply, wiped her eyes, and went back out to the bedroom, where Liam lightly snored.

Olivia noticed Liam had shed his leather jacket, exposing some of the physique she felt on their bike ride. She could see the taut forearms and biceps, both well-covered with tattoos. The black T-shirt he wore clung to his body, letting her see just a hint of the definition in his abs and chest. She stood watching him breathe in and out for minutes with a fascination.

What a waste, she thought to herself when considering her room-mate. *How could a man who looks that good be such an asshole? Why do women fall for that?*

Olivia tried to justify it all to herself when Liam's snoring gave in and became light coughing, enough to rouse him from his sleep. He peeled his eyes open and spied Olivia at the foot of the bed, staring at him.

"Something I can do for you?" he asked.

"Yes... I mean, no... I mean... it's after seven. Maybe we should get something to eat," Olivia rambled, trying to cover up her embarrassment at being caught staring.

"Okay," Liam said, swinging his feet off the bed so he could stand. Then, in one stride, he was next to Olivia, staring down at her. Olivia became mesmerized by his piercing gaze. Liam stood more than a foot taller than her, and the imposing figure rested his palms on her shoulders. Electricity shot through Olivia at the touch.

"You're going to need to move," Liam said quietly. "I need to take a piss."

Liam's crudeness snapped the spell Olivia had fallen under, and she stepped to the side so he could pass. Liam entered the bathroom, and Olivia heard the immediate sound of him urinating.

"You could at least close the door!" she yelled.

Laughter came from the bathroom as Olivia looked and saw the door swing closed.

The toilet's flush and running of the water in the sink followed, much to Olivia's relief. Liam paced back over to his side of the room and grabbed his leather jacket.

"Let's go," Liam said, twirling his key ring on his finger.

The two rode the elevator silently down to the lobby, where Liam again approached the woman at the front desk.

"Hey there, darlin'," Liam said smoothly. When speaking to the woman, Olivia noticed he turned up his Irish accent, making the blond blush immediately.

"What can I do for you?" she asked excitedly.

"We're looking for a place to have dinner and relax a bit," Liam spoke. "We've been on the road for a few days, and I'm missing my Irish surroundings, you know? So is there a place nearby where I can get a Guinness and some Irish food?"

"Really?" Olivia chimed in.

"Shush," Liam said to her, waving off her concerns.

"Well," the clerk responded, "there aren't too many places like that around here. The nearest location I can think of is over in Waxhaw, about twenty minutes from here. Mary O'Neill's Irish Pub. I think it's just what you're looking for."

"Ahh, just the name warms the cockles of my heart," Liam said with a grin as he grabbed his chest. "Thank you so much for the help, Darlene," Liam added as Olivia noticed he took a glance at the nametag the woman wore.

"I can give you directions if you need them," Darlene added happily.

"I think we can handle it from here, Darlene, thank you," Olivia insisted, tugging Liam away from the front desk.

Olivia pulled Liam out the front door and began marching toward the motorcycle.

"What's up with you?" Liam asked, stepping faster to keep up with the stomping Olivia. Olivia spun around and faced Liam when she reached the bike.

"You are what the problem is," Olivia hissed. "The way you treat women... you just think you can charm your way to get whatever you want, and women will just fall at your feet. It's disgusting."

"There's nothing wrong with a little flirting," Liam stated. "I thought women liked to be treated special like that."

"There's a difference between treating a woman well and what you do," Olivia answered. "You're doing it with the hopes of getting into their pants without any thought about them."

"That's not true... at least not all the time." Liam grinned. "Seems to me that you feel a little jealous about it."

"Right," Olivia scoffed. "I'm jealous that you don't treat me like a toy for you to play with and discard. You got me. Can we just go eat, please?"

Liam sighed deeply and got on the bike as Olivia put her helmet on.

"Need help with the helmet again?" Liam smirked.

"Just drive, wiseass," Olivia barked as she strapped the helmet herself. She gripped Liam tightly as he pulled out of the parking lot.

Liam drove on 521 North to South Carolina 75. They crossed just over the border into North Carolina before arriving at the pub. Liam parked the bike out front, and Olivia trailed behind him as they walked into the place.

The pub immediately reminded Olivia of Millie Malone's, the Irish pub she worked at in Harriman. It had the same cozy feel, and the bar area was filled with patrons while many of the wood tables were occupied with diners. A waitress walked over to Liam and Olivia as soon as they entered.

"Good evening," she said cheerily. "Just the two of you?"

"Yes, ma'am," Liam asked. "Do you have room for us?"

"We are a little crowded tonight because we have music," the waitress replied. "I can sit you outside where the band will be if you'd like. I know it's October, but it's still quite warm tonight."

"What kind of music is playing?" Liam asked with trepidation.

"Irish folk music," she responded. "An artist named Aoife Scott. She's from Ireland and..."

"Oh, I know who she is, darlin'," Liam said, clapping his hands and smiling. "Yes, we'll sit outside!" he exclaimed.

"You're in for a treat," Liam said to Olivia as they followed the waitress through the maze of tables to the outside deck.

"Oh, goodie," Olivia said with an eye roll.

"Stop being a thorn in my arse," Liam scolded. "This is going to be heavenly."

The waitress sat the couple at a table in the corner, facing the area where the band was setting up.

"There she is," Liam said quietly, pointing to the redhead standing behind where the microphone stood.

Olivia broke out in laughter as she glanced at the menu in front of her.

"What's so funny?" Liam said, glaring at Olivia.

"You are." She laughed again. "You're totally fangirling over her."

"She's a fabulous singer," Liam defended. "Much better than anything that Britney girl sings."

Olivia laughed harder, causing a snort to escape.

"How out of touch are you? Do you know anything about current music?"

"I know enough not to listen to it," Liam growled.

The waitress reappeared at the table and asked about drinks.

"A pint of Guinness for me," Liam said triumphantly.

"I guess I'll have the same." Olivia sighed.

The waitress looked at Olivia warily.

"I'm going to have to see some ID from you, honey," the waitress added.

Olivia instinctively reached for her purse to get her driver's license when Liam reached over the table and grabbed her hands to stop her.

"She'll have a Coke," Liam interrupted. "She's always trying that." Liam smiled.

The waitress smiled and walked off while Olivia shot a stern look Liam's way.

"What the hell?" she asked, jerking her hands away from him. "I wanted a beer."

"You can't go showing your ID around here," Liam rebuked. "No one can know who you are. We can't leave a trail anywhere."

"I hate to tell you, Lurch, but you stick out like a sore thumb everywhere we go," Olivia replied. "If anything, they'll spot you before me."

"Can we try to at least make this a pleasant meal and enjoy the food and music without all the constant backtalk?" Liam asked.

The waitress delivered the Guinness and placed a glass filled with Coke in front of Olivia. She smiled broadly, took the wrapper off the straw, and took a sip.

"Hmm, yummy," she said sarcastically.

"Ready to order?" the waitress asked.

"I'll have Shepherd's pie," Liam told her.

"I'll have the Kilmaine burger," Olivia said, handing the menu to the waitress.

"And can we get an order of the wings, too, darlin'?" Liam asked.

"You bet," the waitress responded. "How hot do you want them?"

"What do you think you can handle, Princess?" Liam asked Olivia snidely.

Olivia stared back at Liam.

"As hot as you've got," Olivia said, accepting the challenge.

"Now we're talkin'!" Liam laughed.

The wings arrived at the table, well-coated with sauce. Just the scent wafting off the crispy skin proved enough to be felt in Olivia's nostrils, but she was not backing down. The waitress placed a stack of napkins at the table as well.

"Enjoy," she told the couple.

Liam picked up a wing and inhaled.

"Oh, yeah," he said, bringing the wing up to his lips. "Are you sure you're up to this?"

"I grew up on Peruvian food and ají sauces, Irishman. So I think I can handle whatever you can throw at me."

Olivia grasped the chicken wing and took a healthy bite. She chewed and swallowed without any issue, feeling a bit of heat and burn, but coping well with it. She smiled at Liam after taking a second bite.

Liam tore into the wing he held, removing the meat deftly in one fell swoop. Olivia watched as he quickly picked up a second one and went through the same process. She rose to the occasion and did the same.

It was after that second wing that Olivia noticed Liam began to sweat. The tops of his cheeks above his beard flushed, and even the tips of his ears reddened.

"You okay there?" Olivia said as she plucked a drumette from the two wings left on the plate.

"Fine." Liam coughed, gulping the rest of his Guinness.

Olivia finished off her third wing and then pointed at the lone flat left on the plate. It was swimming in the spicy sauce.

"That last one is yours." She pointed.

"No, you can go ahead and have it if you want," Liam said, backing off and coughing again. "I don't want to fill up before my meal."

"Your loss." Olivia smiled as she grabbed the wing and polished it off, making sure to suck the sauce off her fingers victoriously as Liam looked on.

"Can I get another pint here?" Liam bellowed, clearly burning. "And some bread?"

Three pieces of soda bread later, Liam's fiery mouth had calmed, and the entrees arrived. Olivia happily munched on her hamburger, gloating in her small victory over Liam. At the same time, Liam polished off a generous helping of Shepherd's pie laden with lamb, peas, carrots, and mashed potatoes. Just as they finished eating, the band started up, and Aoife Scott began to sing.

Olivia was pleasantly surprised by the sweet sound of the singer's voice. With just a small band of a guitar player and a banjo player, they sang through ballads, traditional Irish songs, and more. Every once in a while, Olivia looked over at Liam and saw him singing along or closing his eyes and enjoying the music.

Aoife broke into the next song, which she said was called "The Wallflower Waltz." As she began singing the tune, Liam leaped up from his chair and stood in front of Olivia, holding out his hand.

"Let's dance," he said to her, taking her right hand in his.

"This isn't the kind of dancing I do," Olivia said as she struggled to remain seated.

"Let me lead, and you won't have a problem," Liam insisted, pulling her up.

Liam's size dwarfed Olivia as he put her left hand firmly in his while placing his right hand on her hip. He gingerly led her around the small makeshift dance area, waltzing and smiling down as they moved. Olivia obediently followed his lead and caught on to the steps quickly. Before she knew it, they were gliding around. She felt giddy inside as they moved to the music.

The entire porch area had broken out in applause when the music stopped, including Aoife Scott and the band. They had been the only ones dancing, and Olivia flushed with embarrassment. At the same time, Liam took a bow before leading Olivia back to their table.

"Where did you learn how to dance like that?" Olivia said with surprise.

"My ma," Liam said proudly. "She insisted my brother and I learn proper dancing. She always said dancing was a great way to impress a woman and make her feel special."

"Sounds like a smart lady," Olivia said as she sipped her second Coke. "I'd love to meet her someday."

"Ah, well, that would be quite something," Liam lamented. He picked up the glass of Connemara whiskey he had ordered and sipped it. "She passed a long time ago. I was just a teenager."

"Oh... I'm sorry... I didn't know," Olivia said compassionately.

"No way you could know, right?" Liam replied. He took another sip of his drink and put the glass down. "She would have liked you, for sure. You're tough and don't take shite from anyone... even if you aren't Irish."

Olivia smiled at Liam as he picked up the check the waitress had left and used cash to pay the tab.

"We should go," Liam said, standing up from the table and glancing at his watch. "It's after ten, and we need to get to the airport at four."

Liam walked to the front of the stage as Aoife sang and bowed to her as she blew him a quick kiss before making his way out.

Once they were on the bike and headed back to the hotel, Olivia dutifully put her arms around Liam again as they drove. She held tightly as the vibrations from the motorcycle worked through her body.

They arrived safely back at the Carriage Inn and walked through the door side by side, laughing about the night they had. Darlene was still behind the front desk when they entered.

"How was Mary O'Neill's?" she asked.

"Perfect!" Olivia answered before Liam could say anything as she moved toward the elevator.

When they arrived at the room, Olivia kicked off her sneakers and went to her backpack.

"I'm going to jump in the shower and change," she said to Liam as he took off his boots.

"Knock yourself out," he offered with a smile.

Olivia showered and readied herself for bed, slipping into the tank top and sleep shorts she had for nightwear. She tied her hair back once more and smiled at herself in the mirror, pleased with the way she looked and how well the evening had gone. Just that brief outing made her forget about all the anxiety that had surrounded the trip so far.

Olivia stepped out of the bathroom and moved toward the beds when she stopped cold. Liam lay on his bed, the bed cover pulled down, clad just in his black boxer briefs. She did all she could to hold in a gasp as she took in his giant form. Muscles rippled over his body, and Olivia saw that tattoos not only covered his arms but a good part of his chest as well. She had never seen a man with such a definition before, and she couldn't help but stare.

"Everything good?" Liam asked her when he caught her staring. "This is how I sleep. I hope that's good with you."

"It's fine," Olivia said, her voice trembling as she sat on her double bed. She quickly pulled the blanket down and slid under the top sheet, the blanket immediately feeling like it would be much too warm for how she felt at the moment. Finally, she reached over and turned off the light between the two beds, leaving the couple in darkness.

Olivia did her best to control her breathing to make herself calm down.

"Liam?" Olivia said quietly.

"Hmm?" he grunted.

"Thank you for tonight," she offered. "It was just what I needed to relax some."

"No problem," Liam said sincerely. "I do have something I want to tell you too."

Olivia held her breath with some anticipation.

"What's that?" she managed to get out.

"I won't challenge your toughness when it comes to wings again. You won that one. I'll get you next time. Now go to sleep."

A giggle escaped her lips as she melted into her pillow.

Chapter 7

The incessant beeping of a cell phone pulled Liam out of a pleasant sleep. Exhaustion had caught up with him last night after dinner, and he wanted nothing more than to roll over and get back to his dreams. He squinted at the numbers on his phone and saw it was almost 3:00 a.m. The ride to Charlotte Airport would be about forty-five minutes, so they would have to get moving right away.

An annoyed groan escaped his lips as he looked over at Olivia, still sound asleep on her bed. She lay on her side, facing away from Liam. Even with just the sliver of light from the parking lot peeking through the curtains, he could make out the curve of her back and the bronze legs she bared in her sleep shorts. The longer Liam lay there staring at Olivia, the more feelings began to stir inside him. Finally, he became acutely aware that he was clad only in his black boxer briefs and pushed himself into the bathroom, remembering to close the door this time so that he could compose himself.

He emerged a few minutes later in better control of himself. As Liam turned the corner from the bathroom entrance, he spied Olivia standing up, facing away from where he was. She was just putting on her jeans and caught a glimpse of her slowly pulling them over her behind. He suppressed the groan he felt in his throat and instead tried to come up with something to say to let Olivia know he was back in the room.

"Good, you're up," he said abruptly. "We need to get on the road."

"Yeah, I heard you in the bathroom and thought I would get dressed quick so we could go," Olivia replied. She sat down to pull her sneakers on before turning to Liam.

"You look like you're half asleep," Olivia mentioned.

"Four hours of sleep really doesn't cut it for me after days like this."

"I thought with the Sand Hogs and the Cosantóir, you were used to staying up until all hours of the night." Olivia smirked.

"Well, that starts to wear on you after years of doing it," Liam admitted as he put his boots on. "The younger guys can still do stuff like that. I tend to find other ways to expend my energy nowadays."

"I bet you do," Olivia told him as she rolled her eyes.

Olivia plucked the Winnie the Pooh from the bed. She stuffed it into her backpack before declaring to Liam that she was ready to go.

"You have your ticket?" Liam said before they left the room for the last time.

"It's electronic—on my burner phone," Olivia replied.

The duo made their way out of the hotel and to Liam's bike. The air was chilly in the darkness, and Olivia shivered a bit as she waited to get on the motorcycle.

"You don't have a jacket or something?" Liam chided.

"I didn't think this was going to be a long trip," Olivia responded. "I only had two days' worth of clothes."

Liam shook his head and grumbled before digging into one of the side compartments of the bike. He pulled out a green hooded sweatshirt and tossed it to Olivia.

"Wear that," he commanded.

Olivia slipped it over her head, and the sweatshirt went down to her knees. Her arms didn't show through the sleeves.

"It's a little big," she said, her voice muffled by the hood of the sweat-shirt that concealed her face.

"It's either that or freeze on the back of the bike for forty-five minutes. Your choice," Liam told her as he put his helmet on and handed Olivia hers.

Liam looked on as Olivia pulled the hood of the sweatshirt back and put the helmet on. The sweatshirt looked more like a baggy dress on Olivia, and Liam couldn't help but crack a smile.

Once on board the Harley, Liam headed out up 521 North to cross into North Carolina and get to the airport. Traffic was virtually nonex-istent at that time of the morning. The sun was still hours away from rising on a Monday, and there were even fewer people out and about.

Liam got to Charlotte Airport a bit before 4:00 a.m. and parked his bike in short-term parking. The couple made their way through the near-empty airport, with many areas not even opened yet. They waited just outside the security checkpoint to meet Beatriz and Daniela so Olivia could say goodbye.

Liam spied the Starbucks nearby, and it was open, so he ventured over to grab a cup of black coffee. He also bought a can of Coke, partly a joke, to give Olivia and a couple of snacks if she was hungry. The entire time he waited at Starbucks, he kept a close eye on her, watching Olivia as she sat, tapping her feet nervously.

When he walked back and handed her the can of soda, Olivia chuck-led.

"I thought this was funnier than coffee, but if you want one, I can..."

"No, no, this is perfect," Olivia said as she popped the can open.

Liam sat and sipped his coffee until the sound of pattering feet nearby caught his attention. He looked up and saw Daniela running full speed at Olivia.

"*¡Tía!*" the little girl shouted as she wrapped her arms around Olivia.

Liam rose from his seat and saw Beatriz moving cautiously, with a man and woman walking behind her. As they approached, Liam recognized the man as Don.

"Everything okay?" Liam asked as the group got together.

"No problems," Don assured. "We had a trail car follow us just to make sure all was well, and no one seemed to be following us. Emily will be traveling with them to Houston, and she will fly back once we know they are safely on their way to Peru. I don't want to be a jerk or anything, but we need to say goodbyes now to get Beatriz and Daniela through security. Anyone needs a ticket beyond that point, so they will be safer."

Liam watched on as Olivia said a tearful goodbye to her sister. They spoke softly to each other in Spanish. Liam could tell Olivia did all she could to assure Beatriz that this was the best solution for her and Daniela's safety. Olivia then bent down to Daniela, hugged her tightly and kissed her, and handed her the Winne the Pooh to travel with. Daniela hugged the bear and then turned to look at Liam. She paced over in front of him and stood, curling her finger so that Liam would crouch down to be about her size.

"*Adios*, Gigante," Daniela said sadly.

"Goodbye, Little One," Liam said, patting her on the head.

Daniela reached out and gave Liam a hug, surprising him. He gently put his arms around her to hug her back, patting her on the back.

"Here," he whispered to her, handing her two packages of peanut butter cups. "For the plane ride."

"Thank you," she whispered back with a smile, stuffing the candy into her jacket pocket. She then handed the Pooh bear to Liam.

"For you," she insisted.

"I can't take your bear," Liam told her, pushing it away.

"You need it so you won't be lonely," Daniela replied. "Mama said *Tía* is leaving you too. So now you have a friend."

"Yes, yes, I do." Liam smiled. "*Slán abhaile.*"

"What does that mean?" Daniela said with a laugh.

"It means safe home," Liam told her. "That's my other language, just like you have another one."

"Maybe you can teach me one day when you visit," Daniela asked.

"Maybe," Liam replied.

Beatriz came over and gathered up Daniela and hugged Liam.

"Thank you," she whispered in his ear as she sobbed. "Make sure she stays safe."

"I'll do my best," Liam vowed.

Don and Emily hustled Beatriz and Daniela toward the security checkpoint for International flights. At the same time, Olivia and Liam watched for as long as they could. Liam finally broke the silence.

"We need to get you to your flight," Liam said softly, placing a hand on Olivia's shoulder.

Olivia simply nodded as she continued to wipe tears away from her face.

"They'll be good, right?" Olivia asked as they walked briskly toward the domestic checkpoint.

"I think every precaution has been taken to ensure that," Liam told her.

Once they reached the security area for domestic flights, more people waited around, putting Liam a bit further on guard. Again, he scanned the crowd, making sure he didn't spot anyone or anything unusual.

"You... you should probably go and get in line for security," Liam said, pointing to the line that had already formed.

Olivia looked up at Liam, her eyes filled with tears.

"I'm... I'm scared," Olivia admitted to him.

"Dammit, woman, you're the toughest girl I know... even tougher than a lot of the biker groupies I've come across in my years. If anyone can handle this, it's you. So go back to New York and get somewhere safe. I'll be back home tonight, and I'll check on you, I promise. Okay?"

Olivia nodded and hugged Liam tightly. The feel of her body pressed tightly to his warmed Liam, and he held on for an extra beat to keep her close.

"*Slán abhaile*," he whispered to her.

Olivia took two steps back from Liam, still facing him.

"Besides, I need to get my sweatshirt back from you. You look feckin' ridiculous in that," he scoffed, eliciting a laugh from Olivia.

Liam stood watch as Olivia moved onto the security line. All seemed fine as she made slow progress toward the checkpoint. Only when Liam heard a man and woman yell, "Watch it," he turned to see what was going on. A few paces back from Olivia was a rugged, bearded man moving through the crowd toward her. A hint of recognition crossed Liam's mind, and he began to move.

He made it two steps before Liam felt a tug on his jacket.

"Going somewhere?" a young Hispanic smiled at him. Liam shot a look to his other hand and saw he held a knife in it. Reacting quickly, he grabbed the hand on his jacket, twisted it, and held it in an armbar before Liam leveled the heel of his boot directly into the young man's knee. Anyone watching could see the kneecap twist and move in the man's jeans before he crumpled to the floor in agony.

Liam sprang toward the security line with the other Caiman, just one person behind Olivia. When the crowd heard the injured man cry out, people turned to look, including Olivia. Liam locked eyes with her and shouted.

"Move!" he said to Olivia, waving his arm to the right. He saw Olivia notice the man behind her now, but she was frozen with fear.

Liam gripped a purple carry-on bag from the woman next to him, took two steps, and swung with all his might, knocking the Caiman and the two people next to him to the ground. The glint of a blade skittered across the airport floor, away from the reach of the biker Liam had knocked down.

Liam grasped Olivia's hand and dragged her with him. He caught another glimpse of the Caiman on the floor. The man smiled at Liam to confirm Liam's suspicions.

"We need to run," Liam said, holding tight to Olivia's hand. She did her best to keep up with him, and once they were outside and got to Liam's bike, he wasted no time in getting the helmet onto Olivia's head. Then, he hopped on the bike and started it up, driving off from the airport without saying anything else.

"What happened?" Olivia cried. "Are Bea and Danni safe? What's going on?"

"I don't know about your sister and your niece," Liam admitted as he spoke into the helmet microphone, driving faster. "Let's pray they got to a safe area."

"Were they Caimans?" Olivia asked.

"Not just Caimans," Liam answered solemnly. "That was Marcos... they call him The Butcher."

"*El Carnicero*," Olivia whispered.

"What?" Liam asked.

"*El Carnicero*... it means the butcher... I've heard Benny mention his name before, and not in good ways."

"I can confirm for you that his name is never used in a good way," Liam answered. "If he's coming after you, it's because Benny told him to."

"What are we going to do?" Olivia panicked.

Liam swerved the motorcycle onto I-85 North and sped faster than he ever had with a passenger on board. He noticed the tighter grip of Olivia's hands as they tried to wrap around his waist.

"I know where we can go," he said confidently.

Chapter 8

L iam drove for hours, right through sunrise and beyond, while barely saying a word to Olivia. Constant looks in his side mirrors to see if it looked like they were being followed were the norm for most of the trip. Only when Olivia started to fidget a bit on the back of the bike did Liam speak up.

"If you keep twitching around like that, you're going to send both of us spilling onto the pavement," Liam grumbled.

"I'm sorry," Olivia exclaimed, "but three hours or so on the back of this thing isn't easy. Besides, I have to pee. So we need to stop."

"We really shouldn't," Liam argued.

"Your choice," Olivia answered. "But in about two minutes, I am going to soak this seat, and then we'll both be miserable."

"Like I'm not already," Liam complained.

He signaled to get off at an exit just outside of Rocky Mount. He pulled into the first gas station he could find and parked at the pump, turning the bike off. Olivia dismounted in a flash and ran toward the storefront before Liam could even say anything to her.

He dutifully picked up the gas hose to fill up the bike while he waited for Olivia and filled the tank. Liam kept a careful eye on the roadways nearby for any signs of anyone who might be on their tail but saw no one. As he went to put the pump back and walked toward the store to pay for the gas, his phone rang. A quick look told him it was Finn.

"Hey," Liam said into the phone.

"Are you two all right? What the heck happened?" Finn asked.

"Caimans tried to ambush us at the airport. They went right after the girl. Did the sister get off all right?"

"Yeah, they made it to Houston," Finn said. "I guess there was some ruckus with people trying to get into the secure area after she passed through, but they're fine. They are waiting for the connection to Lima now."

"Finn, do you know who The Butcher is?" Liam said solemnly.

"Can't say I do," Finn replied, "but he doesn't sound like someone I want to know."

"He's not," Liam replied. "Have Da or Preacher fill you in on him. He's the one after the girl, and he won't stop until his job is done. We need to hide out for a little bit before coming back."

"That sounds like a good plan. Where will you go?"

"I know a place that's safe," Liam responded. "I can't tell you where for our safety. You have to trust me. I'll reach out if I need to or when I can."

"How the fuck do they keep finding you?" Finn asked.

Liam pulled his wallet out to pay for the gas and knocked the Winnie the Pooh bear out of his pocket. He stared down at it as it sat on the floor before he scooped it up. He gazed at the plastic brown eyes of the bear.

"I have a few theories on that. I'll get back to you. Talk to you soon."

"Keep me posted. Be safe, brother," Finn said as he hung up.

Olivia reached Liam just as he moved back from the counter.

"I feel much better, thank you." Olivia sighed. "Is everything okay?"

"Come outside," Liam ordered, leading Olivia out by the elbow.

"Take it easy," Olivia said, yanking her arm away as they reached the front of the store. "What's going on?"

"Where did the kid get this from?" Liam asked, shaking the bear in front of Olivia's eyes.

"I don't remember exactly," Olivia said. "She got it as a birthday present."

"From who?"

"I don't know. It came with a bunch of presents to the apartment."

Liam marched back toward his Harley and stood next to it. He reached into the sheath at his hip and pulled his knife out, taking a close look at the bear. He then deftly pried out the left eye of the bear. As it came free, a small button from behind it popped out and hit the ground.

"The fucker has been tracking you the whole time," Liam said as he and Olivia stared down at the beacon. Liam stomped it with the heel of his boot before tossing the tracer in the nearby trash.

"That should at least buy us some time," Liam told Olivia as he slipped his helmet back on.

"Why... why would that be in there?" Olivia questioned.

"Because Benny wants to know where his daughter... and probably your sister too... are at all times. We don't know how long that has been in there, but my guess is it's been a while. If the little one had taken this on the plane with her, they would know exactly where they were going and when they would get there. That should solve part of the problem."

"It should be everything," Olivia said. "Without tracking us, he can't find me. We should be fine now."

"I wish it were that easy," Liam conceded. "The Butcher... he's a hired killer. He doesn't get paid until he's finished. So he won't just walk away from you. Besides, you're a challenge for him now. You got away once, and he hates to lose. My guess is he'll do whatever he has to so he can find you and make an example of you."

Liam saw Olivia visibly shaken by his statement.

"I'm sorry, but you need to know the truth of that."

"What... what am I going to do?" Olivia asked fearfully.

"We're going to use the extra time we have to hide out, regroup, and devise a plan. We've already spent too much time around here. Get on the bike so we can go. You have to trust me now. Let me do what I'm good at."

Liam sat on the bike, and Olivia hesitated for a moment. He held his gloved hand out to her before she took it, and he led her toward the back of the bike. Once she was on, they were out onto the highway heading on 64 East as fast as Liam could.

Several hours later, Liam crossed the Virginia Dare Bridge and headed to the Outer Banks. Traffic slowed a bit, but a Monday in October proved much more manageable than the same day in July. Liam did his best to remember the landmarks he knew from the area as they made their way along the ocean side of South Virginia Dare Trail. He slowed the bike down as they moved past the spacious luxury houses on each side of the street before Liam finally ducked the motorcycle down a side street that had a No Outlet sign posted with a Private Beach Access sign just under it.

He pulled the Harley into the driveway of a large brown home positioned on the beachfront. Once the bike was placed under the carport next to the garage, he turned the engine off and dismounted. Olivia followed suit.

"Where are we?" Olivia asked as she removed her helmet.

"Shhh," Liam said, holding his index finger up to his lips. He walked over to the door that led to the garage and stared at it.

"Ah, feckin' keypad lock," Liam complained. He fished into his pocket, looking for something.

"Liam, we're in enough trouble already," Olivia said in a hushed tone. "Breaking into someone's house in daylight may not be the best move. Let's get out of here."

"Quiet!" Liam hushed before grabbing his keys from his pocket. He looked at a key fob and then punched in the number 121688. He heard the lock on the door release and turned the handle to open it.

"Get in," he hurried.

"No," Olivia said staunchly. "We're going to get caught."

"We will if you don't get in," Liam said, ushering her inside. "Hear that beeping? That's the alarm that will go off in thirty seconds if we're not inside."

"Jesus! Let's go!" Olivia shouted.

Liam pushed her back in and shut the door. He walked over to the control panel on the wall and punched in a code to silence the alarm.

"How do you know the codes to get in here? Someone you robbed, beat up, or blackmailed along the way?" Olivia said.

"Not exactly," Liam said. He walked up the wooden steps and opened the door that led to the house. He flipped the lights on and tossed his keys onto the oak bar that lined the far wall of the room before making his way around the bar.

"What are you doing? We need to get out of here!" Olivia insisted.

"Want a drink?" Liam asked. "I'm parched."

He bent down and opened the mini-fridge under the bar.

"Slim pickings," Liam said as he tossed Olivia a bottle of water while he grabbed a nitro can of Guinness. Then, he went to the wall behind him and took a pint glass to pour the beer into.

Liam noticed Olivia staring at him as he poured his beer.

"What?" he said.

"Maybe you want to make us some sandwiches while you're at it. At least we can eat before the cops get here."

"I doubt there's any food here," Liam said as he took a long draw on his Guinness.

"Ahh, that's the stuff." He grinned.

Liam came from behind the bar and walked past Olivia to the leather couch positioned on the side wall, facing a big-screen TV. He put his feet up on the leather ottoman in front of him.

"Are you going to sit?" he asked Olivia, pointing to one of the chairs near the couch.

"Why bother? I'll be standing with my hands up soon enough."

"The cops aren't coming," Liam assured.

"How can you be so sure?" Olivia asked, crossing her arms.

"They have no reason to," Liam answered.

"I'm sure the locals patrol these mansions offseason," Olivia insisted. "They'll notice we're here."

"Probably," Liam said, sipping his beer and smiling again.

"I'm so glad you are enjoying yourself through all this," Olivia scoffed as she finally sat.

"Will you stop your worryin'? There's nothing wrong with us being here," Liam insisted.

Olivia shook her head in disdain.

"Go over to that shelf over there and have a look at the pictures." Liam pointed.

Olivia rose from her chair and looked at the various framed photos on the shelves and the wall. Many were black and white and some older color photos. Still, others were newer, including Liam holding a giant tuna he had hooked on a fishing trip.

"That's you," Olivia said as she grabbed the frame off the shelf. "So, you know the owners?" she asked with relief.

"Know them?" Liam laughed. "I am the feckin' owner!"

"This is your house?"

"Girlie, I've been making a lot of money for a long time now. What do you think? I just pissed it all away on booze and women? You can only try to do that for so long." He laughed.

"So this is where you have your orgies with the rest of the Cosantóir?" Olivia scowled.

"Hell no!" Liam answered. "I wouldn't let most of those pigs anywhere near this place. This is like my Fortress of Solitude."

"Your what?"

"Fortress of Solitude... you know, like Superman?"

"I have no idea what you're talking about."

Liam shook his head sadly.

"Superman has his secret place to go when he needs time away from the world. This is my place like that. A couple of the brothers know about it, but most don't. I come down once or twice a year for a few days when I want it. The rest of the time, I rent it out to tourists. They pay a fortune to stay here. This house is a moneymaker for me. We'll be safe here."

"Why didn't you just tell me that from the beginning?" Olivia yelled.

"What fun would that have been?" Liam said. He polished off his Guinness and rose from the couch. "Besides, it was fun to see the shock on your face when I said I owned the place."

"I wasn't shocked," Olivia said, glancing down at her feet.

"Yes, you were," Liam insisted. "You figured how could a lunkhead who digs tunnels for a living ever afford a place like this without knowing anything about me. My brother may have a law degree, but that doesn't mean he's smarter than me. I've worked hard all my life and have earned everything I have. Nothing's been handed to me."

"Okay, I'm sorry," Olivia told him. "I misjudged you. You're right. I shouldn't have jumped to conclusions like this. People do the same thing to me all the time, and it bugs the hell out of me. They think, 'Oh, she's just a waitress, or she works at a convenience store, she must not be able to do better than that.' They don't know anything about me or my situation."

"Seems like we have more in common than you may have thought," Liam said as he walked past Olivia. He patted her on the head as he went to get another Guinness from the fridge.

"So, what's the plan then?" Olivia asked as she finally opened the bottle of water and guzzled most of it.

"We can relax here for a few days and make sure your sister and niece are safe," Liam began. "Then we make a plan to head back to New York. I'll keep in touch with the Cosantóir to see if things have cooled down any, and we can figure out the best way to get you home."

"Okay," Olivia said. "One problem—I don't have anything here. I have one day of clothing, which I'm wearing, no toiletries, nothing."

"So, we'll get you some clothes," Liam said. "There are plenty of stores open year-round here now. I'm sure you can find a few things. We'll have to get supplies in for the house anyway."

Liam began to pour his second Guinness while Olivia stared at him.

"Now what?" he complained.

"So let's go," Olivia said, waving toward the door.

"Seriously?" Liam said. "I can't relax for a few minutes? I just saved your life and drove six hours to get here."

"Come on," Olivia insisted. "I need to get out of these dirty clothes, take a shower, and change before I can feel comfortable. It won't take long, I promise."

Olivia walked over to the bar and picked up Liam's keys, twirling them on her finger. Liam slammed his glass down on the bar.

"Christ," he said, shaking his head before snatching the keys from Olivia.

"This is why Superman never brings Lois to his Fortress," he mumbled as he headed for the door.

Chapter 9

Olivia walked out of the house to the carport. She made it over to the motorcycle before she noticed Liam was not behind her. She peeked her head back inside the open garage door.

"Liam?" she asked.

"Over here," he yelled before flipping on the light in the garage. The fluorescent glow illuminated the room.

Liam was folding back the gray tarp covering the vehicle in the center of the room. Underneath was a pristine, black Pontiac GTO convertible.

"Whoa," Olivia said, taken aback by the polished beauty of the auto.

"This will make getting around a little easier for us," Liam announced proudly. "It will undoubtedly be easier on your ass than my bike."

Liam glanced over and smiled as Olivia frowned at him.

"Nice," she answered sarcastically. "Can I drive it?"

Liam burst out laughing, holding his sides.

"Are you feckin' kidding me? Do you know how much this car cost me to restore? Do you think I would let just anyone drive it? You're nuts. Besides, it's a stick."

Olivia walked over and stood in front of Liam, staring up into his face.

"I bet I can handle a stick better than you," she said with a grin.

Olivia saw that she caught Liam off guard, and he stared at her intensely for a moment before breaking his gaze.

"I'll bet you can"—he smiled back—"but this one's got a lot of power to it. I doubt you're up to the challenge. I wouldn't want you to get hurt."

With that, Liam opened the passenger door so Olivia could climb in. A rush of heat crossed her body as she slid across the red leather seat, and Liam shut the door. Olivia instinctively reached for the shoulder belt to fasten but found none there.

"Where's the seat belt?" she asked as Liam got in.

"Only lap belts in this beauty," Liam announced proudly.

"They didn't believe in safety in the sixties?" Olivia added.

"No airbags either, darlin'." Liam smiled. "You're at the mercy of the driver."

"How reassuring," she told him as she fastened the lap belt.

"You just rode six hours on the back of a motorcycle with me without airbags or seat belts. It was just you holding on to me. I think you can make it ten minutes down the road in the car."

Olivia nodded while thinking about the time on the back of the bike. At first, she seemed to clutch on to Liam out of fear. However, as they rode along, she grew more comfortable, and her comfort from holding on rose.

They drove the short distance to one of the nearby strip malls, seeking out a small boutique positioned in the corner, surrounded by surf shops and souvenir stores.

Olivia stared out at the store as Liam turned the engine off.

"Are you getting out?" he interrupted.

"Uhm... I don't have any money to buy anything. I only brought a little cash with me," she said, blushing.

"Don't worry about it," Liam reassured. "I'll cover you. Let's go and get this over with."

Olivia got out of the auto and paced over to the front door of the store. She pulled the door open and was blasted with frigid air from the air conditioning in the store. The place was packed full of clothing of all kinds, nicely arranged on spacious racks and displays on the walls.

Olivia dared not glance at any of the pricetags for fear of what she might find. As someone who lived on a tight budget, she had long made do with the clothing she had, adding to her wardrobe only when absolutely necessary.

A bathing suit on a mannequin caught her eye immediately. Even though it was something she didn't need, she loved the look and cut of the black one-piece and moved over to see it up close. She walked around it once, examining it before seeking out a price tag more out of curiosity than anything else. When she didn't find one, she turned to the older woman behind the counter, who closely monitored Olivia's movements.

"Excuse me," Olivia stated politely.

The saleswoman didn't even look over to acknowledge her and idly flipped pages on the magazine in front of her.

"Excuse me!" Olivia asked again, with more force.

The clerk slowly raised her head to see Olivia.

"I don't see a tag on this bathing suit," Olivia asked. "Could you tell me how much it is?"

The woman peered over the reading glasses she wore and examined Olivia and then the suit.

"If you have to ask, you likely can't afford it," she scoffed. "Perhaps you want to try the Super Wings down the street."

Olivia's body flushed deep red before she turned to go toward the front door. Liam reached out his hand and grabbed her.

"Let's just go," Olivia said quietly in a cracked voice.

"Fuck that," Liam answered.

He marched over to the front counter and stood in front of the woman, slamming his hand down to cover the magazine she read before he slowly crumpled the pages in his palm.

"The lady asked you a question," Liam growled. "The least you can be is civil and give an answer."

The woman stepped back from the counter with her eyes widening.

"You assume we can't afford to shop here because we're not snooty yuppies with sweaters draped over our shoulders? Or is it because I'm in leather and tattoos, and she has darker skin? Who's the owner of this shack?"

"I am," the woman said, trying to stand up for herself.

"I'm guessing you'd be grateful for any type of business this time of year down here," Liam yelled. "Your store is empty on a Monday in October. You can't afford to be a snob."

Liam reached inside his leather jacket rapidly as Olivia saw the woman cringe and cower. Then, she watched Liam pull out his wallet.

"See this?" he said, slamming down a stack of hundred-dollar bills on the counter. "This is what you won't be getting today."

Liam scooped the bills back into his palm and stuffed them in his wallet before turning on his heels and marching toward Olivia.

"Let's go," he barked, taking Olivia by the hand.

Olivia stepped quickly to keep up with his pace, glancing back to see the store owner with her jaw hanging open. Olivia gave a casual wave to her as they left the store.

"I should go back in there and..." Liam said as he opened the car door.

"I don't think you need to do anything else," Olivia told him as she slid inside the GTO. "I think she got your point. Let's just go back to the house. I can wash what I have, and it will be fine."

"To hell with that," Liam responded as he started the car. "We're getting you clothes. Come on."

The tires squealed as the car pulled from its parking spot and raced down the road. Liam drove fast, bypassing several other small malls as Olivia looked on and recognized the determination in his face.

"Thank you for that," she told him.

"For what?" he asked. "That woman was a bitch. She deserved it."

"Still, you didn't have to stand up for me."

"No one should talk to you that way," Liam added. "Don't put up with it. You have no problem sassing me when you want to. Do the same with others. I thought you were tougher than that."

"I am," Olivia vowed. "She caught me off guard. But, trust me, it won't happen again."

"Good!" he answered emphatically.

Liam swerved the car into another parking lot that held just a single shop in it. Olivia read the shop sign and saw it was Footprints in the Sand.

"I don't know why I didn't think of this place right away," he said as they got out of the auto.

Liam flung the shop door open, hearing bells jingle as he did, so Olivia could walk in first. The shop was smaller than the previous one but had an eclectic selection of items. A tall blonde who stood just to the left folding some T-shirts looked up and smiled.

"Hi, folks." She beamed. "Come on... Liam, is that you?" she said with laughter.

" 'Tis me in the flesh," he said with a bow. Olivia stood by as the woman came over and hugged him tightly.

"I was wondering when you were going to drag your sorry ass down here again," she said, slapping his shoulder. "It's been what, at least a year? So why are you hiding from me?"

"Not hiding, Alicia. Just been busy, I guess. How about you?"

"I've been good. The business was outstanding this season. It was more than enough to see me through the slow part of the year. So…" Alicia said, peering around Liam to gaze at Olivia, "what brings you in here?"

"Oh… my friend here," Liam said, stepping aside, "needs some stuff. We came down spur of the moment, and she doesn't really have anything. Can you set her up with a few days' worth of stuff?"

"Of course." Alicia beamed. "I'm Alicia," she said, extending her hand toward Olivia.

Olivia grasped it and shook it. "Olivia. Sorry."

"Don't be sorry," Alicia added. "The Irish boy here is not big on manners all the time. Charm yes… manners, not so much."

"That sounds about right." Olivia chuckled.

"Now that you two have bashed me, maybe you can get down to it," Liam replied. "Get her whatever she wants, Alicia. I'll take care of it."

Liam turned back toward Olivia.

"I'm going to run over to the Food Lion and get some groceries for the house, and then I'll be right back. You'll be safe with Alicia; I promise."

Olivia nodded and watched as Liam moved out of the store to his car.

"Okay," Alicia spoke, grabbing Olivia's attention. "Let's get you some clothes. Look around, grab what you want, and bring it to the dressing room if you want to try anything. I'm right here if you need me."

Olivia moved about the store, gazing at the different items, styles, and colors. She looked at a skirt or top more than once, turned to the price tag, and then returned the clothing.

"Don't worry about the costs, honey," Alicia assured her from across the store. "If Liam said he's got you, he does. Besides, he knows I'll give him a break on the price."

"I guess you two go a long way back?" Olivia asked tentatively.

"Oh yeah... Liam and I have known each other for at least fifteen years. We've had some fun times." Alicia laughed.

"Oh?" Olivia asked with a tinge of jealousy.

Alicia giggled some more.

"Not like that," Alicia assured. "I was with one of the Cosantóir for a few years. I spent a lot of time at Hog House and hanging out with the club. Then, when Brian passed away, Liam was there for me. He was a good friend. He helped me get set up down here and start my life over."

Olivia grabbed a beaded top and held it up against her body, glancing into a nearby mirror to see how it looked.

"That's cute," Alicia said, walking up behind her. "Go try it on."

Olivia went into the dressing room and stripped off her top.

"How long have you known Liam?" Alicia asked from outside.

Olivia pulled the top into place and adjusted it.

"Not very long," she admitted. "Just a few days, really."

"Wow," Alicia said softly. "You must have made some impression on him. I've never had him bring a woman in here for anything."

"Really?" Olivia replied. "I thought it was more of a pity thing."

"Trust me, Liam doesn't pity anyone. He's more of a 'by your own bootstraps' kind of guy. I could tell by the way he looked at you it's sure not pity."

Olivia grinned and swelled with confidence.

"I definitely want this," she said of the top. "Do you have a skirt to go with it?"

"Of course," Alicia told her. "I'll gather a few other things for you as well."

Olivia spent the next forty minutes trying on different clothes and choosing items and accessories enough to fill three shopping bags before

Liam reappeared. She watched as he sauntered to the front counter, where Olivia and Alicia stood chatting.

"Only three bags? I think I got off easy," Liam said, looking at the counter.

"Olivia got some nice things, and we got the chance to chat. It was a good time," Alicia told him.

"Well, how much does this good time cost me?" Liam asked Alicia. Alicia handed him a sales ticket, and his eyes grew wide.

"Christ, is this with my discount too?" he said with shock.

"Stop it," Alicia insisted. "You're going to embarrass Olivia. She's worth it. You want her to look nice, don't you?"

Olivia looked over at Liam and saw he fumbled for an answer.

"Whatever," he said, pulling out his wallet and handing over a few hundred to Alicia.

"Thank you, sir." Alicia grinned. "I'm heading over to the Secret Island Tavern tonight if you guys want to meet me. They've got a killer DJ playing for some good dancing."

Olivia looked at Liam hopefully.

"Really? I hate places like that. We should just crash at the house."

"Come on," Alicia whined. "It will be fun. They have Guinness. You can mope in the corner while we dance."

"Please?" Olivia asked softly. "I sat through your Irish singer night," she reminded.

"What time?" Liam grumbled.

"I'll be there around nine," Alicia replied. "It was great to meet you, Olivia. Try to get Grumpy here in a better mood before he comes out."

"I'll do my best," Olivia added happily as she grabbed the bags off the counter and practically skipped out the door to the car.

Liam tossed the shopping bags into the trunk where the groceries he had purchased also lay. Olivia kept smiling until he sat down in the car beside her.

"Thank you," she chirped. "I was able to get some clothes, and Alicia is really nice."

"You're welcome," Liam gruffed. "Yeah, she's a wonderful gal. I'm glad she's doing well."

Olivia peered at Liam as he drove.

"She said you were a big help to her when her boyfriend died."

Liam shot Olivia a look that startled her.

"She told you about that?" he said with shock.

"I mean... I asked how she knew you, so Alicia explained that she was with one of the Cosantóir and that he passed away. That's all she mentioned about it."

Olivia noticed the stern gaze and stronger focus Liam had on the road.

"It was messy stuff back then with Brian," Liam spoke. "He was a good guy. We were still young... in our twenties... not much older than you are now. Brian worked hard and played hard... probably too hard. He got involved in gambling—cards, dice, sports betting, you name it. He would get his paycheck from the Sand Hogs and piss it away, sometimes in hours. Then he borrowed money from the wrong people and couldn't pay it back in time. You don't really want to hear about this."

"No, I do," Olivia insisted.

Liam roughly pulled the car into his driveway and then to the garage before jerking the vehicle to a stop.

"Listen." He snarled. "Brian borrowed money from a guy who used the Caimans as his recovery team. When he didn't pay, a few guys came and roughed him up pretty good. They broke three of his fingers and a couple of ribs, so he couldn't work, and told him they'd come back.

Then, one day on a ride back from Rhodes late at night, a car sideswiped him off the road heading toward Tuxedo. Cops say he ended up unconscious on the train tracks, but there's no way he could have gotten there unless someone dragged his body over. The Caimans—including The Butcher—showed up at his funeral and watched from across the street. When I saw The Butcher smiling as we came out of the church, I lost it. I went over and socked him in the mouth a few times and knocked a couple of his teeth out. He got me good on the leg with his blade before my brothers dragged me away. When I saw him again at the airport and saw the gold teeth he flashed when he smiled at me... The point is that these are bad dudes after you and your sister. They're guys you don't want to fuck with, and you need to take that seriously. I made sure Alicia understood that, which is why she left Harriman. You need to understand the same thing. It's not a good idea for you to go back there."

Olivia sat back after Liam's impassioned speech and took in the gravity of his tone.

"I can't let them chase me away like they did to Bea," Olivia defended. "I have a life to lead, with plans and—"

"Don't you get it?" Liam barked. "You won't have a life if they catch you! If Benny doesn't have you outright killed immediately, God only knows what he'll do to you. You'll end up drugged up somewhere, having your body sold every which way until you wish you were dead. That's the way he works."

"So I'm supposed to run for the rest of my life?" Olivia asked. "How is that living? I'd always be looking over my shoulder, wondering when it was going to happen. No... I'm doing this my way."

Liam shook his head and got out of the car, popping the trunk to grab the groceries. Olivia followed him out and grabbed her shopping bags, then went into the house. The two climbed the stairs with the thud of Liam's boots as they hit each step the only sound.

When they reached the top floor, Olivia took in the spacious living room and dining area along with the kitchen. Liam placed the bags on the island counter in the kitchen's center. Then, he began to put items away in the cabinets and fridge.

"You can take the bedroom over there." Liam pointed. "It's across the hall from mine. You have your own closet and bathroom."

"Thanks." Olivia nodded as she carried her items into the bedroom. The room had a king-sized bed, a dresser, a closet, and a TV on the wall. The room looked twice the size of what she had back home. There was also a sliding glass door that led to a patio outside the bedroom so that she could look right onto the beach and the ocean.

Just as Olivia finished stowing away the last of her new belongings, Liam filled her bedroom door.

"Everything okay?" he asked.

"Yeah, fine," Olivia told him, unsure of what else to say.

"I'm going to lie down for a bit to rest. If you're looking for anything to eat, there's some stuff in the fridge. I wasn't really sure what you wanted, so I might have overbought. Help yourself."

"Thanks." Olivia watched Liam walk toward his bedroom.

"Liam?" she yelled, halting his movement.

"Thank you... for all of this. I know you're putting yourself out there and in danger for a person you barely know. I want you to know I appreciate it. I hope you can see why I'm doing it."

"I can't see why you're doing it, but you're welcome." He sighed.

Liam closed his bedroom door, leaving Olivia standing in the doorway of her room, watching.

She turned back toward her room and lay on the comfortable bed.

I'm doing the right thing, right? she asked herself.

A soft knock on the door that steadily escalated to louder knocking roused Liam from his slumber. His dreams crept across his mind filled with many visions—some violent, some calm, and some passionate—and all included Olivia in some way. Finally, he pried his eyes open in the darkness just as a sliver of light appeared from the hallway.

"Hey, I didn't mean to wake you up, but it's almost eight fifteen," Olivia said quietly.

"Hmm... it's okay... I should get up," Liam groused. He reached over and flipped on the lamp next to his bed, squinting from the brief flash it brought to the room.

"Oh... I'm sorry..." Olivia said as she backed out of the room and shut the door.

Liam wiped his eyes, unsure as to why Olivia left so abruptly until he looked down. He saw he was clad in just his boxer briefs and that those briefs were at full attention thanks to his dreams.

"Shite," he whispered to himself as he climbed out of bed and went to the bathroom.

Under normal circumstances, Liam didn't care a bit if a woman walked into his room or that he had a raging hard-on in his pants. However, this time it felt different. He immediately turned on the shower, making it cooler than what he usually liked, stripped off his briefs, and got under the pulsating water.

"Ahhh, Christ!" he yelled as the cold water pelted his body. Once he gained better control of himself, he turned the water up to finish cleaning himself up. He left the shower stall and wiped the fog off the mirror to look at himself when done.

"Get a hold of yourself, boy-o," he said out loud, rubbing his face.

Liam returned to his room and dressed in fresh clothes, pulling his regular black boots on before exiting his room and heading out toward the rest of the top floor of the house. He saw Olivia sitting in one of the oversized beige recliners facing the window looking out over the ocean. She turned back to him when she heard his footsteps.

"I didn't mean to walk in on you like that," Olivia apologized again.

"No worries," Liam replied, attempting to brush it aside like it was nothing. Instead, he watched closely as Olivia stood. She wore a beige beaded halter top that came down just below her breasts and a pair of skin-tight leather pants. He inhaled quickly to compose himself again.

"That's what you're wearing?" he managed to croak out.

"What's wrong with it?" Olivia said, looking down. "This is perfect for dancing. Look at you," she shot back. "Do you own anything other than black T-shirts and jeans?"

"I probably have some blue T-shirts in there," Liam replied. "People aren't going to be staring at me because of what I'm wearing."

"Nothing wrong with a bit of staring, is there?" Olivia smiled slyly. "You're doing it right now." She laughed.

"Let's just go," Liam replied, snatching his keys off the counter in frustration.

They drove the ten minutes down the road before pulling into the parking lot of the Secret Island Tavern. Liam looked shocked at the number of cars in the parking lot for a Monday in October. The crowd proved much more extensive than he thought it would be.

As he and Olivia walked toward the front door, he spotted Alicia standing outside, waiting for them.

"You came!" she announced with surprise, giving Olivia a hug. "Wow, you look hot in that," she remarked. "Doesn't she, Liam?' Alicia asked with a smirk.

"Yeah, thanks for helping pick out the clothes," Liam complained. "We're trying not to stand out in a crowd, you know."

"Stop being so uptight," Alicia replied, grabbing Olivia by the arm, so they walked in ahead of Liam.

From the moment Liam crossed the threshold into the club, he regretted being there. The loud, incessant bass of the music reverberated everywhere to the point where he had to close his eyes just to think. The dark lighting accented with the flash of strobes seemed destined to not just bring the dance floor to a frenzy but to induce a seizure or two as well.

Liam got over to the bar where Olivia and Alicia were stationed, working on getting the bartender's attention. Olivia leaned over the bar, waving to the bartender so that her cleavage was impossible to miss.

"Step back," Liam said protectively, guiding Olivia and Alicia back with his left arm. He put the thumb and index finger of his right hand in his mouth and let out an ear-piercing whistle that could be heard above the ruckus of the music. The bartender snapped his head around and turned to Liam. Liam simply smiled and waved him down to them.

"What'll be, ladies?" said the bartender, grinning at the two women while keeping an eye on Liam.

"Two of the watermelon vodka cocktails, please," Alicia uttered. Alicia turned to Olivia.

"Trust me, you'll love these."

The bartender then cast a glance at Liam.

"You know how to pour a Guinness?" Liam asked him.

"Of course," the bartender said, arching his eyebrows.

"Well, I guess we'll find out," Liam replied.

The bartender walked off to get the drinks as Liam scanned the room. There were no signs of trouble—just a lot of young people sitting at tables or dancing. The DJ stood on a platform stage in the back of the room in front of the dance floor, where Liam saw guys and girls pressed against each other.

"Can you grab the drinks?" Alicia asked Liam. "We're hitting the dance floor."

"Yeah... whatever," Liam answered. "I'll find a table."

The bartender appeared with two pastel cocktails with small slabs of watermelon sticking from them. He also put down a pint of Guinness in front of Liam. Liam picked up the pint and examined it, noting the slow cascade and creamy head that marked the signs of a good pour.

"Nice job, chief," Liam said.

"Thirty dollars," the bartender commented.

"Feckin' highway robbery," Liam mumbled, passing over two twenties to the young man.

"Keep it," Liam told him. "Just pay attention to the ladies and me, and you'll do all right."

"You got it." The young nodded.

Liam cruised his way over to a hightop off to the right near the dance floor, working his way through the maze as he tried to avoid spilling anything. When he reached the finish line of the stool, he sighed in relief, put the drinks down, and enjoyed his beer.

He caught sight of Olivia and Alicia dancing with each other, moving along with whatever mix the DJ had on at the moment. Liam became mesmerized by Olivia's movement, the way she shook her hips or bumped against Alicia. Liam told himself he was watching her for her protection, but inside he knew it was more than that.

After several songs and half of his Guinness, the ladies appeared at the table. Each grabbed their drink, clinked glasses, and gulped down their cocktails.

"Oh man, these are good," Olivia crowed as she finished her drink. "Can we get more of these?"

A waitress happened by, and Alicia corralled her to order another round.

"Don't worry, Scrooge," Alicia said to Liam. "I've got this round."

More drinks zipped to the table, and Olivia snatched hers up, gulping at it again.

"Slow down there, Princess," Liam chastised.

"Come on, loosen up, Liam. Have some fun," she scoffed.

"My idea of fun is going back to the house. Unfortunately, this is just a fast way to vomit and get a headache."

"You're telling me you aren't the least bit interested in watching some of those pretty women out on the dance floor?" Alicia asked him. Liam saw Olivia stare at him, waiting for him to answer.

"Can't say I noticed any," Liam said smugly as he started in on his next draft beer.

"You're full of shit," Olivia said, slurring her words a bit as she sipped more of her drink. "Look at that girl there. She's perfect."

Liam followed where Olivia was pointing and spotted the redhead in a short black skirt, torn fishnets, and a see-through top.

Liam shrugged his shoulders, not looking to encourage anything.

"You're telling me you wouldn't want to dance with her?" Olivia asked. "Or are you just afraid to ask because she'll say no?"

Liam narrowed his eyes at Olivia, stifling his anger.

"You like her so much; you go dance with her," he said, throwing down the gauntlet.

"Okay," Olivia said, accepting the challenge. She finished her cocktail and made her way out, so she was right next to the redhead. They danced around each other for a bit as Liam looked on.

Liam noticed Olivia's eyes lock on his as he gazed at her. Then she started to move more seductively, getting closer to the redhead, so their bodies were intertwined. Olivia turned her back to her dance partner and raised her hands over her head, waving them slowly. Her beaded top rose as far as it could, exposing the undersides of her breasts. The redhead had wrapped one of her arms around Olivia's waist to glide her fingertips across her bare stomach. He spied the redhead lean in and kiss Olivia's neck, and Olivia broke into a smile.

Liam fidgeted in his chair, working with all his might to contain himself.

"Boy, she can move," Alicia said in awe.

"I guess," Liam said nonchalantly.

"I never saw you with someone like her, Liam," Alicia said, sipping her cocktail. "She's beautiful, but she's everything you usually avoid in a woman."

"What's that supposed to mean?" he said, taking offense.

"Come on... remember who you're talking to," Alicia replied. "I saw who you brought back to the Hog House. It was never the same woman most weeks, and it was never someone who would challenge you in any way. Olivia keeps you off-balance. Maybe it's just what you need."

"Don't worry about it," Liam assured. "Nothing is going on between us. I'm just helping out. She'll be gone in a few days, like the others."

"If you say so." Alicia nodded. "I guess what's going on out there now doesn't bother you, then?"

Liam looked where Alicia was pointing. The music throbbed in his ears, and he saw now that not only was the redhead grinding against

Olivia's backside, but a young man had positioned himself in front, with his hands moving up and down on Olivia's waist and steadily gliding higher. Olivia just kept swaying, eyes closed, caught up in the frenzy of the music.

Liam slammed down his empty pint glass and dashed to the dance floor. He grabbed the young man by the collar of his shirt and jerked him back.

"You're done now," Liam said, scowling down at the trembling man.

Olivia had kept moving but opened her eyes and saw Liam in front of her now. She reached out and grabbed his hips, dancing up against him as he stood stoic. The redhead behind her had now backed off, leaving Liam with Olivia.

"Dance with me." Olivia leaned in and said to Liam.

Liam pulled Olivia close to him and grasped her hips, causing her to gasp. Then, instead of dancing with her, he hoisted her up over his shoulder and walked off the dance floor with her.

"Hey!" she yelled. "I want to dance more!"

"We're done here," Liam barked. He walked over to where Alicia sat.

"Thanks for the fun time," Liam told her as he scooped up Olivia's purse and headed toward the door.

"Put me down," Olivia said, pawing at the back of Liam's T-shirt.

"In a minute," Liam yelled back. A young man with a hipster beard and beanie stepped in front of Liam as he neared the door.

"I don't think she wants to leave, man," the guy said to him.

Liam looked him up and down and saw that he was small, clearly drunk, and trying to impress someone. He looked over and saw a young girl sitting at a table, keenly watching.

"Look, pal," Liam said, shifting Olivia to his other shoulder. "I know you want to show off in front of your lady there and all, but you really caught me on a bad night. So, scurry back over to your table, tell your gal you did your best, and I ran off, and you won't have to spend the night in the ER. Fair enough?"

The young man nodded rapidly and stepped aside so Liam could exit.

He stormed to his GTO, grateful he had left the top down on the convertible. He dumped Olivia into the front seat and raced to the driver's side to start the engine and leave.

"What the fuck?" Olivia yelled once she had righted herself in the passenger seat. "I was having fun!"

"That was enough fun for the night. It was time to go."

"Don't you ever do anything that's remotely a good time?" Olivia screamed.

"You think this is some feckin' vacation we're on here?" Liam shouted back. "People are trying to kill you. Hell, they're probably lookin' to do the same to me. You can go get felt up by some woman on your own time."

"Ahh, so that was it." Olivia laughed, closing her eyes and letting the fresh ocean air rush by her face as they drove.

"What was it?" Liam asked.

"You didn't like that the girl was into me, and then that guy. You're jealous. I gave you a fair shot to dance with her and then with me. You turned both down. Your loss."

"Christ, you're so drunk right now you don't even realize what you're sayin'," Liam scoffed as they pulled into the driveway and then the garage. "Feckin' lightweight."

Liam walked around to the passenger side of the car and opened the door. Olivia sat still with her eyes closed, smiling.

"Are you getting out?" Liam said with frustration.

"I'm listening to the music," she said, laughing and swaying.

Liam pulled Olivia out of the car and over his shoulder once again, patting her backside in the tight leather pants she wore. Then, he marched up the three flights of stairs to the top floor of the house and pushed open the door to her bedroom before flopping her body onto her bed.

"Stay there," Liam ordered before he walked over to his bedroom and into the bathroom. He gathered up some Tylenol and then went to the kitchen, getting a bottle of water out of the fridge before heading back into Olivia's bedroom. He saw that she had kicked off the chunky heels she had on and was lying on the bed laughing.

"Here," Liam said, handing her the pills and the bottle of water. "Take these, drink your water, and sleep it off."

Olivia sat up and popped the white tablets into her mouth, followed by a healthy swig of the cold water. She then rushed her head back down to the pillows and laughed some more.

Liam turned and headed to the doorway, going out to the kitchen and grabbing the bottle of Jameson he had bought while out to pour himself a glass. No sooner had the liquid hit the ice cubes in the rock's glass when Liam heard his name called.

"Liam?" the voice called out in a sing-song tone. "Ohhh, Liam?" Followed by a giggle.

Liam put down his drink and walked to Olivia's doorway. She was still flat on the bed.

"What?" he asked with an edge to his voice.

"I need your help," she said sincerely.

"With what?"

"I can't get my pants off," she told him. "I need you to help me."

"You've got to be friggin' kidding me with this," Liam said as he turned to go.

"No, wait!" she yelled. "I really do need help. I can't get them off. It will be too hot to sleep in these things. And what if I need to pee?"

"For the love of God," Liam grumbled.

He walked over to the bed and watched as Olivia unbuttoned the pants and eased the zipper down as far as it would go.

"Okay, give 'em a pull." Olivia laughed.

Liam tugged hard on the pants, lifting Olivia's body off the bed, but barely budging the pants. Olivia burst out in wild laughter.

"I'm glad you're amused," Liam said as he tugged some more, flipping Olivia's body over so that she was on her stomach now. Then, finally, Liam reached up and pulled on the waist of the pants, getting them over Olivia's backside to reveal the tiny black bikini panties she was wearing. Liam inhaled deeply at the vision before him.

"Roll back over," he ordered as Olivia turned onto her back once again.

Liam grasped the pants edge closest to Olivia's feet and tugged hard. Not only did he get the pants most of the way down, but he had pulled Olivia's body to the edge of the bed right before him. Liam spied Olivia get up on her elbows to watch him. When he failed to react, she slid to the bottom of the bed and stood up, her body next to his. She pushed the leather pants down the rest of the way, leaving her in just her top and panties.

"My hero," she said softly, running her hand behind Liam's head and through his hair. "I think you deserve a reward," she cooed.

Before Liam could act, Olivia had pressed her body and lips to his.

Chapter 10

1⁰

The moment Olivia's lips touched his, Liam surged. His body knew what it wanted, even if his brain told him it was a bad idea. Olivia broke her lips from his slightly and grinned at him. Her right hand worked its way down from his pecs and over his abs until it reached the buckle of his belt. Her hand deftly undid the buckle while Liam's eyes stayed locked on hers.

"Don't start something you have no intention of finishing," Liam told her, grasping her hands in his.

Olivia wrested her right hand away from his grip, reaching down and cupping him through his jeans.

"It doesn't feel like you're as annoyed as you seem," Olivia purred.

"I don't want to be accused of taking advantage of a drunk virgin," Liam answered back.

Olivia threw her head back and laughed, lying on the bed as she did so.

"I'm no virgin," she said seductively, "and I'm aware of what I want and what I'm doing."

Olivia crooked her index finger at Liam, calling him to the bed like a Siren calling a sailor to sea.

That was the last invitation sign Liam needed. He pulled his black T-shirt over his head and shed his boots as quickly as he could.

"Keep going," Olivia egged him on as she watched him strip down.

When he got down to his boxer briefs, Liam began to climb onto the bed to be with her. First, he knelt between her legs and placed his hands on her thighs, rubbing them on the inside. Liam felt the shivers and goose bumps course through Olivia's body from his touch before his hands moved around to her backside to remove her dampening panties. Liam then pulled her closer to him before he kissed Olivia just above the soft strip of hair previously covered to elicit a moan from her lips.

Liam used a combination of his lips, tongue, and fingers to tease and tantalize Olivia into a frenzy without penetrating her at all. Instead, he grazed all around her, circling in slowly with his fingers and mouth until Olivia clearly couldn't take much more.

"God, please," she moaned breathlessly.

"Please, what?" Liam asked slyly, flicking his thumb just across the hood of her clit so Olivia gasped louder.

"I... I need something... I need you," Olivia groaned.

"Need me to what?" Liam replied, thoroughly enjoying himself now as his index finger glided across the wetness of her without going in.

"Oh, fuck," Olivia said softly, feeling frustrated and aroused beyond her dreams. "I need you inside..."

Liam eased an index finger inside, causing Olivia to grip the blanket on the bed between her fists. Then, he curled his finger deeper, striking a spot inside that radiated more heat through Olivia's body. Liam watched her body's reactions to his touch and movement as she ground against the palm of his hand with now two fingers inside her. Within moments, Olivia was groaning loudly and clenching on him as she came.

As Liam eased his fingers out and the pleasure began to subside in Olivia's body, he knew their tryst was far from over. He rose from the bed and shed his boxer briefs, letting his cock free from its cage. He reached down to his jeans and grabbed a condom from his pocket. Olivia already stretched to him as he placed himself back on the bed.

"Don't worry"—Liam smiled—"I'm not done yet."

Liam rolled himself between Olivia's legs once more, kneeling and leaning forward to reach the halter top she still wore.

"This needs to go," he said hungrily, peeling the top over her head and tossing it to the floor.

He placed his hands on Olivia's hips and tugged her forward, so the two sat facing each other. Then, Liam lifted Olivia off the bed with little effort and brought her right to his body, lowering her slowly onto his hard cock. Liam watched her reaction as he entered her, closing her eyes tightly and groaning as she felt every aching inch of him inside.

With Olivia's legs wrapped tightly around his waist, Liam moved his hips, thrusting slowly at first before building to a rhythm that sent electricity through both their bodies. The sweat building between them grew as they moved as Liam licked and kissed Olivia's neck more and more. He could hear Olivia gasping for air as she moaned.

"Please... I'm so close..." Olivia begged into his ear.

"Not yet," Liam whispered back, his left hand moving to her right breast and grazing her nipple with his thumb, causing Olivia to push against him more.

Liam felt Olivia's fingernails digging into his back as she sought to hang on, doing her best to hold out for him. She brought her mouth to his shoulder, muffling a deep moan as her eyes tightened closed. He knew she was the precipice, and he was ready to push her over the edge.

Liam leaned forward, bringing Olivia down onto the bed beneath him so he could look at her. It only took one long, slow thrust before he saw her body tense and hold on to him. The look of ecstasy on her face as she cried out proved more than enough for Liam as he exploded, pulsing inside her.

Liam rolled to his right and lay back on the bed, catching his breath as he heard Olivia trying to do the same. Within seconds, he found Olivia's head resting on his shoulder as she ran her hand over his chest.

Liam remained quiet as Olivia's breathing returned to a normal pace, and before he knew it, soft snores were coming from her as she lay next to him.

Unsure of what to do next, Liam stayed still, staring at the ceiling. All he could hear were the sounds of the ocean waves outside and the soft, content slumber Olivia was in.

Do you know what you're doing? he thought to himself as he moved his right arm around Olivia to hold her closer.

Sunrise peered through the curtain in Olivia's bedroom, bouncing off the mirror over the dresser enough to rouse her from her sleep. As her eyes fluttered open, a dull ache coursed through her head and body. Olivia looked to her left to see Liam lying there, naked and fast asleep without a blanket. Temptation filled her head, and Olivia wanted to reach over and touch him again, recalling the previous night's epic adventure. However, the peaceful look on Liam's face caught her attention more than the enormity of his body. She lay next to him and just watched his chest rise and fall, examined the contours of his chest and abs, and took in the muscle definition he had that made a trail down below his waist to the cock that had given her so much pleasure.

Olivia experienced a rush of warmth through her body. She thought back to the previous night but held back from acting on anything. Instead, she hopped out of bed, searching out the panties Liam had tossed aside, and pulled them on. She discovered Liam's black T-shirt on the floor and picked it, donning that instead of something of her own. She grasped the collar of the cotton T-shirt in her hands and held it up to her face, taking in Liam's manly scent as she smiled. The T-shirt came down almost to her knees, but the idea of wearing something that belonged to Liam was more important than that.

Olivia crept out to the kitchen, flipping the light on to seek out what was there. She got the coffee going and examined the groceries Liam had purchased to see what she might make for breakfast. She was ravenous at this point, not remembering eating much at all the day before.

After gathering some eggs, bacon, and English muffins, she set about making some simple breakfast sandwiches for them. The crackle and aroma of the bacon lifted her spirits as she cooked. Soon, Olivia found herself turning on the satellite radio in the kitchen and listening to music, swaying her hips as she cooked.

Just as she was taking the over-easy eggs off the stove and placing them on the toasted muffins, Olivia caught a glimpse of Liam as he stood at the corner of the kitchen island, watching her.

"Oh, I didn't expect you up," she said, startled by his appearance. She glanced at Liam, shirtless and in his classic boxer briefs. "I was going to surprise you with breakfast."

"You're just full of surprises, aren't you?" he replied with a smirk, causing Olivia to blush.

"I guess so." She laughed.

Olivia passed a plate with a sandwich to Liam and then began to pour coffee. She handed him a steaming mug as she stepped closer to him.

"I didn't plan... But, I mean, what happened last night... I didn't know things would play out that way," she told him as she averted her eyes from Liam's gaze.

"I didn't either," Liam said through a mouthful of breakfast sandwich. "To be honest, you shocked the shite out of me."

Olivia laughed nervously.

"I... I hope that's a good thing," Olivia said as she looked back at Liam.

Olivia pulled up a stool next to Liam at the counter and sat down.

"It was an excellent thing." Liam grinned.

Liam polished off his sandwich in just a few bites and turned toward Olivia.

"Look," he began. "I know it's not what either of us imagined happening when this little trip started..."

"Liam, it's okay," Olivia interrupted. "I know who you are and what your reputation is. I'm not expecting you to call me your girlfriend or anything. I get it."

"That's not what I was going to say at all," Liam answered. "Jaysus, do you really think that's all I'm about? Yeah, I know what everyone sees in me. It's no secret. But that doesn't mean I'm like that all the time. If I didn't want that to happen, it wouldn't have—trust me. Have I slept with women and never seen them again? Yes, I have. I don't have to be that way, though, and I'm not all the time."

"I just don't want you to think I'm pressuring you into anything, is all. It can be what it was."

Liam slammed his mug down on the counter, causing Olivia to jump in her stool.

"Christ, you're even colder than me!" Liam barked.

"I thought you would be relieved that I didn't have any expectations from you. I'm not some teenage girl swooning over the bad boy in school. We obviously both wanted something last night, and we got it. So we can leave it at that. I'm okay with it."

Liam moved over and stood next to Olivia, towering over her.

"And what if I'm not okay with it?" he growled. "What if I want more?"

Olivia began to answer, but before she could get a word out of her mouth, Liam firmly pressed his lips to hers, taking her breath away. Her muffled words were smothered out, and her minor protests of surprise quickly became soft mewls of enjoyment.

When Liam swooped down and scooped Olivia off the stool, she let out a brief squeal. His hand cradled her backside as he carried her over to the couch. Liam sat down, holding her in his lap before his hungry lips met hers again. His hands moved everywhere over her body, exciting her more and more. His stiff cock was beneath her as she put her palms on both sides of his face, kissing him more.

Olivia groaned in surprise when she discovered Liam's right hand under the T-shirt she wore, cupping her left breast. He flicked his thumb around her areola before circling her nipple and brushing roughly across it. She felt his right begin to go lower, across her trembling stomach until it found the waistband of her panties. He pressed his palm tightly against her sex, feeling the heat she gave off as she panted.

"Still ready to leave it at that?" he whispered to her as his fingers went across the thin damp fabric.

Olivia let out another moan, leaning her head back as she closed her eyes, unable to answer.

Liam dipped his hand inside her panties and easily slid fingers inside her, bringing out a long gasp.

"You can tell me to stop if you want," Liam growled into Olivia's ear. "Or you can tell me you want more."

"More," she moaned instantly. "I want more."

Liam chuckled as he moved his left hand off Olivia's hip and down to his briefs so he could pull his cock out through the Y-front. Olivia felt it immediately brushing against the front of her panties, which Liam abruptly pulled aside. Then, he lifted Olivia up with one deft movement and placed her on top of his erection. The moment he slid inside her, Olivia heard a guttural moan escape Liam's lips.

"Yes," Olivia answered as she rotated her hips on his lap, letting the tip of his cock touch her deeply.

It didn't take long before Liam's hands were back at Olivia's waist, holding on to her as they moved in unison. Olivia knew what built up inside her, and she badly wanted release. Still, every time she sped up the tempo of movement, Liam held her in place to slow her down and draw out the experience.

"I know you're there," Liam whispered. "I can feel how close you are. Do you want more?"

"Fuck yes," she cried out. "Please... more."

"As you wish." He chortled.

Liam thrust his hips upward, driving deep into Olivia and pushing her over the edge. She clenched and tightened on his cock, her entire body trembling as she came. The fire within her moved from head to toe as her orgasm went wave after wave, more than enough to make Liam come as well.

Olivia threw her arms around Liam's neck and kissed his throat, Adam's apple, and then his lips as she worked to get control over herself again. Finally, she placed her head on his shoulder as she panted.

Liam took Olivia by the shoulders, pushing her back a bit so that she could look straight into his smoky dark eyes.

"Are you convinced now?" Liam asked.

Olivia nodded, sweat trickling down her forehead as she pressed herself against Liam. His arms engulfed her as he held her tightly.

Chapter 11

The sounds of the shower water running in Olivia's bedroom gave Liam the chance to do the same. The two had spent the morning with each other on the couch and in Olivia's bed once again before they wore each other out. Liam had just exited his bathroom, long dark hair still dripping, and went to his dresser to get clothing for the day when his cell phone buzzed.

Liam plucked the phone off his nightstand and answered when he saw it was Finn.

"Hey, brother," Liam said casually as he returned to his dresser and grabbed a pair of charcoal boxer briefs.

"Everything going okay?" Finn asked.

Liam paused before answering, walking to his bedroom door to shut it if Olivia was out of her shower and could hear what was going on. He put Finn on speaker before he stepped into his briefs.

"You could say that," Liam answered evasively. "I'm keeping her safe."

"Good to hear. I just wanted to give you a quick update. Beatriz and Daniela arrived safely in Lima. They had family there to meet them, along with someone Siobhan coordinated with to make sure there were no issues. We reminded Beatriz not to try to contact Olivia just yet. We don't know the whole story about what's going on. Until we do, we have to assume Benny knows everything about where everyone is."

"I know he was tracking us," Liam replied. "I found the tracer in a stuffed animal and got rid of it before we got too far on the road."

"I'd still take it cautiously, Liam," Finn warned. "The Caimans have been active up here. More than once, they have come around to A Safe Place trying to get information. Several of the brothers have reported noticing them around Monroe and Harriman a lot. They are still trying to find her."

"Which means The Butcher is probably trying to find us down this way," Liam answered with concern.

"Do you think he knows where you are?"

"I can't say for certain," Liam said as he pulled out a green Guinness logo T-shirt and pulled it on. "I'm keeping my eyes and ears open for anything suspicious."

"You can always come back to Harriman," Finn advised. "Strength in numbers, Liam. The brothers are here to back you up."

"I'm not worried about me," Liam answered. "The girl needs protection. I can't just leave her vulnerable, whether it is here or back home."

"You sure weren't talking that way a few days ago," Finn said with surprise. "What's really going on?"

"Nothing you need to concern yourself about, little brother."

"Liam, if you're getting involved with her…"

Liam shut the conversation down immediately.

"Don't you worry about me. Take care of what's going on up there so you can buy me some more time to figure out what is best. I'll be in touch when I need to be."

"But," Finn attempted to add.

"But nothing. Talk to you later."

Liam hung up the phone and went to his closet to grab a pair of jeans. A light rap on his door had him spinning around. Olivia stood before him in a pair of frayed and faded denim shorts and a white T-shirt.

"I heard you yelling into the phone." Olivia said as she approached Liam.

"Just my brother and I getting into it, as usual." Liam sighed. "The good news is your sister and niece arrived safely in Lima. They got to your parents without any issues."

Olivia's eyes lit up.

"Oh, thank God," she said, rushing toward Liam to wrap her arms around his waist and press her head to his chest. "I'm going to call them right now."

"No!" Liam insisted, saying it louder than he had intended. "You can't do that. Not yet."

"Why not?" Olivia responded.

"Because even though they are safe, you are not. We don't know if the Caimans are watching your parents or are listening in on their calls. All it takes is one conversation between the two of you, and people will know where you are."

"So I'm supposed to live the rest of my life not talking to or seeing my family? I can't do that," Olivia argued, sitting down on the bed.

"Not the rest of your life, but for now, yes," Liam answered. "It's just a precaution until I can figure out our next moves. So you need to give me a little time."

Olivia rubbed her hands on her knees, looking down before she peered back at Liam.

"Okay," she acquiesced with a nod.

"Good," Liam chimed in. He began to put his jeans on when Olivia interrupted him.

"So... I guess this means I'm kind of like your prisoner then, huh?" She smiled.

"I wouldn't necessarily call it that," Liam told her as he buttoned his jeans. The light inside his head turned on as Liam understood what Olivia said. "However, that might have some advantages."

Olivia rose from the bed and strode in front of Liam, who had just zipped up his jeans. Olivia's right hand went right for the button and zipper, undoing the task Liam had just performed.

"I suppose I'll just have to go along with what you say... and need." She grinned as she moved her hand inside the denim pants and rubbed his growing cock.

"You're insatiable," Liam groaned.

"And is that such a bad thing?" she cooed, gripping her fingers on him.

"Not at all," Liam replied before scooping Olivia off the floor and bringing her to his bed.

"So much for the shower," Liam huffed as he took off his shirt and tossed it aside, watching as Olivia did the same.

"Maybe we can conserve water afterward and shower together," she replied hungrily, pushing Liam's jeans down while plucking a condom off his nightstand.

After spending the better part of the morning and early afternoon exploring Olivia's body, the two finally decided to get out of bed.

"Can we do something?" Olivia complained. "It's beautiful outside."

"I don't know how good of an idea it would be to spend time around town," Liam cautioned. "Caimans are in New York actively seeking you there, and they know we were in North Carolina. It seems like a big chance to take."

Liam noticed the disappointment on Olivia's face as she slumped onto the couch.

"You've got the beach at your disposal right out the back there," Liam reminded.

He paced over to the couch and sat down next to her, putting his hand on Olivia's knee and gently rubbing with his thumb.

"I'll tell you what," he added. "I can order us some lunch, and we can go walk on the beach and hang out there for a while. How does that sound?"

"It sounds nice," Olivia answered. "It almost sounds romantic. You must be softening up."

"Let's not go that far," Liam replied with a grin. He placed his hand on Olivia's chin and brought her in for a kiss.

"I'll get the food," Liam said as he picked up his phone to order from a delivery app. "Did you happen to get a bathing suit from Alicia's place?"

"I did, but won't the water be too cold to go in?"

"Hell no," Liam told her. "The water is still in the seventies. It's actually nice this time of year. Go get your suit on."

Olivia hurried off to her room to change while Liam put in a Door-Dash order for some sandwiches. Then, he went down to the garage and pulled out a long-unused picnic basket off the storage shelf and packed it with a couple of blankets and towels, along with utensils and some other necessities for lunch. By the time he finished, Olivia had emerged from her bedroom wearing her denim shorts. A sky blue button-down shirt opened enough for Liam to spy the black bathing suit she wore.

"Is that the one from that snooty store we walked out of?" Liam said, noticing the cleavage Olivia displayed.

"Pretty close," Olivia said, pulling the shoulders of her shirt down so Liam could get a better look at the suit. "Alicia had one just like it in her shop, so I picked it up. Do you like it?"

"Put your shirt back on, or we're never getting to the beach today," Liam growled.

"I'll take that as a yes." Olivia grinned.

Liam went to his room to put on a bathing suit and get anything else they might need. Then, ever cautious, he grabbed his knife and sheath and tucked them into the picnic basket along with everything else.

"Wow, you do have knees." Olivia chuckled when she saw Liam in his bathing suit. "I was beginning to think you were going to wear your jeans still."

"Very funny," Liam chided. "Besides, you've seen plenty of my naked body below the waist the last day or two."

"Fair enough." She nodded.

A loud rap at the door had Liam spin his head around.

"Stay here," he said to Olivia quietly. "It's probably just the food." Liam slipped his hand back into the picnic basket, grabbed his knife, and tucked it into the back of his bathing suit.

Liam crept down to the second floor, where the front door was, and pried it open. A young man stood there holding two brown paper bags. When he saw the scowl on Liam's face, he stepped back.

"Just the food delivery," the man said, placing the bags down gingerly on the wood porch.

"Thanks." Liam nodded, snatching up the bags and shutting the door quickly as the delivery person scurried off back to his scooter.

Liam climbed the steps inside and returned to the kitchen area where Olivia sat, waiting.

"Food's here," Liam said, holding up the bags. "Let's do it."

Liam picked up the picnic basket and carried it back downstairs to the bottom floor, where the couple could exit the house and have the door lock behind them. They walked just a few yards before reaching the sand. The soft areas squeezed through their toes before they got to the more rigid sand surface closer to the edge of the ocean.

"I haven't been on a beach since I was a little girl," Olivia said, walking along as the water lapped at her feet so she could squish the sand between her toes. "I forgot how much I love it."

"To be honest, I rarely come down here," Liam replied as he paced alongside.

"Why? It's beautiful."

"Because I'm usually alone when I come to Nags Head. I don't want to be that creepy loner walking on the beach. I sit on the house's back patio, look out, or hop on a charter to do some fishing. More often than not, my days and nights are spent at Fish Heads."

"What's that?" Olivia asked, plucking a shell from the sand.

"A local place—a tiki bar right on the beach. They have a pier you can fish on, a bar, and a restaurant, and they have bands each night. It's a great place, especially this time of year when most of the tourists are gone."

"Can we go?" Olivia asked excitedly.

"Didn't we already go through this?" Liam said, annoyed. "It's too risky."

"You just said yourself that hardly anyone is here this time of year," Olivia argued. "Just for a little bit, please?"

Olivia hooked her arm through his and batted her long eyelashes at him. One look into her brown eyes had him melting.

"Jaysus, you're too much. I'm against it. Let's see how the day goes."

Liam came to a stop on the beach and moved up on the sand, placing the picnic basket down so they had a dry spot to sit and view the ocean.

The beach was deserted, with nothing more than some hopeful seagulls circling overhead and pelicans diving into the water for a lunch of their own.

Liam reached into the wicker basket, pulled out a sizeable checkered blanket, and spread it on the sand. He placed the towels down and then removed some of the food, laying out a spread for the two of them.

"Sit," Liam told Olivia, tugging her down to the blanket so she was next to him.

"What did you get?" Olivia asked as she sat.

"They had a beach picnic special, so I did that. It's some chicken wraps, fruit, olives, cheese, and other stuff."

Liam reached behind him and pulled the knife sheath from the waistband of his bathing suit.

"Did you need to bring that?" Olivia said cautiously.

"We need a knife anyway, and I'm not taking any chances," Liam replied as he picked up an apple and skillfully cut it into slices in seconds. He grabbed a piece and placed it on Olivia's tongue, watching as she crunched down on the crisp Golden Delicious.

"Yummy," she said through a mouthful of apple.

The two dined on lunch as they admired the water, waves, and clear blue sky. When a pod of dolphins rose from the water not far offshore, Liam pointed them out and relished in the delight he witnessed on Olivia's face. The brief respite proved the perfect tonic to help them both relax a bit from the tensions around them.

Liam rose from the blanket and put out his hand toward Olivia, helping her up. He pulled his T-shirt over his head and tossed it to rest with their other belongings.

"Let's go," he bade.

Olivia shed her shirt and unbuttoned her denim shorts, pushing them down as Liam watched. The suit fit her perfectly in all the right places, allowing Liam to take in her beautifully tanned legs to the high cut of the suit on her hips.

"I'll take your staring as a compliment." Olivia laughed.

"Damn, that's a sexy suit," Liam told her, pulling Olivia close to his body. He ran his hands down her body to her waist, gripping her.

"Let's go!" Olivia yelled as she broke free and dashed toward the ocean water.

Olivia waded out into the sea. She was waist-deep before she ducked under a small incoming wave, emerging on the other side of it before turning back to Liam to wave him in.

"Come on!" she yelled.

Liam ran and dove into the water, cutting through the waves and swimming toward Olivia, rising up next to her.

"God, this feels so good," Olivia said over the sound of the waves and water. The two waded out a bit farther until Olivia was treading in the ocean while Liam could still stand comfortably. Liam reached over and pulled Olivia next to him, pressing her wet body to his.

"Yes, it does." He grinned.

Waves lapped around them as Liam went in for a kiss. Olivia had wrapped her legs around his waist to hold on to him tightly. They kept the initial kiss going until a more significant wave struck them and pushed them down, causing both to fall into the water and come up laughing.

The two made their way back to the sand and beach and lay on the blanket and towels Liam had set down for them. The sun was just warm enough to take any potential chill away, and Olivia lay down on her stomach, her head turned so she looked at Liam sitting up on the blanket next to her. Seconds later, Liam felt her hand tracing the outline of the scar on his left calf.

"What's that from?" she asked, running her index finger along the length of the mark from just above Liam's ankle toward his knee.

"I told you about that," Liam replied bluntly. "That's where The Butcher got me after I knocked some of his teeth out. He tried to go for my Achilles tendon and missed. Fucker kept me out of work for weeks. Some day I'll get another tat there to cover it up."

"It's a big scar," Olivia repeated with awe.

"You're not messing around with some teenage bullies," Liam said, looking at Olivia. "These guys mean business. I'm not telling you we need to take these precautions for nothing. They will kill both of us without thinking about it."

"I'm sorry," Olivia spoke, moving her hand away and back down to the blanket.

"There's nothing for you to be sorry about," Liam chimed in. "It was long before I got involved with you and your sister."

"No... I mean for dragging you into all of it," Olivia explained. "I just needed them to be safe, and Siobhan had the best solution. I didn't know it was going to cause so much trouble."

"I don't think anyone knew what they were up against," Liam told her, placing his hand on Olivia's bare back. He could see that his touch left soft finger marks on her bare spots. "You're going to get burned a bit out here," he added as he reached over to the bag he brought and grabbed the sunblock.

Liam squirted some of the lotion into his hands and began to apply it to Olivia's warm skin. He made slow circles on her back and up and down her spine. Olivia arched her back some as the application soon became more of a massage. Next, Liam reached up to Olivia's shoulders, easing the straps of her bathing suit down her arms until they were off her body completely, and continued with his technique around Olivia's shoulder and the back of her neck. He pushed aside her flowing brown hair to gain better access before putting just a tad more lotion on his hands.

His strong palms worked their way down Olivia's body toward her chest. Liam used his thumbs to tug down on the part of her swimsuit just enough to expose the sides of her breasts so he could rub them lightly. A sigh escaped Olivia's lips as he touched her. As tempted as he was to move his fingers underneath her body to touch her, he held off, drawing out the experience.

Liam put more sunblock in his palms and then went to work on Olivia's ankles and feet. His first touch there caused her to giggle and laugh as he grazed the delicate part of her soles. However, once Liam began to hit the pressure points in Olivia's feet, her body relaxed even more. His slow massage worked its way over her strong calves to the sensitive parts behind her knees. Liam watched as Olivia raised her backside a bit and moaned when his hands got closer to her thighs. Liam alternated between light and hard touches with his fingers as he massaged her thighs, so Olivia did not know what to expect next.

When Liam ran his fingers just up and down along the tops of her thighs outside of her bathing suit, Olivia moaned and wriggled on the blanket. Her hips rose as Liam glided the palm of his hand to the front of her swimsuit and traced a finger along her pussy, putting the slightest amount of pressure on her to make Olivia gasp.

Liam accepted the invitation and slid his finger just inside her black bathing suit, dabbing at the wetness that had long formed before he gently slid a finger inside her. As he went deeper and then added a second finger, Olivia groaned loudly, raising her hips again and moving up and down against Liam's hand.

Liam continued to work his two fingers inside and began to guide Olivia's buttocks down with his left hand in rhythm, so she was fucking his hand. Olivia ground herself against Liam's hand with each motion down. Liam saw that she was gripping the blanket beneath her tightly in the palms of her hand as she gasped with each movement. The speed intensified, and when Liam brushed a finger gently up and around Olivia's clit, he knew she was there. Olivia clamped down Liam's fingers, holding them in place as a long moan flew from her lips. Liam pressed down on Olivia's backside once more, holding her tightly in place so that his fingers hit just the right points for her as she came.

Liam eased his fingers out as he watched Olivia's body tremble and begin to regain control. She opened her eyes and turned to look at Liam over her shoulder. He saw sweat running down her forehead that she gently wiped on the towel next to her as he smiled.

"I would go back in the water to cool off, but my legs feel like Jell-O right now," Olivia said hoarsely.

"Good," Liam said proudly as he reached over and grabbed a bottle of water.

"I'd be happy to return the favor," Olivia told him as her left hand moved to Liam's thigh under the black swim trunks he wore.

Liam smiled, but his eyes squinted a bit as he looked to his left beyond Olivia.

Two figures off in the distance stood and watched before moving toward where Olivia and Liam sat on the beach.

Chapter 12

Olivia caught the look in Liam's eyes, moved her hand from his leg, and spun around to look in the opposite direction. She noticed the two shadows coming closer, one much taller than the other. Tension peaked in the pit of her stomach, replacing the pleasure Olivia experienced just moments before. She spied Liam leaning back to pick up his knife and sheath and tuck them into the back of his bathing suit.

"Sit up and get ready to run if I tell you to," Liam ordered. "Go straight down the beach until you see a stairway up to street access. From there, you can go to the right toward my house or to the left and find a store, a home, a cop... anything where you can be safe."

Liam rose and stood in front of Olivia, shielding her as the strangers approached. Then, Olivia saw it was a man and a woman, and the man waved to them.

"Hey there," he said when he was about ten yards away, somewhat out of breath. "I didn't expect to see anyone out on the beach."

The man looked to be in his early forties, fit, short-cropped graying hair, and a deep tan. He wore a tropical button-down shirt over a salmon tank top with a pair of khaki shorts like he was trying to let everyone know he was a tourist. The woman next to him looked no taller or older than Olivia, her blond curly hair waving at her shoulders. Her bright blue bikini top and skin-tight bike shorts got her more attention than the man she was with.

"Can I help you with something?" Liam asked abruptly.

The man stopped a foot or two in front of Liam.

"No, no." He laughed. "I'm just saying hi. We've been here for a few days now at that house there," the man said, pointing at a place just a few doors down from Liam's. "We were wondering if we would have the whole place to ourselves all week."

"Guess not," Liam answered. Olivia noticed how Liam's eyes moved, sizing up the other man while keeping an eye on the girl behind him.

"Well, I didn't mean to disturb you two," the tourist answered. Olivia shivered a bit, wondering if he had seen her and Liam just a few minutes ago. By the quick smile on the girl behind the man, she figured yes.

"I'm Paul, by the way," the man said, extending his hand to Liam. Liam looked down at the tanned hand in front of him and held fast for a moment before putting out his own.

"Aaron," he replied to the man, planting his hand firmly in the other man's. "This is Serena." Liam pointed with a nod toward Olivia.

"Nice to meet you both," Paul replied. "This is my daughter, Josie," he said, stepping to the side so Josie could step forward. But, instead, she gave a shy, casual wave.

"Are you guys down for the week?" Paul asked.

"We were, but we may have to leave early. So we'll see how it goes," Liam said cautiously.

"Oh, that's too bad," Paul replied. "Well, hopefully, you get to stay, and we'll see you around a bit. How was the water?" Olivia noted that Paul was now looking directly at her, and the straps of her bathing suit were still down off her shoulders. She quickly put her arms back through the straps and blushed.

"It... it was nice," Olivia said, straightening her suit. "You'll like it."

"Serena, you should gather up the rest of our stuff," Liam said, looking at Olivia to get her attention. It took her a moment to remember that she should respond.

"Right," she said, stuffing items back into the bag and picnic basket.

After hurrying her packing, Olivia stood up next to Liam. Liam casually put his arm around her, pulling her closer to him to protect her.

"You guys enjoy your day," Liam said to Paul as Liam led Olivia off.

"We didn't mean to chase you off," Paul said sincerely.

"It's okay," Liam said as they moved off. Olivia hustled along to keep up with the long strides Liam made as he moved toward the house. She glanced back to see Paul and Josie had continued on their way down the beach, walking side by side.

"Just keep moving," Liam said as they reached closer to his home and ducked up the street nearest the house.

"Why don't we go right up to the house?" Olivia said, following Liam off the sand, up the steps to an access area.

"Because they don't need to know where we're staying," Liam replied.

"Do you think we need to worry about them?"

"I'm not sure," Liam answered. "They are probably just tourists, but I don't need any friends down here anyway."

Olivia and Liam walked down the driveway, scurrying across the hot surface until they reached the grassy area in front of his house. They ducked down to the home's secluded side, and Liam pushed open the wooden door to the outdoor shower. He held the door open so Olivia could enter. He turned the spigot before she could protest, and cold water began to shoot down on her.

"Ahhhh! It's freezing!" she yelled.

"Gotta wash the sand off before you go in the house," Liam said with a laugh. "My house, my rules."

Olivia watched as Liam stripped off his trunks and T-shirt and climbed into the shower stall with her. He stepped in front of the cold stream of water to shield her from it. Olivia reached up and brushed some of the wet hair from in front of her face to look up at Liam. He went over and began to peel her wet bathing suit down her body, bending down until he got it to her feet so she could step out of it.

"We don't want any sand anywhere." He grinned as his hands worked their way back up her legs to her waist.

"No, we don't," she answered softly, closing her eyes as she felt Liam's hands on her and his lips at her neck.

The rest of the day passed quietly back at Liam's home. Olivia spent time outside in the backyard sunning and overlooking the ocean and the clear blue sky. Liam spent time surveying the area while attempting to relax some before the sun began to set.

Once they were both inside, Olivia resigned herself to mindlessly flipping the channels on the television, looking for something to watch. With no access to the Internet or her cell phone, and Liam cautious about going anywhere, dejection and boredom reigned over the house.

It wasn't until night had settled in that Olivia felt a pat on her shoulder. She spun around, gratefully distracted from watching yet another episode of reality TV, and saw Liam standing there.

"Go get dressed," he told her. "We're going out."

"Seriously?" Olivia asked with excitement.

"Yes," he relented. "If I have to sit and look at you moping around and watching TV endlessly, I'll go crazy. So we'll go to Fish Heads and grab dinner and a drink. It's nothing fancy, and we're not staying all night. Fair enough?"

"Yes!" Olivia yelled with elation. She leaped up, standing up on the sofa so that she was the same height as Liam, and planted a kiss on his lips. "Thank you!"

Olivia jumped over the back of the couch. She went to her room, stripping out of the shorts and T-shirt she wore so she could put on the lilac-colored floral-print midi dress she got from Alicia's shop. She buttoned the dress up in the front and looked in the mirror, undoing a couple of the bottom buttons to make the slit show a bit more of her leg. Olivia tied her hair up in a ponytail. She slipped back into the chunky heels that gave her a few more inches, so Liam didn't completely dwarf her when they stood together.

By the time she reappeared in the living room, Liam was sitting in a recliner wearing black jeans and a dark blue T-shirt. She saw him staring at her and did a slow twirl in front of him so he could get a good look at her.

"What do you think?" Olivia asked, smiling.

"Very nice," Liam answered stoically as he rose.

"That's it? Very nice?"

"What did you want me to say?" Liam responded. "It's a nice dress."

Olivia watched as he plucked his keys and wallet off the counter and stuffed them in his pocket.

"I was hoping for a little more enthusiasm on your part, I guess. I love this dress."

Liam reached over and snatched Olivia, lifting her up into the air and causing her to gasp. He held her up, so she looked down at him.

"It's awesome!" he feigned, opening his eyes wide and grinning.

"Better." She laughed as he slowly lowered Olivia. Liam paused when her feet hit the ground as he wrapped his arms around her and kissed her deeply.

"I love the dress," Liam said softly, "and I can't wait to get you out of it later."

"Perfect," Olivia whispered back, flush from the kiss.

The two walked down to the garage, where Liam pulled out the motorcycle helmets.

"We're not taking the car?" Olivia asked.

"Parking is a bitch over there," Liam told her as he strapped on his helmet. "The bike can fit better. Also, it's only a few minutes down the road."

"But I'm wearing a dress," Olivia told him.

"Shit, you're right," Liam said. He put the helmets back down and walked back over to the GTO. "Next time, we both wear jeans."

"Good... that means we're going out again while we're here," Olivia stated as she slammed the passenger door shut.

"Hey! That's not what I said! You're twistin' my words around."

"Yes, I am," Olivia said proudly as Liam pulled the car out of the garage.

Olivia enjoyed the short ride down the road to the sign that indicated they were at Fish Heads. She looked around and was surprised at the number of cars in the sandy parking lot for a weeknight. Music could be heard playing as they walked up toward the building and through the bait and tackle shop that led to the bar and restaurant. Liam grasped Olivia's hand and led her over to two empty seats at the bar.

Olivia turned around on her stool as soon as they sat to get a view of the band just setting up. They looked older, with a man with gray hair tied back in a ponytail wearing a Hawaiian shirt seemingly leading the band. Olivia turned around to look at Liam as he spied the multitude of beers on tap.

Olivia saw Liam break out in a smile before he yelled.

"Hey there, miss! I can't help but notice there's no Guinness on tap!" Liam had amped up his Irish brogue to a new level to get the bartender's attention. The woman stopped what she was doing and turned to face Liam with a severe look on her face. Olivia expected a confrontation from Liam's bluntness but got just the opposite.

"Learn to drink something else. It's a tiki bar," she shot back before breaking into a smile. "It's been a long time since you dragged your sorry ass in here."

The bartender came down and leaned over the bar to give Liam a big hug.

"I know it's been a while," Liam said as they broke their embrace. Olivia saw the enormous smile Liam had on his face as he looked at the fair redhead behind the bar. Olivia leaned closer to Liam on his stool so their shoulders were touching. Liam looked at Olivia and then at the bartender.

"Fiona, this is Olivia," Liam said politely. "Fiona is an old friend from up our way."

"Nice to meet you," Olivia said with a smile. Olivia knew she was getting looked over.

"Nice to meet you, too," Fiona replied. "If I knew you were in town, I would have grabbed some Guinness for you, Liam. You know you need to give me a heads-up. Your ma would be up in arms over your manners."

"True enough," Liam answered. "It's okay. I'll just take a whiskey."

"And for you?" Fiona asked Olivia.

"Hmmm... something tropical... maybe a piña colada?"

"Are you legal?" Fiona questioned.

"She's legal," Liam piped up.

Fiona arched an eyebrow at Liam.

"Don't feck me over, Liam," Fiona said sternly.

"I'm twenty-one, honest," Olivia told her.

"I'll trust you," Fiona said, "and take it out on him if there's trouble."

Fiona walked off to get the drinks while Liam turned to look at the pier and the band setting up.

"I'm gonna hit the men's room," Liam spoke. "You okay for a minute or two?"

"I think I'll survive," Olivia offered. She watched as Liam rose and headed back inside. Fiona then appeared with Liam's whiskey and put a glass in front of Olivia.

"Here you go," Fiona said with a smile.

"Thanks," Olivia said as she sipped through the straw, getting blasted by the chill of the drink.

"How long have you known Liam?" Olivia asked before taking another sip nonchalantly.

"Oh, we go way back to when we were kids. I grew up just a few doors down from him. There was a group of us, friends through high school and all."

"He... he seems to have a lot of female friends," Olivia added, looking for information.

Fiona let out a hearty laugh.

"That he does," she scoffed. "He's always been a ladies' man. I think he thought he was good at it even when he was a scrawny kid. How long have you known him?"

Olivia hesitated and took another sip.

"Not very long," she confessed.

"I can tell you this," Fiona said, coming closer to Olivia. "In all the years I have known Liam, and since he's been coming here, he's never introduced me to a woman he has with him. They've always been nameless entities. You're the first he's brought forward. In fact, I can't remember him ever bringing someone from back home down here with him. He's always going off about the whole Fortress of Solitude thing."

"Yes!" Olivia roared and laughed, feeling more at ease.

"He obviously thinks highly of you; otherwise, he wouldn't have brought you to meet me."

Liam returned to the bar, placing his hand on Olivia's shoulder before picking up his drink.

"What's so funny?" Liam asked.

"You gave her the Fortress of Solitude speech?" Fiona mocked. "You're still the geeky kid I knew, aren't you?"

"Jaysus," Liam said, shaking his head. "You had to tell her that?" Liam said, looking at Olivia.

"Fiona brought it up," Olivia defended.

The band had begun to play, starting with a version of Clapton's "Wonderful Tonight." Liam reached over and plucked Olivia's hand, taking her out to the small dance floor.

"What are you doing?" she asked with surprise.

"Getting you away from Fiona, so she doesn't start telling you all the horror stories about me."

Liam pulled Olivia closer, and she put her head up against his chest as they danced slowly.

"Fiona said you never introduce women to her," Olivia said, looking up at Liam.

Liam sighed as they moved on the floor.

"It's true," he said with a nod.

"How come?"

"I guess... I guess I've never had anyone with me that I wanted Fiona to meet. It never felt right. Now it does."

Olivia beamed and squeezed her arms around Liam. She crooked her finger so he would bring his face down closer to hers. When he did, she gave him a slow kiss.

"Someone is so getting lucky tonight," she purred.

Chapter 13

13

Liam put his concerns aside for a bit so that both he and Olivia could relax. They enjoyed the Fish Heads atmosphere, having a few drinks, dining on the fresh fish tacos, and listening, singing, and dancing to the cover songs played by Captain Carroway and the Seeded Ryes. The worries of the natural world seemed outside the beach area as the two laughed and enjoyed each other's company.

After the band's rendition of "Margaritaville," Olivia headed off to use the restroom, and Liam sat at the bar by himself for a moment. Then, Fiona approached him at the end of the bar as he drank the last of the whiskey in front of him.

"Another one, Boss?" Fiona asked as she snatched up the glass.

"Nah, I think I'll switch to ginger ale for now, Fiona," Liam stated.

Fiona stood frozen and stared at him before busting out in a laugh.

"What's so funny?"

"She's totally got you." Fiona laughed as she picked up the soda gun and began to fill a glass for Liam.

"What are you talking about?" Liam said defensively.

"Look at you," Fiona said as she placed the glass down. "You're laughing, dancing, and listening to beach music. You're even passing on whiskey and drinking soda."

"It's called being responsible," Liam said as he grabbed the ginger ale from the bar.

"Call it whatever you want, Liam," Fiona said with a knowing smile. "The truth is this girl has you wrapped. Remember who you're talkin' to here. I've seen you most of your life. Responsibility was never something that worried you much. Now, here you are drinking soda and dancing to love songs."

"Ahh, you're daft," Liam said scornfully.

"I think it's sweet," Fiona told him. "I forgot you had a soft, sensitive side. I just hope you know what you're doing."

"What the hell does that mean? And why does everyone keep telling me that?" Liam responded angrily.

"Take some advice from an old friend, Liam," Fiona began. "She's young, and I'm guessing she hasn't seen much about the way you've lived your life so far. So if you really care about her, be careful with her. Don't feck it up by being... well, by being the usual you."

"Thanks for the pep talk," Liam said as he finished the ginger ale and pushed the glass toward Fiona, asking for a refill. "I know what I'm doing."

Liam glanced to his right and saw someone walking toward him. When the figure got a few feet closer, he recognized it as Paul from the beach.

"Fiona," he said with urgency, getting her attention. "My name is Aaron, and Olivia is Serena. Just go with me."

Fiona nodded and watched as Paul slid onto the barstool next to Liam.

"Fancy seeing you here." Paul smiled.

"Just enjoying the nightlife," Liam replied cautiously.

"This place is great," Paul said, looking around. "I love the atmosphere here. I can see why they're so crowded. Can I get you a drink?"

"No, thanks, I just got a refill." Liam held up his ginger ale.

"Is that straight soda?" Paul asked with surprise. "I sure didn't take you for a soda guy. Come on, let me get you a real drink."

Paul waved to get Fiona's attention, and she came down to the end of the bar.

"What can I get you?" Fiona asked with a smile.

"I'll take another Jack and Coke and then get him whatever he wants." Paul pointed at Liam.

Fiona looked at Liam.

"What can I get for you, Aaron?" Fiona asked.

"I'm good," Liam responded. "Get one for yourself."

"Thanks," Fiona said as she poured herself a shot of Jameson after making Paul's drink.

Paul held up his drink to Liam and clinked glasses with him and Fiona.

"Cheers," he said as he took a healthy sip. "Where's your daughter Serena?"

Liam put down his soda and looked at Paul.

"I think we both know she's not my daughter," Liam said emphatically.

"Hey, I didn't mean to offend you," Paul said, putting his hands up. "Good for you, man. She's a pretty girl. You're a lucky SOB. I'm surprised you let her out of your sight in a place like this."

The silent alarm in Liam's head began to go off, but he remained calm and stoic.

"Where's your daughter?" Liam asked Paul as he sipped his soda. "What was her name? Josie?"

"Yeah, that's her," Paul replied. "She went to the ladies' room. Probably just gabbing away. I'm not sure she's too thrilled to have to spend the week with me anyway, but it's the only time we have during the summer. She lives with my ex and starts college in the fall."

Liam glanced in the direction of the door leading to where the restrooms were, anxiously waiting for Olivia to reappear.

Olivia looked into the mirror in the ladies' room after washing up, straightening her ponytail, and making sure her dress appeared just right. A glow of enjoyment passed her face as she reflected on the excellent time with Liam. At that last glance, she caught a view of a familiar face behind her coming from the stall.

The girl strode next to her at the sink, turning on the water and soaping her hands. Olivia's stomach became uneasy, and she turned to the paper towel dispenser to grab a couple to dry her hands.

"You're Serena, right?" the girl asked quietly as she rinsed the soap from her hands.

"Yeah," Olivia answered, recalling the alias Liam had bestowed on her. "We met at the beach... Josie, was it?"

Olivia dried her hands rapidly before crumpling the towel in her hand and gripping it in her fist.

"Yep," Josie answered, shutting off the water. A few other ladies had entered the restroom.

Olivia pulled the door open and stepped outside, and Josie followed right behind her.

"Did you have a nice time at the beach?" Olivia asked, trying to make small talk and get back to Liam as fast as she could.

"It was all right," Josie said, shrugging. "Not exactly a great time with my dad, you know? This scene is much better. At least there's something to do, and there are a lot of cute guys to look at. Are you legal?"

"Legal?" Olivia asked as they crossed into the front shop that led back to the bar.

"Yeah, you know... twenty-one? I wasn't asking if you're legal in the country or anything." Josie laughed. "Geez, we're not all racists."

"No, no, I didn't mean it that way," Olivia said, trying to backtrack. "Yeah, I'm twenty-one."

"Cool. Do you think you can score me a drink? I'm only twenty, and my dad won't get anything for me but soda."

"I don't know if that's a good idea," Olivia offered, stepping out onto the back patio and scanning the crowd to find Liam. "We could both get in a lot of trouble."

"Oh, come on," Josie whined. "They'll think it's for you. I'll wait at our table over there. My dad's not even there right now. You don't look like the goody two-shoes type."

"What does that mean?" Olivia asked, facing Josie.

"I mean, come on." Josie smiled. "Look at the sexy dress you're wearing. And your boyfriend... holy shit, is he hot for an older guy. I'm sure you do the bad girl thing."

"He's not really my..." Olivia began and stopped herself short. "I should get back over to where he is." Olivia wracked her brain, trying to remember the name Liam gave himself earlier.

"It's cool if he's just a Sugar Daddy," Josie said, grabbing Olivia's arm. "I totally get that. I'd do that too."

"Look," Olivia began, attempting to tug her arm away. "I need to—"

The band kicked in and started playing "Get Down Tonight," causing Josie to grab Olivia's hand.

"Let's dance!" Josie shouted, dragging Olivia to the dance floor before she could answer. Before Olivia knew it, she moved to the song's rhythm with Josie dancing in front of her, tossing her hair from side to side. Olivia glanced over to the end of the bar where she and Liam had been sitting, and she saw Josie's father engaged with Liam. So instead of continuing the dance, Olivia moved away and headed to Liam. She noticed he glanced at her as she approached, and he rose from his barstool as Olivia got to him, putting an arm around her as she got there.

"There you are," Liam said with a forced chuckle. "I was wondering where you got off to."

"There was a line at the ladies' room, and then I ran into—" Olivia started as Josie came up behind her, huffing a bit.

"She ran into me," Josie said, smiling. "Where'd you go? I thought we were going to dance?"

"Sorry, I..." Olivia looked at Liam and then back at Josie and Paul. "I guess I'm just not feeling well. Probably the drinks and being out in the sun all day. Maybe we should go."

Liam breathed a sigh of relief when he finally saw Olivia coming toward him. But, when he realized Josie was right behind her and could see the discomfort on Olivia's face, he knew it was time to act.

"Let me settle up our tab," Liam said, turning back to the bar. Liam kept one eye on Olivia as she stood with Paul and Josie as he got Fiona's attention.

"I'm settling up," Liam said. "As quickly as possible."

"You got it," Fiona told him as she went to grab his tab.

When Fiona returned to Liam with the check, he took hold of it and handed her a hundred-dollar bill.

"Have you seen this guy before?" he said as quietly as he could.

Fiona looked Paul up and down and turned back to Liam.

"Yeah, he's been around for a couple of days," Fiona replied. "He's been here for lunch and at night a few times. Sometimes with the girl, sometimes without."

Liam grabbed a pen off the bar and scribbled his phone number on the back of his tab.

"Call me if you see him or if he starts asking about us," Liam said. He patted Fiona's hand.

"Are you in trouble?" Fiona asked.

"Probably," Liam said with a wink and a smile. "Talk to you soon."

"*Fanacht sábháilte*," Fiona whispered.

"Always," Liam replied.

"We're all set," Liam said to Olivia, pulling her toward him.

"Maybe we can get together tomorrow for some lunch?" Paul asked. "The four of us? Right here?"

"I don't know," Liam said. "It really depends on how Serena is feeling. If we're here, we're here."

Liam hustled Olivia away and through the crowd around the stage where the band played until they got to the front house and out the door.

"Just keep walking," Liam insisted, holding Olivia's arm.

When they reached their car, Liam opened the door so Olivia could slip inside. Then, he glanced up the parking lot toward the main entrance to Fish Heads to see if they were being watched. Even though he saw no signs of Paul there, he still had a feeling they were looking.

"That was creepy," Olivia said shakily.

"What did she do?" Liam asked as he drove back toward the house.

"Nothing really, I guess," Olivia told him. "I saw her in the bathroom, and she asked if I would buy her a drink. Then she asked me about you and if you were my boyfriend or anything. After that, she forced me onto the dance floor, and then I came to you."

Liam kept his eyes focused on the road, glancing into the rearview mirror to see if they were followed.

"What did you tell her?"

Liam saw from the corner of his eye that Olivia stared at him.

"I didn't tell her anything," Olivia insisted. "I never answered her."

"That's probably for the best," Liam replied.

"Meaning what?"

"Just that the less they know about either of us, the better, is all," Liam said in a huff.

Olivia sat quietly as Liam pulled the car into his driveway and drove to the garage.

"Do you think they are onto us?" Olivia said worriedly.

"I don't know," Liam said honestly. "Fiona said the two of them have been around Fish Heads for a couple of days. So it could just be a coincidence that they are here this week and stumbled on us. There's something about him I don't trust, though. So I think we may need to accelerate our escape."

"And go where? You said it wasn't safe back in Harriman yet."

"I don't know," Liam said solemnly. He looked over and saw tears in Olivia's eyes.

"Hey, I'll think of something," Liam told her, pulling her close. "I'm not going to let anything happen to you. If we have to leave in the morning, we will. We'll go somewhere, trust me. "

"I feel like... like I'm adrift on the ocean with no idea what's coming next," Olivia cried.

"I've got you... I promise," Liam vowed.

Chapter 14

Olivia happily accepted Liam's invitation to stay with him in his bedroom for the night. Being alone didn't fit with her feelings of unease. The comfort and security of having Liam next to her provided Olivia with just what she needed. Yet, even with his protection, she still struggled to fall asleep, tossing and turning most of the night. A last glance at the clock on the nightstand next to her showed it was nearly 4:00 a.m.

Sitting up in the bed to aggressively fluff her pillow once again roused Liam from his sleep.

"You okay?" Liam asked groggily.

"I guess," Olivia replied, forcing her head back down on the pillow. She turned to her left to look at Liam's face. His eyes remained closed while he was partially awake.

"I'm just having trouble sleeping," she said worriedly.

Liam had pried his eyes open and was staring at Olivia now. He rolled onto his back and slid over toward the middle of the bed so he could put his arm around her and pull her closer. Olivia rested her head on his chest, listening to the calm beat of his heart.

Olivia's right hand toiled on Liam's bare chest, feeling the contours of his muscles under her fingertips. Her hand slid across his taut abs, dipping even lower until she reached the waistband of the boxer briefs he wore to bed. Olivia glanced at Liam and saw his eyes were still closed.

It wasn't until her hand went lower, gripping him through the cotton, that stirring occurred.

The slightest touch through the briefs awakened Liam above and below Olivia's hand. She gave his cock a light squeeze, making it even firmer, and Liam spoke up.

"What are you doing?" he said raspily.

"Just returning an earlier favor," Olivia replied. Her right hand had worked its way inside Liam's briefs so she could feel the hot, hard flesh of him directly. Another light squeeze that moved into slow strokes up and down his shaft got his full attention.

Liam went to move to his side to get his hands on Olivia, but she moved closer to Liam, draping her left arm over his body to keep him in place.

"This is my game," she purred.

Making a fist around his cock, Olivia moved slowly up and down, running her thumb over the engorged purple head. She heard and felt Liam's breath quicken with each move as her thumb dabbled in the precome forming from Liam's excitement. Then, she rapidly rubbed her thumb just under the tip to excite him all the more.

"You're making me crazy," Liam growled.

"Good." Olivia smiled.

Olivia moved her body, never breaking contact with Liam's rigid cock in her hand so that she knelt between his legs. She looked down at him hungrily before giving him a long, slow lick from the base of his cock to the tip, causing Liam to visibly shiver. Olivia peered up at Liam and smiled as she repeated the move.

She pulled off the black tank top she wore to bare her breasts before moving even closer to Liam. She kept her eyes locked on his as she peeled off his boxer briefs and tossed them aside and then quickly did the same with her own sleep shorts. She positioned herself between Liam's legs once again, lowering herself slowly so that her own wetness would glide against his anxious cock. Liam groaned again and reached for Olivia before she pushed his hands away.

"Tsk, tsk," she said, wagging her finger and scolding her lover. "Were you trying to touch me here?"

Olivia brought her hands up to her bare breasts, cupping them in her hands before rubbing her thumbs over her erect, sensitive nipples.

"Or was it here?" she asked coyly. She slid her hand down her body as Liam's eyes transfixed on her. Her hand dipped lower and lower until she ran a finger along her wetness. Olivia let out a light moan as she did this, and then reached her hand back to Liam's cock, sharing that wetness with him as she slid up and down on him.

Olivia relished in the power she felt and what she could do to Liam, controlling his hunger at the moment.

"Enough teasing," Liam said as he reached for her again. Olivia moved just beyond his fingertips and touch.

"Did you want something?" she asked playfully.

"You know damn well I do," he panted as her hand edged him along again.

Olivia grabbed a foil wrapper off the nightstand and tore it open. Then, she slowly unrolled the condom onto Liam, taking extra time to squeeze him and feel him.

"Am I doing this right?" she teased.

Olivia moved onto Liam, straddling atop him, his cock resting just outside her as she rubbed against him again. The head of his cock continually worked against her sensitive clit as they both got closer and closer before Olivia slid Liam inside her, causing them both to gasp together.

Olivia rocked her hips back and forth slower, taking Liam in as deeply as she could. She knew how close she was and felt Liam reaching that point as well. Then, she abruptly slowed things down, dragging Liam to the edge again while she barely moved her hips.

"Say my name," she whispered to him.

"What?" Liam replied. His eyes closed with each excruciating gyration of Olivia's hips.

"I want to hear you say my name when you come, Liam. You never say my name at all. Say it, scream it, please," she asked him as she teetered on the edge herself.

Liam groaned, trying to hold on before he reached down and grasped her thighs as Olivia rode him.

"Olivia... oh Christ... Olivia," he moaned as he surged into her.

It proved all Olivia needed to hear and feel as she came as well, tensing her body before feeling the exquisite release she longed for. She collapsed on top of Liam, pressing her head to his chest once again and this time listening to the rapid heartbeat that filled his chest.

"I think I can go to sleep now." She giggled before moving off to Liam's side. Liam put his arm around her immediately and held her.

"I don't know if I can," Liam added, kissing the top of Olivia's head before she turned her lips to him so he could kiss her deeply.

Olivia had managed to drift off to sleep after her early-morning seduction helped her. The sun came through the windows of Liam's bedroom, and Olivia stirred again. She sat up and stretched with a long yawn. Liam lay still, snoring lightly under a rumpled sheet that had tangled around him.

Olivia quietly slipped out of bed and back to her bedroom, throwing on a pair of shorts and a T-shirt before heading to the kitchen to make coffee for the two of them. The thoughts of the troubles that lay ahead were tossed away for the moment, allowing her the blissful state she stayed in as the coffee readied.

She brought a steaming mug to Liam in the bedroom, placing it on his nightstand. She then squatted down and kissed his stubbled cheek before moving to his lips to rouse him awake.

"Good morning," she said happily. "I made coffee."

"I think it was already a good morning the way you woke me up the first time." Liam grinned. "The coffee is the icing on the cake."

"I'm glad you think so," she answered proudly.

"Did you want some breakfast?" Olivia questioned.

"I think I need a shower first," Liam replied. "I seem to be a bit sweaty and sticky."

"I'll take the blame for most of that." Olivia blushed.

Olivia watched as Liam rose from the bed, standing in front of her and towering over her in his naked form. She couldn't resist placing a hand on his chest and moving down toward his abs.

"I think this is how things started a few hours ago," Liam said, placing a thumb under her chin and turning her face up toward his so he could kiss her.

"Is that such a bad thing?"

"Not at all." Liam smiled. "How about I make you some breakfast after I shower? You can go sit on the back porch, take in the sun and the ocean, and I'll do the cooking."

"You know how to cook?" Olivia asked skeptically.

"Of course I do!" Liam stated firmly. "My ma wouldn't have it any other way. Get outta here!"

Liam gave Olivia a playful slap on the behind to move her along. Olivia returned the favor by hitting the bare flesh of Liam's firm backside.

Olivia watched as Liam walked to the bathroom and turned on the shower. She smiled and walked out into the living room area and turned on the stereo system, putting some music on before she opened the glass doors leading to the back porch that overlooked the ocean.

Keb Mo's "Life is Beautiful" played over the speakers positioned high in the outdoor corners of the house, and Olivia sat down on one of the lounge chairs. The warmth of the sun touched her face, and she closed her eyes as the rays sated and filled her. A light breeze ran across the area, sending goose bumps up Olivia's legs. As she began to relax, she heard a door slam inside the house that startled her. The noise was followed up by a ringing of the burner cell phone she held in her pocket.

Olivia leaped from her chair, reaching for the phone. Only a couple of people had the number for the phone, and she stared at it while it rang in her hand before she flipped it open and answered it. She dared not say anything into it for fear of who it was.

"Olivia?" a voice crackled.

She lifted the phone to her ear and cautiously whispered.

"Beatriz?" she asked.

"Yes!" her sister said excitedly into the phone.

Olivia looked around, wanting to share her happiness with someone before remembering there was no one nearby. She paced down the porch steps and out onto the beach so she would not be overheard.

"Bea! I have been so worried about you! How are you? How is Danni? And Mom and Dad?"

"Everything is fine,' Beatriz replied. "I don't have long to talk. I'm not supposed to even call you, but I needed to hear your voice. We are safe at the house. We haven't left to go anywhere. Dad goes to work each day and picks up groceries when we need things. The people here stay in touch with New York, so we know what is going on, and they say we need to keep hiding for a bit more. How are you? Where are you? They said you are not home yet."

"I'm not," Olivia answered as she moved farther out onto the sand. "I'm still with Liam. He is taking care of me. We ran from the airport and came to the coast. He has a house here at the beach, and we are safe, but we'll be on the move again, probably today. I'm not sure when I will get to go home."

"Maybe... maybe you should come here," Beatriz told her. "Be with us back home. I know Mama and Dad would love to have you here, and Danni misses you terribly. At least you would be safe."

"I don't know," Olivia said cautiously. "I like my life in New York. And now... well, I think now I have more reason to stay."

"Why?" Beatriz questioned.

"It's... it's complicated," Olivia told her sister.

"It's him, isn't it?"

Olivia said nothing in reply.

"Olivia, I know he's protecting you, and maybe that's why you feel drawn to him, but..."

"But what?" Olivia asked.

"But look at the life he leads," Beatriz told her younger sister. "He doesn't seem like the type of person who just settles down to be with one woman. You are young and have your whole life ahead of you. You can do anything you want. Don't get caught up in some romance that may not really be there. It will break your heart, and then where will you be? Alone and in danger again. Please, Liv, just come home to us."

"I can't talk about this right now," Olivia said, annoyed. "I'm glad you're safe. Give a kiss to Mama and Dad for me, and a big hug to Danni. *Te quiero*."

"*Te quiero*," Beatriz replied before hanging up.

Olivia stood on the beach, facing the ocean, relieved that her family was okay, but torn about what she should do next. Finally, she turned and looked back at the house before slowly making her way back.

Liam took his time showering, savoring the hot water around him before getting out and drying off. First, he spent some time shaving off the stubble and trimming his beard, getting rid of some of the unruly hairs to make it look neater than it had been in a long time. Next, he brushed out his long, dark hair, opting to let it fall toward his shoulders instead of tying it back. He even reached into one of the drawers below the sink, pulled out a Polo bottle he rarely used, and put a bit of cologne on.

He opened up the bathroom door leading back into his bedroom. Steam rushed out of the bathroom behind and around him, filtering into the air of the bedroom. He glanced toward the bed and saw Olivia tucked under the bedsheet, lying down and facing away from him. He grabbed a pair of gray boxer briefs from his dresser and sat down on the end of the bed, facing the mirror on the opposite wall.

"Decided to get some more rest, eh?" Liam asked, reaching over and tapping Olivia's feet under the sheet. "I know I just showered and promised you breakfast, but if you would rather do something else first, I think I can be convinced."

Liam reached down to step into his boxer briefs, felt hands around his waist, and then the hands moved up to his shoulders. He smiled before looking into the mirror.

"Hi there," he said as he sat up.

"Hi back," said Josie, smiling with her arms around him.

Chapter 15

Liam spun around in shock, staring at Josie before he pushed himself off the bed. He saw her kneeling on the bed wearing nothing but a sky blue bra and panties. She smiled up at him as he looked on.

"What the feck are you doing here?" he barked.

"The back door was open, and I was walking on the beach, so I let myself in. I didn't think you would mind."

"Do you routinely let yourself into strangers' homes?" Liam asked. "How did you know this was where we were staying?"

"We're just two doors down." Josie grinned, grabbing a pillow and lying on it. "I saw Serena come out of the house before when I was outside. So I thought I would slip in and give you a little surprise."

"Well, your plan worked; I'm surprised," Liam admitted. He reached for Josie's arm to help her up from the bed. "Now you can go."

"Oh, come on," Josie whined. "You're telling me you're not the least bit interested? I know Serena is pretty, but I bet I could rock your world."

"Not interested," Liam stated firmly. "Let's go."

Liam bent over the bed to pull Josie up, but instead, she caught him off-balance and dragged him onto the bed with her. Within seconds, she had flipped on top of him, proving to be much stronger and more agile than he thought the young woman would be.

"That's better." She laughed as she straddled Liam.

"Enough of this," Liam said as he grabbed Josie's hips to lift her up.

"Are you sure?" she said, pressing her body down to his so that her lips were close to his. She planted tiny kisses on Liam's neck before he shoved her back to her straddling position.

"Get off," Liam growled.

"That's what I'm trying to do," Josie purred. Liam watched as she reached behind her back and undid the clasp on her bra, freeing her breasts.

"Still want me to leave?" She smiled.

"Yes!" Liam answered loudly.

Liam pivoted his hips and rolled over, leaving Josie beneath his body.

"This works too," she said, clasping her hands behind Liam's neck before pulling herself up and attaching herself to his lips.

As Liam attempted to pull back from the embrace, he saw from the corner of his eye that Olivia had entered the room. She stopped abruptly when she saw the kiss breaking.

"What the..." Olivia began before she turned to Liam with an astonished look.

"Oh, you're just in time." Josie grinned. "Join us. I'm sure between the two of us, we can drive him wild."

Olivia appeared crestfallen as Liam removed the hands clasped around his neck and sat up, letting Olivia see that Josie was also topless. He watched as Olivia spun on her heels and dashed out of the room.

"Olivia, wait!" Liam yelled, trying to get up. But, instead, Josie attached herself to Liam's back, keeping him on the bed.

"Who's Olivia?" she said softly into his ear.

"Feck," Liam groaned.

Overwhelmed and stunned by what she had seen, Olivia tore out of the house, out the back door, and down to the beach. She gulped at the air as she marched along the shoreline, the ocean water lapping at her feet. She had heard Liam call her name as she stormed out of the house, but she didn't think twice and kept moving forward.

Olivia worked farther and farther down the beach, turning back occasionally to see if Liam even tried to follow her, to get her back, but no sign of him appeared. Disheartened further, Olivia stopped along her walk and sat on the damp sand, frustrated and saddened.

The cell phone in her pocket vibrated, drawing her out of her state. She reached into her shorts and removed the phone, expecting it to be Liam calling her. She was all set to ignore him, or at the very least lash out at him. But, instead, when she looked at the phone, she noticed the same number as before when her sister had phoned her. Olivia flipped the phone open, breaking into a sob as soon as she went to speak.

"Bea, you... you were right... he... I can't believe it," she said before her sister had a chance to say anything.

"What did he do, Olivia?" the male voice said into the phone.

Olivia sat in stunned silence.

"Who... who is this?" she asked shakily.

"You know who this is," the voice said on the other end, breaking into a familiar snicker she had heard too often.

"Benny? But how..." she said softly.

"Oh, I knew your sister wouldn't be able to resist trying to contact you at some point," he replied. "I have friends in Peru, too, you know. I've been waiting for your sister to call you. She couldn't stop herself, even if everyone told her not to contact you. It's just like when she called me when you were in Virginia. She might complain about me, but deep down, I know she wants me back."

"She called you?"

"When you stopped at the gas station in Virginia, yes." Benny laughed. "Did you think it was just by accident guys showed up there? Fucking Liam had to mess it all up. Otherwise, this would all be over with already. She kept telling me how sorry she was. It was hysterical."

"You're a fucking animal," Olivia barked.

"Yeah, well, that's your opinion," Benny said casually. "Now that you have seen what Liam is like with women, we can bring all this to a close."

"How did you know about what I saw?"

"For someone so smart, you can be dense at times." Benny laughed again. "Who do you think sent them there? If I sent a Hispanic couple, Liam would have been triggered right away, and I would have lost you already. They at least kept him at bay a bit. Once you two slipped out of Charlotte, I sent some feelers out. We found Alicia in Nags Head. It was easy to put things together after that."

Panic crossed Olivia's mind as she worried about the safety of Alicia and what may have happened to her.

"Don't bother trying to run," Benny told her. "The girl will take care of Liam. She's very efficient at what she does. He'll be dead before you get back to the house."

Olivia's stomach filled with fear.

"How do you know I'm not at the house?"

"He told me," Benny said coldly.

Olivia spun around only to see the shadow of Paul looking over her, holding a cell phone of his own in one hand with a pistol neatly tucked into the waistband of his khakis.

"So, who's Olivia?" Josie said into Liam's ear again.

Liam went to rise off the bed only to get jerked back forcefully. A leather belt was now around his neck and steadily tightening. He found himself lying on the bed as Josie shifted her weight and was now on Liam's chest. He watched as she wrapped the belt around each of her hands, strengthening the constriction on Liam's throat.

Liam instinctively reached for the belt, trying to loosen the death grip it had as it cut off his air.

"It's too bad, really," Josie told him as she looked into his eyes. "I would have liked to see how you were. But, unfortunately, I rarely get to take down someone as fine as you."

Josie reached back with her left hand as her right held the belt, grasping Liam through his briefs.

"Feels like you have something worth it back there, too; what a shame."

Liam realized he was getting light-headed from the strangling and had to act fast. When Josie reached back to grab his cock and balls, he moved his legs up as if to somersault, catching the woman off guard. Liam trapped her between his muscular legs and pushed down with all his might to throw her to the ground. He heard her body thud to the carpet as he gasped for air and coughed.

Josie bounced back to her feet quickly as Liam stood up. She swept his legs out from under him with a kick, knocking him to the floor so she could jump on top of him again. She attempted to pin his arms down under her knees.

"Nice move," she said, winded from the fall. "It's nice to see you're not a complete pushover."

"Feck you," Liam spat as he tried to free his arms from beneath her knees.

"God, that brogue is sexy." Josie laughed. "No wonder the girl fell so hard for you. Don't worry; once you're gone, Paul and I will take good care of her until we get her back to Benny."

Josie bent close to Liam's face.

"Care for a goodbye kiss?"

"No, thanks," Liam huffed, thrusting his head forward with all his might and cracking his forehead against Josie's face. Within seconds, her body slumped to the left and off of Liam. He rolled to the right first before gathering himself and reaching over to pull Josie's limp body and turn her over. Liam saw she was still breathing, but it was through her mouth as her nose crushed against her face. Blood poured from her as her eyes fluttered.

Liam rose and went over to the curtains covering the windows and pulled them down. Then, he yanked the cord off and made quick work of securing Josie's hands behind her back. Next, he went over to the bed and grasped the belt, then knelt down next to Josie, looping the belt around her neck and slowly tightening it until she struggled to breathe and her eyes bulged.

"You're feisty for a small little bitch, I'll give you that," Liam said between deep breaths. "Where is she?"

Liam watched as Josie struggled to breathe, thrashing her head from side to side before he loosened the belt a little so she could get some air.

"Go to hell," she gasped. Liam tightened the belt again, going one more notch so that Josie's face started to turn purple.

"You said it yourself," Liam said calmly. "You were bringing her back to Benny. Benny would never pass up the chance to see her face to face before he got rid of her. Where is she now? Where's your house?"

Josie nodded rapidly, and Liam relaxed the belt.

"Three houses down," she rasped. "The yellow one."

Liam let go of the belt, allowing the woman to breathe again. She lay on the floor panting as Liam looked around the room. He spied Josie's clothing tucked into the corner of the room and went through her things. There he found a knife on the floor next to her cell phone. He picked up both and tossed them on the bed before he started to get dressed.

He saw Josie's eyes barely open, watching him as he moved about the room and prepared himself. After he dressed, he grabbed his knife and tucked it into the back of his jeans before doing the same with his enemy's blade. Then, Liam walked out to the kitchen before returning with a roll of duct tape. Next, he grabbed a black sock off the floor and prepared to stuff it into Josie's mouth.

"No!" she shouted, blood spurting from her mouth that had trickled down from her nose. "My nose. I won't be able to breathe."

"Not my problem. I guess you better walk fast," Liam told her before stuffing the sock into her mouth and rapidly placing the silver tape over her mouth. Josie struggled immediately before Liam got her to her feet.

"Let's move," he ordered, dragging her body out the back door and down to the beach.

Josie fell several times along the way, but Liam took no pity on her and immediately got her to her feet to keep her moving. The familiar ring in his right pocket let him know someone was calling on her phone.

"Someone wants to talk to you," Liam said as they marched through the sand. He came to a stop, holding the cord tightly that bound Josie's arms to keep her from falling over. He pressed answer on the phone and said nothing.

"Are you done playing around with him?" Liam heard Paul's voice say into the phone. "I've got her, and we should get going as soon as we can so we can collect on this and celebrate. I got you that slutty red set you liked. I can't wait to see it on you."

"That's no way to talk to your daughter, Paulie," Liam said darkly.

Paul was silent on the other end.

"Hmmm. I can't believe you survived her," Paul said bluntly. Liam kept moving forward on the beach until he saw the yellow house they were headed toward.

"She's got a lot of spunk," Liam told Paul. "A nice body too. In another life, maybe I would have taken her up on her offer."

"Where is she?" Paul grunted.

"She's hanging in there, but I don't give her much time. She's looking a bit haggard right now."

"I'll tear your girl's heart out right now," Paul said into the phone.

"We both know you won't, Paulie," Liam said as he lumbered up the sand to the back door of the yellow house. "Without her, you have nothing."

"Then come and get her," Paul said snidely.

"I'm already here," Liam answered, tossing the phone aside as he opened the sliding glass door on the patio that led into the living room. Liam pulled one of the knives out of his waistband and held the glinting blade to Josie's neck. Her eyes were barely open now, and blood had coagulated at what used to be her nose, making her breathing labored.

Paul appeared in the living room, holding a gun shoved into the ribcage of Olivia. The look on Olivia's face when she saw Liam and Josie showed sheer terror.

"You okay?" Liam asked Olivia. She simply nodded at him, too scared to speak.

"What the fuck did you do to her?" Paul yelled as he viewed Josie.

"I guess she likes it rough," Liam replied. Josie started to slump to her knees, but Liam yanked her back to her feet. "Send Olivia over here, and I'll at least take the tape off her mouth so she doesn't suffocate. You can see she's almost there already."

Paul nodded and waved Olivia away. She darted across the room and stood behind Liam. Liam reached over and pulled the tape off Josie's mouth and the sock from her mouth. She exhaled deeply and then coughed and spat blood out of her mouth. Liam let go of Josie's arms, and she began to stagger toward Paul.

"Jesus, what a mess." He scowled.

Liam spun and looked at Olivia, putting his arm around her to protect her.

"I got you," he said softly.

A gunshot rang through the room and jolted Liam as Olivia screamed. Liam looked toward Paul as Josie's body slumped to the floor. The bullet hole in her forehead gave them all a clear sign of what occurred.

"She's no good to me now," Paul complained, pointing the gun at Liam and Olivia.

"You're a feckin' maniac," Liam offered.

"No, just a pragmatist," Paul said. "She would have been damaged goods now. It would take her months to heal, and she would never be as good as she was before. So I did her a favor. Now send the girl back over here. She's worth too much to me to let you just waltz out of here."

"Not gonna happen, pally," Liam said, directing Olivia behind him. He held the knife firmly in his hand as Olivia moved.

"You need to run," Liam said through his gritted teeth.

"He's going to kill you," she cried.

"Maybe, but not you. Go to the house, get in the car and go. Now!"

Liam watched as Olivia slowly backed out the sliding glass door onto the patio. He heard her steps running on the wood when the gunshot rang in his ears.

Chapter 16

1 ⁶

Olivia had just started down the steps of the patio when she heard the gunfire. Instinct had her stop in place and turn around. Dread filled her mind as she imagined Liam slumped on the floor as Paul stepped over his body to come to corral her. She hesitated at the bottom of the steps, only hearing the seagulls squawking above her and nothing else. She hid down behind the staircase, waiting to see Paul come down, but he never did.

Just one minute seemed like excruciating hours to wait to do anything as Olivia crouched down and tried to control her breathing. One deep inhale later, she forced herself back to the steps and crept up, moving slowly as she attempted to stay out of view. She crawled along the patio, collecting sand and dirt on her knees and elbows as she moved until she reached the glass doorway.

The sliding door remained open, with the breeze billowing the curtain up and down enough that she was able to see a shadow slumped on the floor across the room.

"No!" she sobbed as she entered the living room, running toward the boots that stuck out from behind the couch. Only when she reached the body did she see the large knife sticking out from Paul's chest and the lifeless eyes that stared back up at her. Blood stained his shirt, and small puddles gathered on the floor, becoming more prominent with each passing moment.

"For a hired killer, he's shit with a gun," Liam said as he emerged from the kitchen holding a can of Guinness.

Olivia rushed to him, practically tackling Liam as she threw her arms around his waist.

"Careful there, girl," Liam said, comforting Olivia.

Olivia stepped back and felt the dampness on her face. She glanced at her fingers to see they were stained with blood. Then, her eyes shot toward Liam's direction, where blood was visible through his shirt just below his left shoulder.

"You're shot," she said with worry, guiding Liam to one of the stools around the kitchen island.

"Yeah, someone better had me for sure. I got the knife tossed before the bastard fired," Liam said, struggling a bit with his words.

"We need to call the police and get you to the hospital," she said, searching for a towel to compress against Liam to slow the bleeding.

"I don't think so," Liam groaned as he lifted the Guinness to his lips. "If we do either one, we're fecked. Once we're somewhere where we're at the mercy of the system or others, we have no chance."

"We can't just do nothing. You have a bullet in you, and there's a lot of blood," Olivia said, pressing the towel against Liam.

"We need to get out of this house and back to mine," Liam said. He stood up shakily and put his arm around Olivia's shoulder. "You're going to have to help me."

Olivia struggled with Liam's large frame, nearly falling down the steps leading to the beach before reaching the sand. Each step they slogged through the sand proved difficult, like cement drying around their ankles, with Liam needing to stop several times just to keep his breathing going. The short distance between the houses took them nearly an hour to traverse. Olivia, drenched in sweat, finally got Liam into the house and to his bedroom, helping him slump onto his bed after stripping all the blankets off.

Olivia lay next to him on the bed, trying to catch her breath with her energy sapped. Finally, she sat up and looked down at Liam. His ashen face looked back at her before he opened his eyes and cracked a smile.

"I didn't think you had it in you," he said, wincing as he laughed.

"Liam, I don't know what to do," Olivia said, frightened to the core.

"Take my phone out of my pocket," Liam said as his hand reached for his right front jeans pocket.

Olivia jumped off the bed and went around to the other side to ease the phone from his pocket.

"Find Preacher's number and call him," Liam huffed.

"Oh God, you're not gonna die on me," she shouted, scrolling through the phone rapidly.

Liam coughed and laughed.

"Feck, no. I'm not gonna die on you. Preacher will know what to do. Just call him."

Olivia nervously grabbed at the phone and found Preacher's number and selected it. The phone seemed to ring an interminable amount of times as Olivia waited for an answer.

"Liam, are you okay?' Preacher answered.

"No, no, he's not," Olivia said with panic. "I mean, this is Olivia. Liam asked me to call you. Someone tried to take me, or kill me or something... and they did the same to him. He's been shot. There's blood everywhere..."

"It's not all my blood!" Liam shouted, hoping Preacher could hear him.

"Is that him?' Preacher asked with urgency.

"Yes, it is. I got him back to the house, but now I don't know what to do. Please, I need help."

"Olivia, everything is going to be okay," Preacher said calmly. "Can you put the phone on speaker so I can talk to Liam too?"

"Okay," she replied, her voice cracking. She pressed the speaker button so Liam could hear and held the phone closer to him.

"Liam?" Preacher asked.

"Yeah, I'm here," Liam grunted.

"What happened?'

"Benny had some hired guns here to try and grab the girl and eliminate me. They're both dead. The guy shot me when Olivia ran. I'm pretty sure it went clean through, just under my left shoulder. I don't think it's as bad as she's making it sound. There's more blood on me from the others than my own."

"Still, you're going to need to take care of that. But first, you need to get to a hospital or a doctor."

"I can't chance it," Liam added. "If they admit me, they're going to call cops and keep me, and she'll be helpless. Benny knows that. We need Plan B."

"And what might that be?" Preacher asked. "I can get down there with help, but it's going to be many hours before that can happen. You need attention now."

"Call Alicia," Liam said.

"Alicia Barrett? What can she do?" Preacher asked.

"She's down here—she has been for years. She probably knows someone who can help me—a doctor, nurse, EMT, vet, something. She knows everyone."

"I don't know if you should call her," Olivia piped up.

"Why not?" Liam asked as he shifted on the bed.

"Because... because Benny knows who she is and where she is," she answered.

"How the feck do you know that?" Liam questioned.

"He called me... just before Paul took me. Benny called me," Olivia admitted.

"How did he get your number?"

Olivia looked down at the floor before answering.

"Beatriz... my sister... she called me this morning. I know she wasn't supposed to, but she had to talk to me. I needed to know she was okay. Benny must have tapped my parents' phone, and he traced me. He told me they were coming for me... and you too... and they knew about Alicia. That's how they found us."

"Christ, woman!" Liam yelled. "What were you thinking? You're leading them right to us, and now Alicia is in danger too."

"What was I supposed to do? Not answer the phone? I needed to know how she was. I... I didn't know any of this was going on... I'm sorry..." she said in a mix of tears and anger.

"Okay, that doesn't matter right now," Preacher intervened. "We need to figure out the best way to get help to both of you."

"Fiona," Liam said, moving the blood-soaked towel from his wound and grabbing a pillowcase to use as something fresh to stem the bleeding.

"Fiona is there too?" Preacher asked. "Christ, Liam, how many people have you got down there?"

"Just coincidence. Fiona was here long before Alicia. I can get to her. Maybe she can help."

"Okay, you work on that and let me know that you're okay. We'll have some brothers down to you ASAP. It's going to take about ten hours or so. Can you hold on that long?" Preacher asked.

"It's going to take more than this to get rid of me," Liam scoffed.

"Okay. I'll get in touch soon. I'll pray for you... both of you," Preacher added before he hung up.

Olivia put the phone down on the nightstand and stared at Liam. She saw the anger in his eyes.

"Liam," Olivia started.

"We don't have time to get into this right now," Liam snapped. "You're going to have to go and get Fiona. She'll be at Fish Heads setting up for the day. Tell her I need her help. Before you come back to me, go to Alicia's store and check on her. Make sure they haven't hurt her."

"Okay, but your wound... what do you need?" Olivia said, touching his arm.

"Nothing!" he barked. "Nothing. Just go," he said in a quieter tone.

Olivia walked out to the kitchen and grabbed Liam's car keys off the counter. She wiped tears from her eyes before she made her way to the staircase.

"And don't you dare do anything to my GTO!" Liam yelled.

Olivia sped off toward Fish Heads, trying to concentrate on the road as her hands shook from all that had occurred. She tore into the gravel and sand as she pulled up toward the main building and rushed inside looking for Fiona. She came across a young woman, no older than herself, wiping down tables. The woman stopped and stared at Olivia.

"I need Fiona," she said breathlessly. "Is she here?"

The girl yelled out for Fiona, who came out from the bar area and spotted Olivia.

"Shit, what happened to you?" Fiona said as she looked at Olivia. It was then Olivia realized how she must look. Her body was covered with dirt and sand, and blood stained most of her shirt and half of her face.

"Please, I need you to help me. It's Liam," Olivia said in a hushed tone.

"Tara, I need to go. I'll be back when I can," Fiona said hurriedly as she rushed behind the bar to grab her bag.

Fiona trailed behind Olivia as they got to Liam's car. Fiona stopped and looked at the vehicle.

"You're driving Liam's car," Fiona said solemnly as she got in the passenger seat. "Oh, God, what happened to him?"

"It's not good, but I have one other stop to make first," Olivia answered as she sped out of the parking lot.

Olivia explained the entire story to Fiona as they drove toward Footprints in the Sand. She told Fiona about her sister, the airport, Benny, and what happened to Liam, covering as many details as she could while still moving toward Alicia's shop.

Once they got into the parking lot, the two women got out of the GTO and raced to the store's front door. Unfortunately, the door was locked, and all the lights were still off. Olivia rattled the door several times and knocked loudly, hoping Alicia was in the back and would come out with the commotion.

"Do you know where she lives?" Olivia said anxiously.

"No, I don't," Fiona answered. "We barely know each other. We met a few times because we both know Liam. Shouldn't we get to him? We can come back later and find her."

"No, I need to know she's okay," Olivia insisted, shaking the locked door several more times.

It was then that a dark Corvette pulled into the parking lot, revving its engine next to where Olivia had parked. She reached over and grabbed Fiona's hand, fearful that it might be more trouble seeking her out. The car engine turned off, and the door opened slowly, with Alicia climbing out.

"You're here awfully early," Alicia added, grabbing her keys. It was then she noticed how Olivia looked. "What happened?"

Olivia rushed over to Alicia and hugged her tightly.

"Thank God you're okay," she said.

"Why wouldn't I be?" she asked with concern. "Where's Liam?"

"We'll explain on the way," Olivia told her as she led Alicia to the GTO.

Olivia recapped the saga for Alicia, filling her in on all the details and what happened to Liam. Then, they made a quick stop at the local Walgreens and picked up as many first-aid supplies as they could, unsure of what they might need. Alicia also made a couple of phone calls, finally tracking down a doctor friend who agreed to meet them at Liam's without knowing all the gritty details.

Olivia, Alicia, and Fiona arrived back at the beach house. Olivia raced up the stairs to get to Liam's bedroom. When she burst into the room ahead of the others, she saw the bed empty with blood-stained sheets and towels spread out.

"Liam!" she shouted, looking around the top floor as Alicia and Fiona arrived with the bags of supplies.

"What?" he barked from behind the bathroom door. "I needed to take a piss. I wasn't going to wet the bed, for Christ's sake."

Olivia was relieved when Liam opened the door, standing there in just his bloody T-shirt and boxer briefs.

"It was a bitch getting those jeans off," Liam admitted.

Olivia shook her head and put her arm around Liam's waist, leading him back to the bed as Alicia and Fiona came in.

"Oh good, the gang's all here," Liam joked as he lay on the side of the bed with the least blood on it.

"Jesus, Liam," Fiona said, looking at his wound. "I'll go grab some more towels."

"I'm glad you're okay," Liam said sincerely to Alicia as she sat on the bed next to him.

"I called in a favor," Alicia told him. "A doctor friend is coming over in a bit to check you out. Don't be a dick when she gets here. She works at the hospital."

Fiona rushed back in with a pile of towels, replacing the soaked towel with a fresh one. Olivia looked on just from the foot of the bed.

"Well, how about that," Fiona said as she put pressure on the wound. "Your dreams are coming true, Liam. You've got three gorgeous women in your bedroom taking care of you."

Liam choked out a laugh before it made him grimace. He looked up and met Olivia's eyes, but she turned away immediately.

"I'll get you some water, some clean sheets, and the rest of the first aid stuff."

Olivia darted out of the room and to the kitchen. She reached into the fridge, grabbed a few bottles of cold water, and brought them to Liam's room. She left before he would look at her again, going into her room to grab the extra sheets in the closet. Before she did that, she walked into the bathroom and caught a glimpse of herself in the mirror.

Her face was smeared with dirt and blood, as her hands and shirt were. Her hands shook as she turned on the tap in the sink and tried to wash off some of the grime and dried blood she saw. When it didn't come off quickly, she scrubbed harder and harder, with more incredible determination. Finally, she turned the water off, grabbed the nearby towel, and instead of drying her hands, grabbed it and screamed into it.

Chapter 17

Irritability reigned the moment for Liam once the women arrived. Fiona, Alicia, and Olivia had their own ideas of what would be best to do until the doctor came to treat Liam's wound. He constantly looked at Olivia even though she barely made eye contact with him. After the revelation that Benny had contacted her because of a call with Beatriz, Liam had been enraged. All the hard work he had put into keeping her safe seemed to go out the window with one brief phone call.

The doctor showed up at the house and, upon examining Liam, tried to force the issue of going to the hospital. However, the bickering and yelling back and forth among Fiona, Alicia, and the doctor became more than Liam could stand.

"Enough of all of you!" he barked. "Doc," he said, turning to Dr. Reiki Wada. "If you can't or aren't willing to do anything, okay. Just make a decision, so I don't have to listen to all this. The pain in my side is radiating to my head and my arse!"

"Liam, we're just trying to help," Alicia responded.

"Then go get me some whiskey or something because nothing you three are saying is helping me right now."

"I've got the bleeding packed off, but he really needs to get to the hospital to close him up properly and be watched to make sure there are no complications or infections," Dr. Wada added. "I can give you something for the pain to help you relax."

"Yes, please!" Liam bellowed.

"Stop being such a baby," Fiona told him.

"A baby? I've got a feckin' bullet hole here that I should never have had, I'm in pain, I can't have a drink, and I'm lying in a blood-soaked shirt and bed. When do I have the right to complain, Fiona?"

"He's right," Alicia said to the group. "Give him something, Rei, at least to shut him up."

Dr. Wada nodded before giving Liam an injection, something he had no choice about. Within seconds his body relaxed, and his eyes were fluttering closed.

When he finally did wake up, he was alone in his darkened room. Night had settled in, and none of the women, including Olivia, were anywhere present. Liam shifted in the bed, hoping to get up, but his body was heavy and lethargic. He couldn't swing his legs out of bed to even attempt to stand up. It was then that he caught a glimpse of a shadow sitting in the chair off to the left of the room nearest the windows. A glow from a cigarette appeared at the mouth level of the shadow. Liam squinted but could not make out who it was.

"Whoever you are, you've got some balls for smoking in my bedroom. Even I don't do that. So put that fuckin' thing out."

"As you wish," the gravelly voice responded. Liam caught a hint of recognition in the voice and tried to sit up. Before he could move, he saw the hand lower the glow and snuff it out, followed up by a loud female scream.

Panic struck Liam as he attempted to move but couldn't. His leaden body went nowhere, and all he could do involved thrashing his head.

The shadow rose and neared the bed, lifting another form off the floor. It was then that the moonlight hit just right to reveal Marcos—The Butcher—standing at the foot of the bed. In his right hand was a large blade, and trapped in his left arm was Olivia, frightened and with a burn mark on her shoulder.

"You can watch me kill her before I gut you." Marcos laughed.

"You feckin' son of a bitch!" Liam yelled, still struggling against himself to move. "Touch her, and I will rip your heart out!"

"Too late." Marcos smiled before dragging the knife-edge across Olivia's throat, letting blood spill out all over the bed before Marcos tossed her limp body aside.

"NO!" Liam shouted.

"Now you." The Butcher grinned, flashing his gold teeth as he leaped forward to the bed to drive the knife into Liam's chest.

"Olivia!" Liam screamed.

"What? What's wrong?" Olivia said, dashing into Liam's bedroom and jumping onto the bed next to him.

Liam's wild eyes scanned the room, barely lit by the one lone light over the empty chair in the corner. He panted furiously as Olivia put her arms on him, guiding him back down to the pillows.

"I saw him..." Liam said with panic. "He was there." Liam pointed to the empty chair across from him. "I watched him kill you."

"I'm still here," Olivia reassured, gently stroking Liam's cheek. "I'm not going anywhere." Olivia rested her head on his shoulder as Liam gained control over his breathing.

"I'm sure it's the medicine Dr. Wada gave you," Olivia told him. "We finally convinced her to patch you up, and she gave us some drugs and prescriptions for you. I'll have to change out the dressing on your wound soon, but you can go back to sleep if you want. You need to rest to get your strength back."

"I think I need to stay awake for a little bit," Liam answered. "What time is it?"

"Almost eight," Olivia answered. "You've been out for a while. Fiona and Alicia are resting right now. We've been taking turns checking on you. I talked to Preacher again. Some of the Cosantóir should be here very soon. We're safe."

"For now," Liam grumbled. It's a matter of time before the Caimans get tired of waiting, and Benny orders them to strike. After that, it could get ugly—for all of us."

"Well, it's a good thing we have your ugly mug here already," a deep voice boomed. Darryl, the largest member of the Cosantóir, walked in with a smile on his face. "Christ, man, you look like shit."

"Thanks, brother," Liam said, clapping his right hand with Darryl's.

"I thought Superman came to the Fortress of Solitude to relax, not all this," Darryl told him.

"Oh geez," Olivia said softly, rolling her eyes.

"Demon, this is Olivia," Liam said, pointing. "She's the one I'm protecting."

"I'm sorry he's doing a half-assed job of it," Demon said with a wink.

"Please tell me it's more than just you who came down," Liam said as he rested his head back on one of the propped up pillows.

"I'm here, Whitey's here, and Declan," Darryl explained. "Conor didn't want to send too many down here. He's worried about back home, too."

"What's going on back home?" Liam asked with alarm.

"Fucking Caimans, man," Darryl said, shaking his head. "I think they are getting restless looking for everyone."

Darryl had glanced at Olivia and then turned back to face Liam.

"They've been making noise, threatening people all over town, trying to shake things down. There have been incidents at A Safe Place, a couple of bars and restaurants in town, and they even showed up at job sites and Hog House."

"They did something at the house?" Liam inquired, sitting upright.

"Nothing more than some slashed tires and hassling a couple of brothers, but it was enough to get attention. Even the local cops and troopers are taking notice."

"This is all my fault," Olivia lamented as she rose from the bed.

"It's not your fault Benny is a maniac," Darryl assured her.

"No, but it's my fault my sister left, that we're here and that Benny knows about it, that he's messing with everyone, and who knows what else," Olivia bemoaned.

"She's right," Liam said matter-of-factly.

Wounded, Olivia turned and left the room.

"That was a callous prick thing to say, man," Darryl chided.

"Why? It's true," Liam offered. "We wouldn't be involved in any of this if it weren't for her."

"She's protecting family, Liam. That's what we do too. That's why I'm here. From what Preacher and Finn told me, she's done everything she should and more, especially when it comes to helping you now. Without her, you would've bled to death in that dude's house. But, man, Finn told me you were into this girl. So what's up with you?"

Liam winced as he repositioned himself on his pillows.

"I know... I mean, I am, I think... why did Finn even tell you that? It's no one's feckin' business but mine."

"Don't go pulling that lone wolf shit with me, brother," Darryl said, crossing his arms. "I've known you too long, and we've been through enough together. I saw her when I came into the room with her head on your shoulder and the way you were holding her. That's no crime.

Sounds like you've needed each other a lot through all this. Ease up on her. She's protecting you now."

Liam nodded slightly.

"I'm going back out to get settled and grab something to eat. You need anything?" Darryl asked.

"Nah, I think I'm good. Thanks, brother," Liam responded. "Can you ask her to come back in?"

"Sure thing," Darryl said.

"Hey, Demon!" Liam yelled before Darryl left the room. Darryl turned to look back at Liam.

"Tell Declan and Whitey they better not mess up or take any of my shit. I don't want those slobs trashin' the place."

"No promises, man." Darryl smiled. "They're already playing pool down there and hanging at the bar."

Liam pushed himself back onto the pillows before noticing Olivia peeking around the doorframe.

"Hey," he said softly.

"Hey," she replied, stepping into the room.

Liam patted the spot on the bed next to him, and Olivia slid across the bed, sitting next to his hip.

"I'm... I'm sorry," he said, trying to look Olivia in the eyes. "I've been an asshole. It's not fair to blame this on you."

"Thank you," Olivia whispered and smiled. Liam felt her fingers mingle with his left hand on his waist. Olivia tugged lightly on his fingers, pulling them up to her lips to give them a kiss. The move caused Liam to grimace.

"Oh, I'm sorry," she gushed, putting his hand back down.

"It's okay," Liam said. "It just tugged on the stitches, I guess."

Olivia rose and moved to the other side of the bed to look at the dressing.

"Let me get some clean bandages to change that," she offered, walking over to the tote bag on the dresser that contained supplies.

Liam watched as Olivia gingerly unwrapped the wound before taking some sterile wipes and clearing away more of the dried blood and anti-septic around the stitches.

"If this is just an excuse for you to get your hands on me, it's working." Liam laughed.

"Liam, stop," Olivia said playfully. "I'm trying to do this." She gently pushed Liam's right hand away from its position of cupping her back-side.

"You know, playing nurse-patient could be fun," he growled.

"I think you have some healing to do first before you let your imagi-nation run wild. Dr. Wada said you need a few days to heal."

"You mean I'm stuck in bed for a few days with nothing to do but have you take care of me?"

"That's one way to look at it." Olivia finished putting fresh gauze on his wound. She leaned in close as she finished up and cut the gauze, placing a soft kiss on Liam's lips.

"Suddenly, this doesn't seem so bad." Liam smirked.

Olivia sat with Liam for a while, talking with him and cuddling with him gently while working to keep him from getting too frisky with her and her body. Then, after taking his next round of meds, he let out a few yawns when Olivia moved to get up off the bed.

"Where are you going?" Liam said, reaching for her.

"You need to get rest," she said, gathering up some of the dirty towels and sheets in the room.

"You're just going to leave me alone... like this?" he said as he looked down below his waist.

Olivia laughed when she looked over, seeing he was clearly aroused.

"You're too much," she told him. "I have to take care of some other things first. I'll be back in later to check on you. If you're still awake then, I'll think about it."

"Oh, I'll be up!" he yelled as Olivia left the room. She walked down the steps to the second floor, where the washer and dryer were located, and placed the soiled items in the machine. She leaned back on the washer as it started, sighing and wiping her forehead.

"Everything okay?" Fiona startled Olivia.

"Yeah, he's doing all right. He seems a little weak, but his meds should be kicking in soon so he sleeps some more. I'm just trying to wash some of these things, and then maybe I'll see if anything else needs to be—"

Fiona raised her hand to stop Olivia.

"Olivia, you don't have to do everything," Fiona remarked. "Christ, you went through a lot today, too. Give yourself some time to decompress. Go take a shower, get some food, have a drink... sleep. You need it."

"I feel too revved up to do anything," Olivia admitted. "I feel like if I stop, the reality of all this will catch up with me."

"It's okay to think about yourself and your needs, you know," Fiona told her as she put her arm around Olivia and guided her out of the laundry room. The two walked together slowly up the stairs.

Fiona led Olivia back to her room and opened the door, flipping the light on.

"Nice digs," Fiona commented. "Now, go clean yourself up. It will make you feel better. Bartender's orders. If you need anything, holler."

"Thanks." Olivia sighed. She shut the door when Fiona left and marched to the bathroom, turning on the water for the shower.

Olivia stripped out of the dirty and stained clothing she wore all day through the tribulations of what had occurred. She noticed a few scratches and marks on her legs and arms, but beyond that, she seemed well.

The moment the hot water hit her skin, she began to heal. Just watching the terra cotta colors of the dried blood, sand, and dirt leave her body and spiral down the drain lifted her spirits. She washed herself off more than once, getting rid of all she could until Olivia felt she had done her best.

After drying off and brushing out her damp hair, she went into the bedroom and lay back on the bed, staring up at the ceiling fan slowly rotating. She closed her eyes and exhaled, placing her hands on her bare belly. She practiced the breathing she had done when she was a child, and Beatriz would get her to breathe to control her emotions.

Olivia visualized happier times, being at the beach back home in Peru as a young girl with her parents and Beatriz. Her mother packed a modest lunch, her father brought fishing poles to fish in the surf. She and Bea would run through the water and watch the surfers catching the more giant waves, counting to see how long each person could stay up on their boards.

Olivia recalled that October always was one of the best times of year in Peru. Part of her longed to be back there right now, safe with her family around her, instead of where she found herself.

Reaching into her dresser drawer, Olivia pulled out a yellow tank top to wear. She also slipped into a pair of gray cotton bikini panties and her sleep shorts before lying back on her bed. The temptation to just close her eyes proved great, and she forced herself to sit up and walk out of the room.

Olivia stopped in the hallway and saw Fiona sitting on one of the couches in the living room, drinking a beer with Declan.

"Feel better?" Fiona asked.

"Much, thanks." Olivia smiled.

"Can I fix you something? A drink? Some food? You must be starving," Fiona stated, starting to rise from the couch.

"No, no, I'm good, thanks," Olivia insisted. "I think I'm just going to..." her voice trailed off as she pointed at Liam's room.

"Gotcha." Fiona smiled. "Get some rest."

Olivia nodded and slowly opened the door to Liam's room. The dim light over the chair was the only glow in the room, and the soft snore coming from Liam's mouth let her know he slept calmly. Olivia crawled on the bed and nestled up against Liam's body, taking care to try not to rouse him.

"I was wondering if you would be back," he grumbled, snaking an arm around Olivia's body.

"Is it okay if I sleep here? If you need space, I can..."

Liam pushed his index finger up to her lips.

"Stay. Please," he asked.

Olivia smiled and got as close to Liam as he could, draping a hand over his abs.

"You know," he whispered, "you can still do what I asked before."

"I thought you were going to take care of that yourself," Olivia said, stifling a giggle.

"I will if you will," Liam challenged.

"Who says I didn't already?" Olivia chirped, reaching up to kiss Liam's cheek and snuggle in again.

A groan escaped Liam's lips as his arm held her even closer, making Olivia smile broadly before closing her eyes.

Chapter 18

Liam spent a few days convalescing in his bedroom. At the same time, his Cosantóir brothers did what they needed to so that Olivia and the others stayed safe. Fiona had the flexibility to call out of work for the week and stay at the house. Liam pressed upon Alicia to do the same and close the shop for the week, but she insisted on working. After much back and forth, Liam gave in only if one of the brothers accompanied her to the shop. They had someone stationed there from when she arrived until closing when she returned to Liam's place.

Dr. Wada visited when she could, surprised by Liam's progress and healing. Liam still felt weakened but worked at walking around the house and the beach as much as possible to build himself up. He had walked by the place where Paul and Josie had been, wondering if the police had ever shown up to investigate anything. Finally, following several passes without any indications, he decided it was time to act.

"I think we need to check out that house," Liam spoke as he sat in the living room with Darryl, Declan, and Whitey. "No one has seen any sign of the cops showing up, and Benny hasn't tried to contact Olivia again. He has to know something went wrong by now."

"I don't think that's such a good idea," Olivia added to the conversation. "What if they have people there waiting? It could be a trap."

"We have to at least get close enough to see," Liam answered.

"What about if I just walk by the house and look?" Olivia said.

"No way," Liam replied adamantly. "If there is someone there and they see you, who knows what they might try. That's too risky. You can't do it alone."

"I'm a lot tougher than you think, Liam," Olivia added. "And I've been in the house. So I at least know where people might be."

"She does have a point," Whitey said as he ran his hands through his silver hair.

"Fine, but I'm going with you," Liam insisted. "You're not doing it by yourself."

"No offense, dude, but you're weak as a kitten right now," Darryl added, leaning forward in his chair. "I think even Deck here could take you right now."

"Hey! Feck off, Demon," Declan defended.

"Deck, come on," Darryl argued. "He's got eight inches on you and about seventy-five pounds. You'd have no chance."

"I know," Declan added, looking at Liam. "But still, it's a cheap shot."

"How about this," Liam said, bringing the conversation back to where it needed to go. "Olivia and I will stroll by the front of the house, Whitey and Deck go the back way on the beach. Then, we meet back up and see if we notice anything."

"Fair enough," Darryl agreed. "I'll keep watch here over the girls until you're back."

The pairs set out in their respective directions, each carrying a flashlight so they could look casually and signal if they needed to. Liam walked gingerly down the steps and onto the sidewalk that stretched up and down the street, taking Olivia's hand as soon as they reached the concrete walkway. The two sauntered together and neared the house.

"You okay?" Liam asked as he glanced at Olivia.

"I'm good," she answered bravely, though Liam felt her grip on his hand tighten as they moved closer.

Liam slowed as they reached the portion of the sidewalk directly in front of the dark abode. There were no signs of any lights inside giving off a glow. Liam inched closer, moving to the empty driveway. He shone his flashlight down as he moved, looking to see if there were any fresh footprints or tire tracks anywhere to be found.

"Liam, let's not get too close," Olivia whispered as she held his hand.

"I think we're good," he replied as he kept moving forward, nearing the door that led to the bottom floor portion of the house. Like his home, it was locked and had keypad access.

"Damn," he said as he jiggled the handle.

He saw three quick flashes of a flashlight coming from the rear of the house, indicating Deck and Whitey had discovered something. Liam gathered Olivia, placing her directly beside him as he moved stealthily around the side of the house and into the backyard.

"What do you see?" Liam whispered to Declan as they reached the back.

"There, on the second floor," Declan said quietly. "That window isn't closed. It's just the screen in there."

"Great," Liam said. "Now, all we need is Cirque de Soleil to get up there."

No stairs led from the bottom floor to the second-floor wraparound patio where the open window was.

"I can get there," Olivia said as she scoped the space.

"How? Do you have superpowers I don't know about?" Liam said snarkily.

"Maybe I do," Olivia shot back. "I did cheerleading in high school. If you can get me up on your shoulders, I think I can reach the rails on the patio and pull myself up."

"Forget it; it's not worth the risk," Liam insisted. "And why am I just learning that you were a cheerleader?"

"Save your fantasies for later," Whitey said to Liam. "You really think you can get up there?"

"Yes." Olivia nodded.

"I say we try it," Whitey voiced.

"No." Liam remained firm in his attitude. "We still don't know if someone is here. She could be walking right into something."

"You want answers or not?" Olivia said strongly. "I'm the only one who can get them. I promise I'll be careful. I won't snoop around. If it's safe, I'll come straight down to the door and let you in."

Liam looked at his brothers, who both nodded in assent before he turned to Olivia. Liam saw the determined look in her eyes that presented itself when he first met her.

"Don't test me with this," Liam said, looking straight at Olivia. "In and right to this door, or right back out that window. Got it?"

"I promise," she vowed, crossing her heart.

"So, how do we do this?" Declan asked.

'You two are going to boost me so I can get a foot on Liam's shoulder and boost myself up. Then, Liam will hold me at my feet so I can reach the floor. It's easy."

"I don't know about this," Liam said warily.

"I'm doing all the work," Olivia replied. "You just have to make sure I don't fall, and if I do, you two need to catch me," she added, looking at Declan and Whitey.

Liam moved closer to the porch, and Declan and Whitey positioned themselves behind Liam. They clasped their hands together so Olivia could put one foot into their hands while placing her hands on their respective shoulders for leverage and balance.

"On three, we go," Olivia said, preparing herself. "I hope this works," she whispered.

"What?" Liam panicked. "You've done this before, right?"

"Not in the last three or four years," Olivia said.

Before Liam could react, Olivia counted to three, and he discovered her right foot on his right shoulder. He instinctively grabbed for her leg while her other foot found its mark on his left shoulder. Liam wobbled a bit before getting a firm grasp to steady Olivia.

"Don't forget, my left shoulder is weaker," Liam grunted. "You need to go fast."

"I'm still a little short," Olivia groaned as she stretched. "Boost me up with your hands."

"No feckin' way. Forget it."

"Liam, just do it!" Olivia ordered.

Liam moved his hands to get underneath the sneakers Olivia wore and lifted her up, groaning more as he did it. He felt his left arm faltering and giving way and let go before he was ready.

"Shite!" he yelled as his hands came down empty. He looked up, expecting to see Olivia tumbling down toward him, but instead, he saw her pulling herself up and over the railing of the porch.

Olivia turned as Whitey shone his flashlight up to where she was. She gave a smile and waved to the brothers below.

"Nicely done," she whispered.

"Just go in," Liam implored, wanting to get this done rapidly.

He watched as Olivia removed the screen and climbed through the window and into the darkness.

The trio stood and waited, with the nearby waves crashing on the shore the only sounds in the air and the shuffling of their feet on the bits of sand outside the door.

"It's taking too long," Liam said impatiently.

"Give her a minute," Whitey assured.

"No, something's wrong," he insisted, reaching to the sheath at the back of his jeans and removing his knife. Liam turned to the door, ready to pry it open with his knife or break the glass pane to gain entry when he was startled by the ghostly image at the window.

There stood Olivia, flashlight under her chin, giving an eerie glow to her smiling face. She unlocked the door and opened it.

"You think this is just a big feckin' joke?" Liam said sternly as he brushed past Olivia and into the house. Declan and Whitey followed closely behind him.

"I thought it was funny," Liam heard Declan whisper to Olivia.

"I didn't notice anything when I came down," Olivia said, trying to turn Liam's mood.

Liam edged up the staircase, taking his time and looking around to see if he noticed anything alarming. All seemed quiet, and they reached the top floor without any issues. Liam scanned the living room and kitchen areas where the fights had occurred, but he saw no signs of struggle or blood.

"Someone cleaned everything up," Liam said as he squatted over the floor where he knew Paul's body lay bleeding. "It was no simple house-cleaning job either. They knew what they were doing."

Liam walked toward the back door where he had entered the day of the fight, checking the wall and doorjamb for marks.

"There should be a bullet hole here somewhere, but there's nothing," he remarked.

"Professional cleaner," Whitey said. "Benny must have had them come in. It had to be at night, or we would have noticed something."

"You guys go search the bedrooms," Liam told Whitey and Declan. "See if you find anything they may have left behind."

Olivia turned and looked at Liam as his eyes worked around the room, looking for clues.

"So, what does all this mean? Maybe it's good they are all gone, and everything is cleaned up. Benny hasn't tried to contact me or anything. Maybe he's giving up."

"Not likely," Liam said solemnly. "More likely, he didn't want any trace of trouble to alarm the rental company so that they called the cops. Just because we haven't heard from him doesn't mean he's throwing in the towel."

Liam spied Olivia looking down at the floor, dejected and frightened.

"I'm sorry, but you need to know the truth," Liam told her, taking her hand. "We still have to be vigilant. He's planning something."

Declan and Whitey returned to the living room where Liam and Olivia stood.

"Those rooms are spotless," Whitey remarked. "You'd never know if someone is in there. I didn't see a speck of dust. They cleaned out whatever those two had with them."

Liam walked into the kitchen, scanning the counters before getting to the refrigerator and grasping the door handle.

"If you want a snack, we can go back to the house," Whitey joked.

Liam pried the door open, and the refrigerator light cascaded across the room, casting his tall shadow on the far wall.

"We should go," Liam said before closing the fridge door.

"Yeah, I could eat too," Declan said as he turned to face Liam.

"That's not why we should go," Liam said.

Olivia shone her flashlight at Liam to reveal him standing there with a can of Guinness in his hand with the handle of a butcher's knife protruding from it.

Chapter 19

Olivia returned to Liam's house with Liam and his brothers, pacing across the sidewalk casually so that no one suspected what they were up to. When they reentered their safe haven, the group immediately fielded questions from Darryl, Fiona, and Alicia. Liam explained the situation thoroughly, letting the group know he felt they were still in danger.

"Don't you think it's time we went to the police with all this?" Alicia asked.

"And tell them what, Alicia?" Liam replied. "The two people I was involved in the killing of are no longer in the house I broke into. Oh, by the way, I have a criminal record, and if you search my house, you'll find I have weapons I transported and carry concealed."

"They have to be able to help us in some way," Alicia stated. "We can't just live looking over our shoulders for the rest of our lives until someone gets us."

"Remember what they did to Brian?" Liam shouted. "They don't care about the cops; the Caimans care about their mission, whatever it happens to be at the moment. Right now, that mission is to eliminate Olivia and anyone who gets in their way of doing it. The cops are not going to sympathize with a motorcycle club or the women they are with. So their philosophy is just to let the clubs kill each other off. It's less for them to worry about and less paperwork."

"That's a pretty shitty way of looking at it," Fiona responded.

"Yeah, it is," Liam admitted. "But it's the truth. My job is to make sure nothing happens to any of you."

Olivia saw Liam's gaze transfixed on her as he spoke.

"For now, no one leaves the house without a partner. We can get everything we need delivered here without a problem. So you want some sun, go out on the back patio and get it, but have someone with you."

"You do realize at some point I have to go back to work... we all have to do that and be able to live our lives," Fiona complained.

"I know we do," Liam admitted. "We just need a little more time to sort this out. I need to go and rest. That little acrobatic routine took a lot out of me."

Olivia saw Liam rise and move toward his bedroom, and she immediately followed him in, closing the door behind her.

"Are you okay?" she asked with concern.

"I think so," Liam told her as he stripped out of his T-shirt. He glanced down at the smaller bandage now covering his wound. "Stretching like that maybe was something I wasn't ready for."

"I'm sorry," she apologized, helping Liam and guiding him down onto the bed.

"No, it was a good idea," Liam replied. "It was the only way we were getting in without attracting attention. You were fantastic."

Olivia sat on the bed next to Liam, taking his large hand into her petite one.

"Liam," she began with an inhale. "I've been thinking... maybe... maybe I should leave here."

"If you want, we can go somewhere else," Liam answered, unbuckling his belt so he could slide out of his jeans. "I can plot out some spots we can ride to along the route back home. We can take our time, hide out and just be with each other until things start to cool off a bit."

"No, no... that isn't what I meant," she said seriously. "I meant maybe I should leave... by myself."

Liam flashed a puzzled look to Olivia before answering.

"No, that's a bad idea," Liam stated.

"No, it's not," she quickly answered. "Benny is only looking for me. I'm just dragging everyone else down with me. The longer I stay with you all, the more peril it puts people in."

"And you think going back to Harriman will make all that go away? As soon as he finds you there, he'll make a move."

"I wouldn't go back to Harriman," she said, resigned. "I would go home... to Peru."

"You were so dead set against that from the start," Liam said with shock. "Why is it okay all of a sudden?"

"Because I realize it's the only solution that makes sense. It's the only way for me... and everyone I care about... to be safe."

"So you're just willing to up and go like that and leave everything behind. All you said you wanted to stay for and build your life for yourself for... all of that meant nothing?"

"You're the one who told me that going to Peru was the best move, remember?" she yelled.

"That was before..." Liam shouted back.

"Before what?"

Liam sat still for a moment as Olivia saw the intense stare he gave her.

"Before this," he said, moving forward to kiss her hard on the lips. Liam took her in his arms and held her, kissing her more passionately, until he rolled over, bringing Olivia's body beneath his.

"It was before I started to—"

Olivia brought a hand up to his lips to silence him.

"Please don't say it," Olivia begged. "It will just make things more complicated."

Liam nodded and bent down, kissing Olivia again. He hungrily went at her, his hands roaming everywhere to remove her clothing. Olivia clasped her hands around Liam's face, drawing his mouth and lips to her breasts. Each kiss, lick, and nibble sent jolts of electricity through her body, making her arch up to reach Liam faster and be closer to him.

Being careful not to touch him where his wound was, Olivia moved her hands down from Liam's chest to across his rippling muscles to where his boxer briefs hugged his body. Her hands went immediately to the waistband, pulling the briefs down so she could feel the length and strength of his cock.

Olivia wrapped her legs tightly around Liam, drawing his erection to her. Liam hesitated, reaching for the nightstand.

"No," she whispered. "I want you... this way... right now."

"We shouldn't," Liam panted, reaching again before Olivia pulled his arm back to her.

"Now," she moaned. "Please."

Liam eased inside her, causing Olivia to gasp loudly. He steadily increased his rhythm as she held him tightly between her legs, her feet nearly touching each other as they squeezed his body.

Olivia looked up at Liam and saw his eyes were closed as he tried to hold on with motion.

"Look at me," she said softly as another moan escaped her lips. "I want to see you watching me."

Liam's eyes flew open as he thrust again. Olivia barely controlled herself, groaning and biting her lower lip.

"Keep watching," she gasped out, peering at him through the slits of her barely-open eyes now.

When her orgasm hit, Olivia arched her back off the bed, clamping on Liam and holding on for dear life. Her body flamed as it washed over her, her contractions driving Liam over his own edge. Feeling him inside her like that caused Olivia to hold him even tighter, if possible, as she wished for the pleasure to never end.

Liam's sweaty body collapsed onto Olivia's at first as they pressed against each other, kissing over and over. Liam hid his face into the pillow over Olivia's left shoulder before he turned and planted slow kisses on her neck and shoulder.

"I love you," he whispered.

Olivia stared up at the ceiling, tears forming in her eyes.

"I told you not to say it," she whimpered.

When she woke in the morning, Olivia found Liam sitting up, scanning his cell phone. She rolled over and propped herself up, her head resting in the palm of her hand, as she snaked her right hand down the top sheet and gave his thigh a squeeze.

Liam glanced over and grinned at her.

"Good, you're up," he said. "We have something to do this morning. Get dressed."

"What are we doing?" she asked as she watched Liam's naked form make its way to his dresser.

"Have you ever fired a gun before?"

Olivia sat upright in the bed, pulling the top sheet over her bare breasts.

"No. Why would I have?"

"Not everyone has," Liam answered as he donned yet another black T-shirt. "I wanted to know if you were aware of how to handle one before we go to the range."

"The range? What are you talking about?"

"I'm going to teach you how to shoot. But, first, go put some clothes on." Liam smiled. "If you're too embarrassed to walk to your room naked, here." Liam pulled another black T-shirt from his drawer and tossed it to Olivia.

Olivia grasped the T-shirt and pulled it over her head. The shirt wore like a baggy dress on her body, but it covered her well. She hopped off the bed and went out the bedroom door, crossing the hall to her room.

"Morning!" Fiona said from her position on the couch. She smiled at Olivia as she sipped her cup of coffee.

Olivia pushed some hair out of her face with her fingers and blushed before she entered her bedroom. She hurriedly grabbed some clothes to put on. As she went to take Liam's shirt off, she lingered in it for the moment, relishing that she was wearing something of his. She tossed the T-shirt on her bed and got dressed to go to meet Liam. When she left her room, she tied her hair back in a ponytail as Liam sipped some coffee himself.

"What are we doing now?" Olivia asked once again.

"We're going to the Gun Shack to use their range," Liam told her.

"I don't know if I'm okay with this," Olivia questioned.

"You need to know how to protect yourself if you have to," Liam said honestly.

"What about everyone else?" Olivia challenged.

Liam let out a belly laugh.

"Whitey and Declan are fine, and I know Alicia and Fiona have used guns before."

Olivia looked over at the couch, and Fiona just nodded.

"It's true," she replied. "I've had a license since I was a teenager. I used to hunt with this hoodlum when we were younger."

"I don't have a permit or license or whatever," Olivia stated, hoping it would get her out of the situation.

"You don't need to in North Carolina to go to the range," Liam told her. "You're just doing target practice—nothing more. It's a contingency plan—in case of emergencies. So stop hemming and hawing about it. We're going."

Liam walked over and grabbed Olivia's hand, leading her down the stairs.

"Have fun, you crazy kids," Fiona added as the couple left the house.

Liam marched Olivia over to his motorcycle, which was now flanked by two other bikes.

"It's a short ride; we'll take the bike," Liam told her, passing her the helmet. "Do you remember what you have to do?"

"Helmet on, feet on the pegs, and hold on for dear life," Olivia said begrudgingly.

"Close enough." Liam laughed. "You don't always seem to mind holding on for dear life," he added.

Olivia felt her body blush as she sat on the bike behind Liam, putting her hands firmly around his waist.

The air proved to be warmer and stickier than Olivia anticipated as cloud cover ruled the morning. Nevertheless, Liam made the short drive to the Gun Shack's location and pulled into the nearly empty lot. Olivia followed closely behind as they walked into the establishment, and Liam went over to the counter. Olivia tried to follow Liam's conversation with the older gentleman behind the counter. Still, frequently to her, it felt like they were speaking gibberish.

Liam paid the man the appropriate rental fees for time and gun use and led Olivia out to the range. They were the only two located at the range for the moment. Liam passed a set of protective goggles to Olivia, who strapped them on. She then grabbed the necessary earwear to use as she stood waiting for further instructions.

Olivia shifted her feet back and forth, pacing in place before Liam came over to the stall with a small gun.

"This is a Walther PK380," Liam explained, holding it in the palm of his hand. The gun looked like a small toy for a child in Liam's large grip. "Too small for me, but I think it will be ideal for you. "It's semiautomatic, easy to load, use, and aim. It doesn't have a significant recoil or anything, and it's easy to conceal if you have to."

Liam held the gun out in front of Olivia.

"Take it," Liam bade.

Olivia reluctantly plucked the gun from Liam's hand and held it cautiously. She was surprised at how simple it was to handle and how comfortable it felt in her tiny hands. Liam walked her through how to properly load the gun as they stepped into the stall. He demonstrated where the safety was, how to use it, and how to fire the weapon.

"Okay, let's see what you've got," Liam said, taking a step back and putting his ear covering on.

"You want me to shoot it?"

"That's the idea," Liam told her.

Liam took Olivia's hands in his, showing her the proper grip to use.

"Hold it like this," he explained. "Don't cross your thumbs like that. You'll cut your support thumb on the slide if you leave it like that.

So instead, keep the support thumb on the same side as your support fingers.

"Your first shot will take some pressure, but the ones that follow can use a lighter touch. Be deliberate about what you are shooting at and when it happens. It's not like the movies or TV. You're going to feel it when you shoot, but it's not going to be like it would if you were using a revolver. Don't put your finger on the trigger until you are ready to fire. Use a firm grip—I know you know what that is—breathe easy, and fire."

Liam stepped back again to allow Olivia to try. She stared down the range stall to the target that seemed ridiculously far away. She lifted the weapon in her hand, holding it properly, and saw her hands shaking a bit. She lowered the gun and put it back on the table in front of her.

"I don't know if I can do it," she shouted.

"I know you can," Liam retorted. "Now pick it up and do it. Do you want to protect yourself against who knows what out there and have some peace of mind? This is how it's going to happen. Do you think Benny or The Butcher care what you think or feel? They just want what they want from you—dead or alive. Do you want them to just take everything from you?"

"No!" Olivia yelled back.

"Then show them that."

Olivia picked up the pistol, released the safety, took aim, and fired. The recoil was less than she thought it would be, but the rest of the event proved nothing like what she expected. Even with protection, the noise was loud, and the rush of air she felt come back toward her surprised her. She also wasn't sure if she had kept her eyes open through the process or not.

Olivia placed the gun down and then looked at Liam. He stared back at her before he smiled slightly.

"How was it?" he asked.

"It scared the hell out of me," she said honestly. "How was the shot?" she asked, looking down the range toward the target.

"You nicked the bottom of the paper," Liam replied.

"Sorry," she said with disappointment.

"What are you sorry about? That's better than most people do on their first try. You're not going to bull's-eye every time, or even once. I don't need you to. I just need you to fire this thing with some confidence so you can stop someone coming at you if you have to. It's a lot different when your adrenaline is pumping, you're scared, and someone is coming at you with a weapon or pointing a gun back at you. This gun doesn't have a lot of stopping power."

"Then why am I even bothering to learn this?" Olivia complained.

"Because it can be enough to save your life. Just knowing how to use it makes all the difference. It's enough to make the other person scared into making a decision if he sees or thinks you can fire it properly. So let's go again."

"Really?" Olivia asked.

"Yes, really. I paid for an hour here, and practice makes you a hell of a lot better than just firing one shot."

Liam pointed back down to the target.

"Think about if you have to protect yourself... Alicia or Fiona... your parents, your sister, Daniela... hell, even if you had to protect me. You can do it."

Olivia let out a big sigh and turned toward the target once more. She picked up the gun, aimed toward the target, took a slow breath in, and squeezed the trigger as she let air out. She followed that second shot immediately with a third and then a fourth. All three shots hit the target, and while not in the bull's-eye, they were better and grouped.

"Nice!" Liam exclaimed.

Olivia stayed focused and emptied the rest of the cartridge into the target before stopping. Liam sent the target back toward them so Olivia could see for herself how she did. Most did well, bringing a smile to her face.

"Feel better?" Liam asked.

"Yes and no," Olivia admitted. "It does get easier, but I don't want to have to know how to do this."

"Honestly, I wish I didn't have to teach you," Liam told her. "But, at this point, we're running out of options, and I need to make sure you're safe. How do you feel about the gun itself? Can you handle this model?"

"I think so, yes."

"I'll make sure to get one for you," Liam advised.

"Isn't there a waiting period or something?"

"I have a permit in North Carolina. I can have it before we leave here today," Liam told her. "Let's practice some more."

Olivia reloaded the Walther successfully, under Liam's watchful eye, and then pointed to the new target.

"I hate you for this, Benny," she whispered as she pulled the trigger.

Chapter 20

Olivia spent the better part of the hour practicing and following Liam's advice to the point where she felt comfortable holding and using the pistol he had selected for her. Finally, after their shooting time, Liam returned to the retail shop to purchase the weapon and the necessary ammunition. Olivia stood by, watching the cash transaction, all the time wondering in the back of her mind if it would ever come to the point where she might need to use the gun.

The couple proceeded back to Liam's house, where he presented her with the firearm and accessories.

"Keep it in your room for now—somewhere hidden but where you could get it quickly if you need to. You want to be able to load it fast and use it right away."

"Thanks," she answered as she took the Walther from Liam's hands. She walked across the hall and into her bedroom, putting the gun in the nightstand drawer where she could reach from the bed if circumstances warranted. Liam had followed close behind her and watched as she stored the weapon. Then, he approached Olivia, taking her in his arms.

"I know you're not comfortable with this, but I think it's important right now," he said to Olivia. "Once everything is settled, if you don't want it anymore, I can take it back from you."

"We'll see," Olivia replied, burying her head on Liam's chest as she hugged him.

"I have to tell you," Liam said quietly, out of earshot of anyone who might hear them from the living room, "it was pretty feckin' hot watching you fire the gun."

Olivia felt Liam's hands slip down from her waist toward her backside, where he gave her a little squeeze.

"You need to make up your mind what you want." Olivia grinned. "Prisoner, nurse, cheerleader, gun-toting woman... you have an active imagination."

"Oh, you bet I do," he whispered into her ear, nibbling on it.

Alicia came by and knocked on the open door to Olivia's room, catching the attention of Liam and Olivia.

"Sorry to interrupt," Alicia said. "Fiona and I are going out on the patio for a bit to get some sun. Want to come?"

"Who's gonna be out there with you?" Liam asked.

"Don't worry, warden; Declan will be there watching us," Alicia added, rolling her eyes.

"Sure," Olivia responded. "Let me get changed, and I'll meet you out there."

Alicia closed the bedroom door as she left. Olivia broke the embrace with Liam and turned to her dresser to grab her bathing suit. When she spun around, Liam had sat on the edge of the bed.

"What are you doing?" she asked.

"I thought I would just stay and enjoy the show." Liam smiled. "Go right ahead." He waved with his left hand.

"Don't you have something more important to do?"

"Not more important than this," he told her. "I did say you had to have someone keeping an eye on you at all times. No sense taking chances."

Olivia shook her head before turning and facing Liam. She slowly peeled her T-shirt over her head, tossing it at Liam once she got it off. Then, she rotated back around, unbuttoned her jeans, and began to slide them down, arching her backside out as the denim eased over her cheeks. Finally, she stepped out of the jeans, leaving her in just her bra and panties.

Olivia strutted over to where Liam sat on the bed and straddled him, kissing his neck before squatting down and running her hands from the insides of his thighs downward. Liam reached to touch Olivia, but she slapped his hands away, turning her away from him once again so this time she could rub her back seductively against him.

"Customers can't touch the dancers," she said teasingly.

She stood with her back to Liam, reaching behind and unclasping her bra before taking a few steps from him and spinning around. Olivia allowed her bra to fall to the floor but kept her breasts covered by placing her left arm over to cover her left breast while her hand covered the right.

She approached Liam once more, staying right in front of him as she pulled her left arm back, baring her breasts right at his eye level. She inched achingly closer to him, mesmerizing Liam until a knock on the door prompted Olivia to cover her breasts.

"Come on, Olivia! Let's go!" Fiona yelled from the other side of the door.

"Guess your time is up," Olivia said as she placed her left hand on Liam's cheek and gave him a light kiss.

"Oh, you've gotta be kiddin' me," Liam said with frustration.

"Sorry," Olivia said, plucking her bathing suit off the top of the dresser and moving to the bathroom. "Now you can add sexy stripper to your list." She smiled as she shut the bathroom door, leaning against it and giggling once she got inside.

Olivia heard Liam rise from the bed and stomp over to the bedroom door. It banged as he flung it open, and it was followed quickly by a yell.

"I hate you, Fiona!" Liam screamed.

The shout was followed by a slamming of Liam's bedroom door across the hall. Olivia chuckled more to herself as she finished putting on her bathing suit, reveling at the moment.

Olivia, Fiona, and Alicia all sat outside for the better part of the morning and early afternoon, enjoying the warm sun that had appeared. As much as the three of them tried to cajole Declan into letting them down on the beach, he resisted them, insisting they all stay at the house in case of any trouble. Declan made sure they had everything they needed to make the most of it, including tropical drinks if they wanted one that he would whip up.

"If you ever decide you want to give up Sand Hog life and live at the beach, Deck, just let me know, and I'll get you a job at Fish Heads," Fiona said as she sipped the latest banana daiquiri concoction that Declan created in the blender.

"I think I do pretty well working in the tunnels, thanks," Declan offered.

"I don't know," Fiona added. "On a summer weekend, I can pull in about a grand in tips sometimes."

"No shit?" Declan said with wonder.

"Forget it, Deck," Alicia told him. "Look at her. It's how she looks in that bathing suit that gets her all the money. I don't think it will work the same for you."

"I don't know; I'm in pretty good shape," he scoffed.

"Well, let's see it," Fiona said. She turned up the music playing on the outdoor speaker. She started clapping her hands before Alicia and Olivia playfully joined in.

Declan seemed to blush but then stood up and started moving to the music. He stripped off the plain white T-shirt he wore to reveal his six-pack abs and smooth chest.

"Damn," Fiona stated. "Who knew you were hiding that under there!"

Fiona rose off her lounge chair and started dancing with Declan, putting an arm around one of his shoulders as they moved together. Alicia turned the music louder and grabbed Olivia's hand so the two of them could dance together as well.

Just as Declan had placed a hand on Fiona's waist and was dipping her back, the music came to an abrupt halt. The group looked over and saw Liam scowling as he had depressed the on/off button on the speaker.

"I'm glad you all are having such a feckin' good time here," Liam blasted. "How many times do I have to say it's not a feckin' party or vacation? Do you realize what we're dealing with here? Knock it off!"

Liam stormed back into the house as Olivia looked on. Whitey had appeared in the doorway as Liam pushed past him.

"What crawled up his ass?" Declan asked Whitey.

"He just got a call from Preacher and Finn," Whitey replied. "Some trouble back home."

"What happened?" Olivia inquired.

Whitey turned toward Olivia and went to respond but stopped himself.

"I don't know that I should say," Whitey added.

"Whitey, what's going on?" Olivia pressed.

"The Caimans," Whitey relented. "They busted up the Quick Chek where you work last night. They completely trashed the place and then roughed up a couple of the employees. One is pretty bad."

"Do you know who?" Olivia asked anxiously.

"I'm not sure; I didn't get any names. All I know is it was a woman."

"Christ," Alicia said softly.

"There's more," Whitey continued. He looked back at Olivia again.

"They messed up Erin's Edibles food truck, right in her driveway. The whole truck was torched, and they stuffed a note in her mailbox."

"What did the note say?" Olivia said, fearing the answer.

"Olivia, you don't need to hear all this," Whitey said, turning to go back inside.

"Tell me, Whitey!" she insisted, running over and grabbing his arm.

"It just said, 'We know, and you're next,'" Whitey told her.

Olivia pushed past Whitey and went into the house, searching for Liam. She finally found him on the bottom floor, sitting at the bar and talking with Darryl.

"This shit's getting ugly," she heard Darryl say as she reached the bottom of the steps.

"I know," Liam growled. "But I can't risk taking her back."

"It's the only way all of this is going to stop, Liam," Olivia stated, interrupting the conversation. "You know it's true."

Liam swiftly spun on his barstool to face Olivia. The words she wanted to say were sticking in her throat.

"There are still other things we can do," Liam said. "We just need time..."

"How long are you going to keep saying that?" Olivia yelled. "There is no more time. They will kill people important to me, and I'm just supposed to sit here at the beach and pretend it's not happening. It's the only thing to do."

Olivia dashed upstairs to her room and grabbed her backpack from the closet. Within moments, Liam had pushed her bedroom door open and was snatching the bag from her hands.

"What the hell do you think you're doing?" he barked.

"I'm getting some stuff together so I can leave," Olivia said as she grabbed a handful of clothing from the dresser. "If I go back, this will stop. You and I both know it."

"Bullshit. We don't know it for a fact. I'm not letting you leave."

"I'm a big girl, Liam," Olivia replied. "I don't need your permission to go."

"I'm glad you're so independent now," Liam said sarcastically. "How are you going? You have no money, no vehicle, nothing. Without me, you would have died at the airport."

Olivia stopped arguing and stood in the center of the room, dropping the handfuls of clothing in her hands.

"I can't keep doing this," she said softly. "Too many people I care about are getting hurt."

She looked directly at Liam, locking eyes with him.

Liam took two steps over to Olivia and embraced her. Then, the sobs she worked hard to hold back started to flow from her.

"It's killing me that I don't have a better way to help you," Liam told her. "But I know I can't let you leave here... or me."

Liam spent the better part of the next hour consoling Olivia and eventually convinced her not to do anything rash. Finally, she reluctantly agreed, putting aside thoughts of leaving for one more day so that Liam and the Cosantóir could come up with a plan. She sleepwalked through the rest of the day, not really concentrating on anything or paying much attention to what went on around her.

Liam was fast asleep by late evening when Olivia still lay in bed with him, her eyes wide-open. The distant rumble of thunder echoed through the room, and the occasional flash of lightning lit up the windows as she watched and listened. Finally, Olivia rose from the bed and moved to the glass door that led out to the porch on the front of the house outside Liam's room. She saw a few drops of rain spatter on the glass pane of the door. Another clap of thunder startled her, but it was the telltale faint ringing of her cell phone that garnered the most attention. She rushed over to the nightstand and plucked the phone up, seeing it was the number her sister had used to reach her.

Olivia answered immediately but said nothing at first.

"Are you tired of all this yet, or do I have to keep going?" Benny said into the phone.

"Why are you doing this? Those people had nothing to do with any of it," Olivia pled as she slinked out of Liam's bedroom to keep him from waking.

"Because I don't like to lose," Benny said. "You know how you can end all this."

"How?" Olivia asked.

"Get your ass back to Harriman so you and I can deal with this face to face. You agree to that, and all this stops. You have my word."

"And that's supposed to mean something? You lie at every turn," Olivia spat out.

"You don't really have a choice, do you? I can guarantee you that your friend Erin will be an obituary in the newspaper if you aren't back here tomorrow. And for every day after that, I'll take out someone else you know and care about. No one's unreachable, you know. Liam just got lucky. So what's it going to be?"

Olivia stood silently in her room, listening to the rain falling harder.

"Fine," she agreed. "I'll come, but I don't know how I'm going to get there by tomorrow."

"I've taken care of that," Benny answered. Go to the front of the house and look out a window."

Olivia moved into the dark living room toward the glass doors leading to the patio high above the driveway. She saw a car idling outside that briefly flashed its headlights. Moments later, a figure stepped out, rain falling around it, and lit a cigarette.

"How do I know he won't kill me and then everyone here as soon as I walk out there?"

"You don't." Benny laughed. "I can tell you that if you don't come out, he's coming in and killing everyone there while you watch before he brings you back to me. Your choice."

Liam rolled to his right in the bed, relieving some of the discomforts he felt from his scar before a loud jolt of thunder got him to open his eyes. Daylight barely crept into the room since a thunderstorm raged outside, but it was enough to illuminate the space. He looked over and saw the other side of the bed was empty with the bathroom light on and the door ajar.

"Are you getting like me now and leaving the door open while you go?" Liam yelled. "You just broke me of the habit, but if you're going to start doing it, I will too."

Liam waited a moment but got no reply from Olivia.

"Hey, you okay in there?" he said, a more concerned edge to his voice.

When no answer came again, Liam got out of bed and strode over to the bathroom door, pushing it open. The bathroom was empty.

Liam dashed out of his bedroom and went to Olivia's, flinging the door open. The bed was perfectly made, just as it had been, and there was no sign that she was there.

The top floor of the house was silent, and Liam ran down the steps to the second floor, calling her name.

"Olivia!"

Fiona came out of her room down the hall while Darryl peeked out of his.

"What's going on?" Darryl said with a yawn.

"I can't find her." Liam panicked.

"All right, I'll search outside," Darryl said, knocking on Whitey's and Declan's respective doors to get them up.

"Get up, brothers. We got trouble," Darryl yelled as he went down to the third floor.

Liam went back upstairs, checking the front and rear porches, getting wet, and tracking his footprints through the house as he moved from one side to the other. His next thought was about his car.

He raced back to his bedroom and found his keys sitting on his dresser, just where he had left them. Sitting on the dresser next to them was the Winnie the Pooh bear, its left eye still torn out but with a pink sticky note attached to its soft right foot. Four words were scrawled on the note:

Estar Seguro mi amor

Chapter 21

Olivia moved cautiously from the house to the driveway, making sure not to rouse anyone as she opened and closed the door behind her. She grabbed only what fit in the backpack she originally had with her when the trip began and got into the front seat of the dark sedan. She slid in and shut the door, hearing the click of the automatic lock as soon as she closed the door.

One look at the driver let her know it was The Butcher sitting next to her. While she didn't get a good look at him when he attacked in the airport, all it took was the crooked smile that revealed the gold teeth Liam had discussed to inform her of his identity. In addition, he was shorter than she had imagined, with a squat form and no discernable neck. Still, the closely shaved head and the piercing eyes he focused on her when he smiled were enough to keep Olivia as far to the passenger side as she could get.

The Butcher said nothing to her, backing out of the driveway and driving off. He spoke briefly, but Olivia realized he was talking into the Air Pod he wore in his ear.

"*La tengo*," he remarked.

Olivia assumed he spoke with Benny to let him know they were en route back to Harriman. She stared out the window, seeing nothing but the dark sky as they crossed the bridge that left the Outer Banks behind them and had them moving north. Her brain processed what options

she may have along the way, and she clutched her backpack between her
ankles for security.

After about an hour of nothing but silence, Olivia looked straight
ahead and spoke.

"*¿Me vas a matar?*" she asked solemnly.

The Butcher chuckled at the question.

"I speak English," he said in a gravelly tone. "I was hired to kill you, yes.
But, unfortunately, plans have changed. Benny wants to see you first."

A small amount of relief washed over Olivia as she realized she at least
would make it to New York before anything happened. After that, all
she could hope for was that Liam and the Cosantóir might figure out
something to do before Benny no longer had use for her.

The car drove across the long Bay Bridge Tunnel, revealing nothing
but choppy waves and cloud cover. Olivia didn't even have the option of
bailing out of the car with the doors locked and out of her control. They
continued on in silence well into Virginia and nearing the Maryland
border before Olivia spoke up again.

"I need the bathroom," she said as she saw the sign for the approaching
Welcome Center in Maryland.

"Not my problem," Marcos said, remaining stoic and staring straight
ahead.

"It will be when I piss all over the front seat of your car, and you have
to smell it for hours. I'll just be a couple of minutes."

Marcos shook his head as he pulled the car into the rest area parking
lot and parked right up front. He glanced around, noticing few vehicles
around them and a few trucks parked off to the side. He turned the
engine off and clicked open the lock. Olivia hastily undid her seat belt
and got out of the car, finding Marcos following each step she made until

she reached the ladies' room door. She went to push it open, but Marcos grabbed her arm first.

"Don't fuck with me," he warned. "In and out in three minutes, or I'm coming in after you. If you talk to anyone or try to get away, you'll pay for it. I can't kill you yet, but that doesn't mean I can't hurt you real bad. Go."

Olivia moved into the bathroom and scanned around. There was no sign of anyone else in the room that she could get help from, so she slipped into the nearest stall and locked the door, sitting down on the toilet. She lifted her small backpack onto her lap and rummaged through it, finding a sample tube of lipstick. She grabbed it and wrote on the door in front of her, leaving her name, asking for help, and mentioning the Cosantóir.

Olivia stuffed the lipstick back into her bag and saw the Walther she had taken from her room before leaving the beach house. The idea of taking the gun out now and trying to get away crossed her mind until she heard the restroom door swing open and footsteps coming toward her. She flushed quickly and exited the stall before Marcos could see what she had done, confronting him right by the sink.

"Let's go. Now," he commanded.

"I'm coming," she insisted. "Can I at least wash my hands?"

"No," he said, dragging her toward the door as an older woman walked in. The woman gave Marcos a confused look as Olivia widened her eyes, hoping to get the woman's attention. They crossed gazes for a moment, and Olivia prayed the woman caught the despair in her eyes.

Marcos marched Olivia back to their car, gripping her arm tightly as they moved past an older gentleman likely waiting for his wife. He glanced at them as they walked by, with Marcos giving the man a sinister flash of his gold teeth. Marcos held the door open for Olivia to get in, appearing like a gentleman before slamming it closed and moving to the driver's side of the car to get in.

As they drove away, Olivia looked out the passenger window, noting that the older woman was coming out of the bathroom as they sped off. She pressed her hand to the window, leaving an imprint on it before turning to face forward.

"No more stops until we're back. Is that clear?" The Butcher said sternly.

Olivia nodded and closed her eyes, saying a silent prayer.

Upon seeing the bear on his dresser, Liam knew Olivia had gone somewhere, but he didn't know where that might be. So he sat on the couch, head in his hands, trying to come up with a scenario in his head that did not end badly for her.

"Maybe she went to Peru," Alicia said, attempting to console Liam.

"If she did, how is she getting there?" Fiona asked. "You said she didn't have any cash, right, Liam?"

"She didn't, but I know she had a credit card. She tried to use it on the way down here at a gas station before I stopped her. I don't know if that would be enough to get her a car and a plane ticket, though. She could have gone to any of a half a dozen airports north or south of here as well. By the time we figured it out, Olivia could be in the air already."

"Well, we can at least look," Alicia said, grabbing her phone. "I'll start checking for flights to Peru today. There can't be that many coming and going. At least maybe we can narrow it down."

"And so what if we do?" Liam snapped. "There's no guarantee we could get wherever she is in time to stop her. I don't know how much of a head start Olivia has. Worse, if she used her card, the Caimans will know it. They might get to her before I can, and…" Liam cut himself out, chilled at the thought of what might happen after that.

"Okay, suppose she didn't go to the airport," Fiona replied. "Maybe she's still around the area here. We can search locally to see if she is hiding out somewhere."

"It doesn't make sense that she would do that," Liam answered with frustration. "Why leave here to stay in the area and put herself at risk? Come on! We need to do better than this!"

"The other answer is that she went back to Harriman, Liam," Whitey added. "It's the only thing that might make sense. She said she felt terrible about putting us all in this situation. It was the only solution to everyone's problems."

"But how the feck would she do that?" Liam yelled. "My car is still here. It was the only vehicle here that she could have taken. She's not taking an Uber all the way to New York. Unless…"

Liam stopped and rose from the couch.

"Unless what?" Alicia asked as Liam took long strides toward Olivia's room.

Liam rifled through the nightstand drawer before returning to the living room.

"Unless she was going with someone she didn't trust," Liam said to the group. "The gun is gone. Olivia took the Walther with her. One of the Caimans must have taken her."

"If they took her, why didn't they do something to the rest of us while they had the advantage?" Whitey asked. "We were all asleep; they could've killed each of us."

"Because she went with them willingly," Darryl said as he entered the room.

"Why would she do that?" Fiona asked. "That's insane."

"I know that she did," Darryl said, moving toward Liam. "I just got a call from Conor. Cops in Maryland got a call to a rest stop from a woman. She found a note scrawled on a bathroom door from Olivia saying to contact the club. The lady said she saw Olivia. The description matches, and she said she was with a guy with gold teeth. My guess is they are headed back to Benny."

"The Butcher," Liam stated. Liam ran the palm of his hand down his face to his beard, rubbing his chin. He then darted toward his room, gathering his keys, knife, and gun before returning to the living room.

"I'm heading back north now," he said emphatically. "You fellas stay here with the girls and keep them safe. Don't go anywhere until you hear something from one of the brothers or me."

"Fuck that," Darryl added. "I'm going with you. You can't do this yourself."

"I'm in too," Whitey said, rising from the couch.

"We can't all go," Liam intervened as Declan rose to follow suit. "We need to take care of Fiona and Alicia too. We still don't know who might be around here."

"I'll stay," Declan volunteered.

"Thanks, Deck," Liam said, slapping Declan on the back. Then, Liam pointed to Darryl and Whitey. "You two have five minutes to get ready to leave."

"If they have already gone through Maryland, they have a hell of a headstart on you," Alicia said somberly. "They'll be in New York before you even get that far. That means..."

"Don't even think it," Liam commanded.

Liam went back to his room, stuffed a few items into a duffle bag from the closet, and then turned and looked at his dresser. He walked over and grabbed the Winnie the Pooh Bear and the note Olivia had written, placing them in the bag as well.

"I'm coming," he said softly.

Chapter 22

The farther the car made its way north, crossing the Delaware Memorial Bridge and driving on the New Jersey Turnpike, the more nervous Olivia became. When they merged onto Route 17 north in New Jersey and were going through the more familiar territory for Olivia, the knot in her stomach tightened. She tried not to let the fear show on her face, but she knew it was cracking through.

Olivia tried to think of something, anything, that might buy her some time and slow down Marcos' approach to home.

"Can we get something to eat?" she asked softly.

Marcos laughed heartily, so much so that he broke into a smoker's cough.

"That's a good one." He smiled, gold teeth glittering. "Fuck no."

"Not even a drive-thru or something?" Olivia glanced over at the dashboard and saw the gas line was nearly on the Empty mark.

"You're going to have to stop for gas anyway," she added. "Can I at least get a candy bar?"

Marcos pulled into the gas station/convenience store just short of the New York-New Jersey border. A young man scurried over to the driver's side of the car to talk to him.

"Fill it," Marcos barked, handing him a credit card. He then looked at Olivia. "I'm going in and watching you the whole way," he told her plainly. "I see you move an inch, and you will pay dearly, understand? So what candy do you want?"

"Reese's peanut butter cups," Olivia answered without a thought.

She watched as Marcos walked out of the car, taking the keys with him. He walked backward the entire way to the storefront, keeping a close eye on her.

Olivia glanced in the rearview mirror and saw the young man standing next to the car as he pumped the gas in. Her mind raced about what move she would have time to make to get any type of signal to let him know she was in trouble. Marcos hadn't lied, and he was watching her, giving her no opportunity to act before he was marching on his way back to the car. He opened the driver-side door and climbed back in, tossing two packages of peanut butter cups to Olivia.

"That's all you get," he barked. "Don't ask me to stop for another fucking thing. Piss your pants if you have to; I don't care anymore. We're almost there."

The young man walked over to Marcos and handed him his credit card, ending the gas transaction. Olivia watched as Marcos felt his leather jacket pocket and didn't find his keys. A brief glimpse of panic crossed his face as he realized the keys were not there.

"Fuck!" he yelled. "I must have left them on the counter. Hey!" he shouted to the young man. "Run in and get my keys!"

"Can't do it, buddy," the young man yelled. "I have to watch the pumps. You gotta do it yourself."

"¡Pendejo!" Marcos yelled as he got out of the car, leaving the door open as he scampered back inside the store.

Olivia saw a glimmer of a chance. She grabbed a package of the candy and a pen she saw on the floor and scribbled on the back of the wrapper.

"Hey!" she yelled to the young man, getting his attention.

He walked over, anxious to talk to a pretty girl, and smiled at Olivia through the open driver's door.

"I'm sorry about my boyfriend," she said, trying to compose herself. "He can be pretty jealous and a jerk sometimes. Here, take this," she told him, holding out the candy bar.

"It's okay, really," the guy offered, rejecting the candy with a grin. "I deal with jerks all day."

"No, really, take it," she insisted, thrusting the candy into his outstretched hand. "Put it in your pocket. If he sees you took it, he'll get mad."

Olivia looked and saw Marcos leaving the store with keys in hand. Marcos stopped and then ran over to the car as he saw the young man leaning back from the open door. He grabbed the boy by the jacket and tossed him away from the vehicle.

"Get lost!" Marcos yelled. "Before I beat the shit out of you."

"Jesus, man!" he yelled as Marcos slammed the door shut and started the car.

"Did you say anything to him?" Marcos screamed as he tore out of the gas station and merged into traffic.

"No, I swear," Olivia replied. "He asked if you were my boyfriend. I think he was hitting on me."

"You better not be lying to me, *zorra*," Marcos added. Marcos calmed his breathing as he drove along, slowing down to avoid unwanted attention to the vehicle.

"I'm not," Olivia told him, inching away from his reach.

Marcos smiled at looked at Olivia.

"You'd be lucky to have me for a boyfriend." Marcos chuckled. "I can probably convince Benny to let me have a go or two at you first if you'd like."

Olivia shuddered at the notion and did her best to hide the fear building in her as she saw the road sign for the Harriman exit approaching. She reached into her pocket and pulled out the candy, slowly opening it and taking a bite, hoping it would quell her queasy stomach.

Please find me, Liam, she said to herself.

Liam struggled with concentration on the road as he moved through traffic heading north. He reached the Bay Bridge faster than he ever had before, leaving Darryl and Whitey trailing behind him and having difficulty keeping up with his pace. More than once, Demon had crackled in his Bluetooth to slow down. However, Liam paid little attention to the request and kept moving along.

When they finally reached the Maryland rest area, he pulled in far ahead of the others. He saw right away that the police had cordoned off the building, still gathering evidence hours after Olivia had passed through. He got off his bike and walked around the area, approaching the building guarded by Maryland state troopers.

He walked forward until a trooper put a hand up to Liam's chest.

"Sorry, sir," the officer told him, looking up to see Liam. "The area's closed."

"Aw, come on, man," Liam feigned. "I need to piss bad. I'll just be a minute."

"Can't do it," the officer insisted. "Take the exit a few miles down and use one of the gas stations there."

"What happened?" Liam said, looking over his shoulder, trying to peek if he might see anything helpful.

"It really doesn't concern you," the officer said, getting more forceful. "It's a criminal investigation. That's all you need to know. So move along, or I'm going to have to arrest you for obstruction."

"Yeah, yeah," Liam said as he turned and started to walk back. Darryl and Whitey had already parked and were walking toward where Liam stood.

"Anything?" Darryl said to him.

"Nah, he won't tell me anything. There are cops in the bathroom, though, so something is there."

"Over there." Darryl pointed, getting Liam's attention. An older woman was sitting at a picnic table with two police officers around her, clearly asking her questions.

"That's probably the witness," Darryl said.

Liam had begun marching over to the picnic table when Darryl stopped him.

"Slow down, man," Darryl said. "Why not let me do this?"

"Demon, I want answers," Liam said as he moved again.

"We all do, but you're not exactly in the friendly state of mind right now, are you? I'm the people person here. Give the cops a minute and see if they move away from her."

As Darryl predicted, the police left the woman sitting at the table before an older gentleman walked over and sat next to her.

"Now we go," Darryl said calmly.

Demon led the way, with Liam and Whitey following behind quickly. Darryl stopped across the table from the woman, who looked shaken by the experience.

"Is everything okay?" Darryl said with concern. "My friends and I just pulled in and heard the news. I saw you over here and thought you might need something."

"Oh, it was awful," the woman answered Darryl. "All Gene and I wanted to do was stop in so I can go to the bathroom. I had no idea we would walk into a kidnapping."

"Kidnapping?" Darryl said, aghast. "Man, that's rough. Can we get you something? Maybe a soda or something to help you?"

"That would be so nice." The woman smiled. "I would love a Sprite if they have one. Gene, why don't you get me one?"

The older gentleman went to stand up, but Darryl put his hand up to stop him.

"We got it," Darryl insisted. He nodded toward Whitey, who raced off to the soda machine on the opposite side of the building.

"Did you see who it was?" Liam said, trying not to sound too anxious to get answers. Darryl spun around and glared at him.

"I did indeed," she insisted. "I went into the ladies' room, and this thug was leading a young Spanish girl out of there. I could tell by the look in her eyes that she was in trouble, but that man was so scary that I froze. When I walked toward the stall, I saw written in red lipstick 'I'm Olivia. Help. Call the Cosantóir.' I had no idea who that was. I thought maybe it was a Spanish word or something I didn't understand. When I came out, we saw the car pulling away. I told Gene, and he called nine-one-one."

"Wow, very scary," Darryl said, reaching his large hand across the table to pat the old woman's.

"Did you see the plates on the car, or what kind it was?" Liam interjected.

"Oh, I'm no good at identifying cars. They all look the same to me. Poor Gene here can't see a thing with his cataracts. That's why I do all the driving now."

"Of course," Darryl told her. "It's the safest thing to do."

Whitey returned with the cold can of soda and put it down in front of the woman.

"Here you go, ma'am," Whitey said to her.

"Oh, you boys are so nice. Please, call me Doris."

Darryl rose from the table and smiled. Liam patted him on the shoulder to get his attention. Two of the police officers were pointing in their direction.

"We need to go before they see our colors and jackets," Liam said quietly.

"Doris, I hope you're doing okay and that the rest of your travels are uneventful. Have a blessed day." Darryl smiled at her.

"Why, thank you." She smiled back. "What was your name?"

"I'm Darryl," he said, presenting his large hand to shake hers. He engulfed it within his paw and shook it gently.

"Thank you, Darryl." She grinned.

Darryl rose from the picnic table and led the trio back toward their bikes before the police got to Doris at the table.

"Nice work," Whitey said as he climbed onto his Harley.

"I know how to sweet talk," Darryl said confidently. "You boys can learn something from me."

"At least we know it was her, and they are headed north," Liam added. "Let's keep moving."

Liam revved his bike and left the rest area quickly, flowing into the left lane of traffic as he sped along. However, his concern remained high as to where Olivia might be and what could be happening to her as he drove. Once he reached the New Jersey Turnpike and then Route 17, he began to feel more confident about finding Olivia, but he also had concerns. The day had worn on, and sunset was approaching, meaning he could be running out of time.

Liam didn't know how long his phone had been ringing in his ear before he finally answered it.

"Liam? Christ, I've been trying to reach you for twenty minutes! Answer your feckin' phone," Conor's voice said to him.

"Sorry, Da, I'm a little preoccupied. What is it?"

"We got a call from the gas station at the border on 17. Olivia was there. How close are you?"

"I can be there in five minutes," Liam said as he raced the engine and wove through traffic. He dodged more than one traffic slowdown by riding on the shoulder or between lanes, causing honks and complaints from cars and trucks. Still, he reached the gas station and parked his bike out in front of the convenience store there in record time and well ahead of Darryl and Whitey.

Liam yanked the door to the store open, jingling the bells violently as he walked to the counter.

"I'm looking for Louis," Liam huffed. "Where is he?"

"He's out at the pumps." The plump older man behind the counter pointed fearfully.

Liam charged out and saw a young man standing by idly as he watched the gas pump work.

"You Louis?" Liam said as he got closer.

Louis' eyes widened as he saw the hulking figure moving toward him.

"Yeah, that's me," he said, clutching the gas hose as if it offered him protection.

"You called the Cosantóir a while ago." Liam said, inches from Louis now.

"Yeah, I knew I recognized the name from the newspapers with all that stuff that's been happening up that way. I'm from Tuxedo, and there's always talk around..."

"Louis, get to the point, man. I don't have time for BS," Liam roared.

"Right," Louis answered, reaching into his sweatshirt pocket. He handed the candy bar to Liam.

"A pretty girl handed this to me. She gave it to me as a gift 'cause she said her boyfriend was acting like a dick... which he was. Guy tossed me across the parking lot and ripped my jacket. She sure didn't seem like the type to be with a guy like that. He was bad news. Anyway, when they pulled away, I noticed the writing on the back of the package."

Liam flipped the orange package over and read the writing:

Help. Liam. Call Cosantóir.

"I don't know if she was saying she needed help or this guy Liam needed help, but I knew about the club," Louis said. "I'm pretty good with computers and stuff. I go to RCC and am studying cybersecurity. So I did some looking online and found a phone number for the house, and then they patched me through to this old guy..."

"Conor. He's the leader of the club," Liam said, staring at the candy bar.

"Do you know this Liam guy? Is he in trouble?" Louis asked as the gas pump clicked, indicating the tank on the car was full.

"I'm Liam," he said somberly. "No, I'm not in trouble, but the girl is. How long ago were they here?"

"Wow, it's been a couple of hours, I guess."

"Did you call the cops?" Liam inquired.

"No, just you guys. Is she going to be okay? I did the right thing, right?"

Liam jumped as the horn of the car getting gas blared loudly. He looked over as the tinted window rolled down the gray BMW, and a man stuck his head out.

"Can I get my credit card back and go? Jesus, you two have been going on and on too long," the man complained.

"Oh, I'm sorry, sir," Louis said, putting the hose back in position and grabbing the credit card. Liam snatched it from Louis' hand and held it before leaning his head into the open window.

"The young man was helping me with a problem." Liam snarled. " A little patience and manners go a long way, don't you agree?"

The man recoiled and nodded rapidly, holding his hand out shakily for his credit card. Liam bent the card between his thumb and index finger, folding it in half and cracking it.

"Have a nice day," he said as the man put the window up and sped off.

"Anything else?" Liam said, looking back at Louis.

"I think that was it. I hope she's okay."

"I hope so too, Louis," Liam said, extending his hand. "Thanks for your help. I owe you one."

Louis shook Liam's hand and forced a smile.

"Yeah, no problem," Louis answered humbly.

"I'm serious," Liam said as he started to walk away. Liam turned back to Louis and reached into his wallet. He plucked out a twenty-dollar bill, grabbed the pen from Louis' chest pocket on his shirt, and wrote on the bill. "Here's my phone number. Come by the Hog House anytime, and I'll make it up to you."

"Wow, cool. I will!" Louis yelled and waved before another car pulled in and got his attention.

Liam returned to his bike and kept going farther north, getting off on Route 17M to go in the direction of the Hog House since he was unsure of where else he should go.

"Now, where do I go?" he said aloud. "Where are you?"

Chapter 23

Olivia already acted on high alert in the car, watching everything Marcos did and said, but when she saw the car motor through the Harriman area, bypassing the complex where her condo was, further panic set in. Marcos drove through Monroe, passing all the familiar spots to Olivia, seemingly eliminating any hope that she might see someone—anyone—who might recognize her and see she needed help.

Once the vehicle skirted out of Monroe and moved farther along on 17M, Olivia spoke up.

"Where are we going?" she asked.

"What? Did you think I was just going to drop you at home?" Marcos laughed. "Benny isn't going to meet you anywhere near where the Cosantóir might find you. He's not stupid."

Olivia viewed out the window as they moved from 17M to Kings Highway in Chester before taking an abrupt right into an industrial area. They moved beyond the several large warehouses until another sharp turn to pull in front of a smaller building. Olivia noticed a few cars parked out front alongside motorcycles bearing the Caimans' colors and logo.

Marcos stopped the car and got out before moving to the passenger side and ordering Olivia out of the vehicle. When she failed to react immediately, he pulled her from the seat, leaving her backpack on the floor in the front of the car, holding the only defense she might have had to assist her.

Olivia walked ahead of Marcos up a few decaying stone steps to a heavy steel door. Marcos pounded his fist on the door three times before a young man in a Caiman's jacket opened it, who let them into the facility. Olivia was led through a dimly lit hallway maze of mostly empty office space before they went through two swinging doors that led to the warehouse area. There, tables were arranged and had different people performing tasks, with everything from money counting machines to drug bags lying about or being used. As Marcos marched Olivia toward a staircase on the far side of the warehouse, she noticed an area arranged to look like a bedroom with video cameras around it.

Marcos pointed Olivia to the stairs leading to an office with windows looking out over the warehouse floor. She reached the door, and Marcos knocked, once again gaining access with the help of another of the bikers. Behind a large wooden desk sat Benny, phone to his ear while he tapped idly at one of the laptops that surrounded him.

"Welcome home." Benny smiled as he hung up the phone.

"Hardly," Olivia said softly, eliciting a laugh from Marcos.

"Is she clean?" Benny asked as he rose from the desk.

"I don't know," Marcos replied. "I didn't frisk or anything when she got in the car, but she didn't try to kill me for five hundred miles, so I'm guessing she is."

"No sense taking chances." Benny nodded as he stopped a few feet short of Olivia. Benny pointed to the other biker in the room with them.

"*Cacheala*," Benny ordered.

The man walked over in front of Olivia and began to pat her down, turning out the pockets of her jeans and patting down her legs in the front and back. Next, he stood in front of Olivia and unzipped the sweatshirt she wore, pulling it off her body and shaking it out but finding nothing. He then ran his hands over Olivia's hips, behind her back, and then slowly over her breasts, leering as he did so before smiling.

"*Ella esta limpia*," the man spoke as he turned to Benny. He looked back at Olivia again, grinning more. Olivia smiled back before she spat in his face.

"*Mamón*," she fired back at him. Anger crossed his face as he lifted his gloved hand to slap Olivia, but she didn't flinch at all.

"Back off, Dragón." Benny laughed. "I told you she was feistier than her sister."

"You really don't want to piss off too many brothers, Olivia," Benny said as he moved in front of her. "They can make your time here miserable for you."

"Right. Because it's so pleasant now."

"Oh, trust me, it can be much worse for you." Benny snarled as he ran his index finger on Olivia's cheek. "It's bad enough you convinced your sister to run away."

"Be glad that's all it was," Olivia said. "I told Bea we should cut your balls off while you slept."

"You know, it's not too late for me to walk out of this room and just let Dragón do what he wants with you before Marcos gets a turn," he whispered to Olivia.

Olivia shuddered at the thought as adrenaline and fear fought for control of her body.

Benny rested against the front of his desk and turned his attention to Marcos.

"Where's her stuff?"

Olivia held her breath, fearing they would go back to the car, get her bag, and find the gun.

"I don't think she had anything with her," Marcos answered. All she did was get in the car."

"I didn't bring anything," Olivia piped up quickly. "You just said you wanted me here, so here I am." Relief washed over her as Marcos seemingly overlooked her bag.

"Fuck," Benny said as he slammed his hand on his desk. "How fucking stupid are you, Marcos? You knew what we needed."

"I didn't even think about it. I was focused on the task at hand—getting her or killing them all. I was a little busy," Marcos answered.

"Where is it?" Benny asked as he got right in Olivia's face.

"Where is what?" she replied, not backing down and wondering how he might know she had a gun.

"The fucking bear," Benny growled.

Olivia looked confused before realizing what he was talking about.

"The Winnie the Pooh thing? I left it with Liam. Daniela gave it to him."

Benny turned, letting out a small laugh.

"Of course you did," he said, more talking to himself than anyone in the room. Benny plucked one of the laptops off his desk and threw it with all his might against the far wall, shattering the glass on a picture of the Caimans that hung there and splintering the laptop into pieces.

Olivia jumped back at the same time Marcos and Dragón recoiled.

Liam, unsure of where to go once he reached Orange County again, made his way to his father's house. When he pulled down the driveway and stopped his bike, several club bikes were already parked there. Liam dismounted and walked up the porch steps, where he greeted two brothers guarding the front door.

Liam entered the house to a buzz of activity. He saw Siobhan on her phone on the couch with Maeve sitting next to her. Finn turned the corner from the hallway and spotted his brother standing there.

"Glad you made it," Finn said to him, clasping Liam's hand. "You okay? You need anything?"

"I'm all right," Liam said, exhausted but still alert. "Any word?"

"Nothing recently," Finn told him. "Come in the office."

Finn led Liam down the hall and knocked on the office door before it swung open. Liam spotted his father behind his desk on the phone while Preacher sat in one of the armchairs.

"Thank God," Preacher said, coming over to Liam and giving him a hug. Liam winced at the contact.

"Easy, Preacher," Liam said. "Let's not get all mushy here."

"How's the wound?"

"Not a concern at the moment," Liam answered, brushing it off.

Conor hung up the phone and looked at Liam.

"Nice to see you alive." Conor smiled. "Cops in Maryland and New York keep calling me asking me about why we were mentioned in all this. I keep giving them the runaround, but sooner or later, they might connect the dots. But, of course, I haven't said anything about the kid at the gas station. Did you get there?"

"Yeah," Liam answered. "Olivia left the kid with a note, but it doesn't really say how she was or where they were going. Has anyone spotted anything?"

Conor looked at Finn for answers.

"All we know for sure is that the Caimans have been keeping a low profile all day. There hasn't been any activity or sightings of them," Finn stated.

"So we still have no feckin' idea where they took her?" Liam barked, slamming his fist on the wall.

"Easy there," Conor said to his son. "We're working the best we can, boy. I've got the word out for anyone who sees anything to let me know ASAP. I'm cashing in favors left and right. We'll find her."

"By then, it might be too late," Liam replied. "I'm going to go to the Caimans' Nest."

"The hell you are," Conor said, nodding to Preacher to block Liam's path.

"Don't make me deck you, Preacher," Liam growled.

"Don't make me," Preacher answered back.

"Going up to their territory is a suicide mission that will just start a war, and you know it," Conor said. "You wouldn't get up the driveway before they killed you. Besides, their place is too far from here up in New Paltz. So they must be doing something closer."

Liam turned back to one of the armchairs and slumped down into it, rubbing his temples and then pushing his hands through his hair. "So what am I supposed to do, Da? Just let her die?"

"No," Conor answered. "But we need to be smart about what we do."

"Well, I'm open to suggestions," Liam said, spreading his arms and looking around the room. All sat or stood silent.

It was then that the pocket of Liam's leather jacket began to shake. His phone vibrated and let out a muffled ring. He reached hurriedly into his pocket, worried it might be Declan calling from Nags Head about a problem.

When he glanced at the screen, all it showed was an Unknown Caller. Liam answered anyway.

"Yeah?" he asked, half expecting to hear a recording about his car warranty expiring.

"Are you home yet?" Benny said into the phone.

"Why don't you drive down here and find out for yourself," Liam replied.

Benny laughed into the phone.

"Good one. I hope you had a safe trip. Those rides take a lot of you, especially with a bum shoulder."

"Don't you worry about me, Benny," Liam said. "I'm fit enough to rip your arms off. Where is she?"

"It's touching that you have so much concern for her well-being, Liam, it really is. How is she, by the way? I always imagined that she is an incredible lay. I guess I can take a run at her, but I'd do it before I let the rest of them have their fun."

"You know you're going to die, right?" Liam said, standing up now.

"We'll see about that. But, for now, I think that we have some business to discuss. We each seem to have something the other wants."

"I have no idea what you're talking about."

"Olivia left something with you that belongs to me, and I need it back," Benny told him.

"What might that be?" Liam asked, wondering what he got from her.

"The bear... do you have it with you, or did you leave it in North Carolina? Don't make me storm the house down there and kill everyone."

"The feckin' Winne the Pooh thing? You're joking, right? I found the bug in that thing and destroyed it," Liam told him.

"I'm aware of that," Benny said, exasperated. "The bear is something I need to have. Just leave it at that. If you bring it to me, perhaps we can work something out regarding Olivia."

"That doesn't sound like much of a guarantee," Liam said.

"It's the best you're going to get, Liam. Yes or no? I'm growing impatient with all the fucking around."

"When and where?"

"I need to see that you have the bear first. So I'm going to hang up and text you a number. Send me a picture of the bear, front and back, and I'll text you with the information. Got it?"

"Got it," Liam replied, hanging up.

Liam walked out of the office, with Finn jumping up to follow him. Liam raced out the front door to find Darryl and Whitey arriving on their bikes, parking next to him.

"Oh, Christ, we just got here," Whitey complained. "Don't tell me we're leaving already?"

"Hold on," Liam said as he rifled through his saddlebag to get the bear out.

"Liam, what are you doing?" Finn asked. "What did Benny say?"

Liam placed the bear down on his bike seat and took pictures of the front and back of the doll. Seconds later, a text message came in with a message:

Send the pictures here.

Liam texted the images back to Benny and waited patiently for a reply.

"Not a great time for Instagram pics," Darryl said to Liam, patting Liam's shoulder.

"Give me a second," Liam said, staring at his phone, trying to will a return message to it.

His phone beeped with a reply:

Got it. 11 PM. 1 Elizabeth Drive in Chester. Alone.

Liam held the bear up to the sky, looking at its front where the eye was torn out.

"What are you hiding, little man?" he said quietly before turning the bear over. He looked all over the small bear before deciding to lift up the traditional red T-shirt that Pooh wore to see the Velcro holding the fur together in the back. Liam slipped his fingers inside and felt around before he pulled something out. In his hand was a USB drive.

"What the fuck is that?" Whitey asked.

"What Benny wants more than Olivia," Liam said as he walked back toward his father's office. He burst into the office and spun his father's laptop around.

"What the hell are you doing?" Conor yelled angrily.

"I need to see what's on this drive," Liam said, plugging it in without a second thought. A small window on the computer popped open, asking for a password.

"Fuck!" Liam yelled, slamming his hands down on the desk. "It's locked. Does anyone know how to break passwords?"

Everyone in the office looked around at each other with no one speaking up.

Liam sat back in the chair, staring at the computer screen. Then, seconds later, he leaped out of the chair and was moving again.

"Now, where are you going?" Finn yelled to him.

"Back to the gas station," Liam answered, heading toward his bike.

Chapter 24

After Benny's outburst, he had Olivia escorted to an office at the bottom of the staircase on the warehouse floor. The small office mainly was windows that looked out on the activity with nothing more than a few metal chairs, a desk chair, a desk, and a file cabinet. A small water dispenser on a wooden stand also occupied the space.

Dragón led Olivia into the office and sat her down at the desk chair.

"*Quédate aqui, zorra.*" Dragón laughed.

"No problem, numbnuts," Olivia grumbled.

Dragón stopped and peered at her.

"I guess you do understand some English, huh, *cabrón*?" she spewed out.

Dragón reached behind his back and pulled out a long knife, holding it up to Olivia.

"Enough to let you know what I'm going to do to you if you keep at it," he said in broken English.

Olivia backed up, sitting down in the cushioned desk chair.

"Good girl." He laughed before leaving the office, shutting the door. Olivia spied him pick up a chair from outside the office and plant it directly outside the office door before he sat, foiling any thoughts she had about finding a way out.

Olivia looked around the office, hoping to find anything she might be able to use to help herself. Unfortunately, the file cabinet drawers were locked, along with the two side drawers of the desk. However, she forced open the thin top drawer at the desk's center to look through it. There were a couple of pencils, a stapler, and an old porn magazine, but nothing else. Olivia stuffed the pencils in her jeans pockets and placed the stapler on the desk.

She watched out the one large office window that looked out to the warehouse floor. She noticed several men at one table putting stacks of money into bill counters before bundling each as they completed. Two women clad in just their bras and panties at another table were busy placing pills in bags. She then noticed two other women in silk robes being led across the warehouse floor to the bedroom set just to the left of her office. She looked on as the women were brought to the bed in the set center, where they quickly disrobed. One man stood behind the camera and barked directions to the women while a second man stripped off his clothes and joined the women on the bed. Shortly after, a sex scene developed that made Olivia look away. She heard a knocking on the glass window and turned to see Dragón getting her attention and smiling, pointing at the scene.

"You might want to watch." He laughed. "You'll be there soon enough."

Liam sped back to Conor's house with Louis in tow on the back of his bike. At first, Louis insisted he drive himself there, afraid to get on the back of the motorcycle. It was only when Liam insisted since they needed to arrive quickly that he went along with what Liam required.

When Liam rushed back into the house with the young man behind him, all eyes turned to Louis. Liam saw the young man was nervous but led him toward Conor's office.

"Don't mind them," Liam said, guiding Louis down the hall. He rapped on the office door and entered as soon as Preacher opened it.

"Who the hell is this?" Conor said, pointing at Louis.

"I'm Louis... Louis Ayala, sir," Louis said, presenting his hand. Conor just stared at the hand in front of him.

"Liam, you know no one outside of the brotherhood is allowed in here," Conor said to his son.

"Special circumstances, Da," Liam said, pulling two chairs over in front of his father's desk before turning the laptop around. "This is the kid who can help us."

"Well, I said maybe I could," Louis stuttered. "We did some password breaking in class. But, of course, I'm no expert or anything."

"Go, Louis," Liam said, pointing at the screen.

Louis looked at the computer screen and then turned to his backpack, pulling out a drive of his own and plugging it into the laptop.

"What are you doing?" Conor asked angrily.

"I just need to use some of my tools to break the password," Louis said, holding his hands above the keyboard.

"Da, just let him work!" Liam pressed. He nodded back to Louis.

"I can explain what I'm doing if you really want to know," Louis said as he typed.

"Just type, Louis," Liam added, rushing him along.

Liam and the others looked on as Louis worked his magic and then stopped typing, sitting back in his chair.

"That's it?" Liam asked.

"Well, we just have to wait for the program to find the right password. It should only take a few minutes."

The computer beeped as it hit upon the password to unlock the drive.

"There it is." Louis smiled. He hit enter and opened up the drive, seeing several Excel files.

"It looks like a bunch of spreadsheets," Louis said, checking them over. "It's all money moving from one account to another. Sometimes small amounts, sometimes large ones."

Liam looked closer at the spreadsheets, scrolling up to see more of the data.

"Adirondack Financial Company," Liam read the top line. "Any idea who that is?" Liam asked the room.

"I know," Finn spoke up. "It's one of Tom Downing's companies."

"Christ, this just gets better and better," Liam bemoaned.

"Who is he?" Louis asked.

"Downing is a bigwig upstate. He owns lots of property, businesses..." Finn began before Liam interrupted.

"And he's big into gambling and loan sharking, among other illegal activities," Liam added.

"From the looks of these records, whoever made this file is siphoning off a lot of money from him," Louis said as he scrolled down the page. "He does it steadily, so it doesn't get noticed easily."

"The Caimans have been his muscle for a long time," Conor said. "I can't believe Benny has the balls to steal from him. If Downing ever found out, he'd massacre all of them."

Liam sat back in his chair and stared at the computer screen and then at his father.

"Then maybe it's time he found out," Liam said, patting Louis on the shoulder. "I think I have another job for you, Louis."

The afternoon bled into the evening as Liam laid the groundwork for what he needed to do. Finally, when it got to be about ten-thirty, Liam prepped himself for his trek to Chester. He reentered his father's office, where Louis and Finn sat at the computer.

"I need to go, Louis," Liam told him. "Are we all set?"

Louis let out a sigh and grabbed the USB drive from the computer.

"I think so," Louis said. "I installed the RAT, so we should be good to go."

"Explain to me how this works again?" Finn asked.

"As soon as your guy puts the USB drive in his computer and the computer reads it, the virus will go to his computer. It's going to give me control of his computer to do whatever I want. I'll scroll through his email, find the addresses you are looking for, and send the files."

"And he'll never know?" Liam said.

"That's the beauty of it." Louis smiled. "I can control his camera, his screensaver, his keyboard, all of it. He won't know at all."

Liam grasped the USB drive and tucked it back inside Winnie the Pooh.

"Louis, if this works, you'll be a legend," Liam told him, patting him on the shoulder.

"I'll be right here watching," Louis said. "As soon as I'm in, I'll get to work."

Finn followed Liam out of the office to the front porch and his bike.

"I know Benny wants you alone, but some of us are coming along. Darryl, Whitey, and a few others will be nearby if you need us."

"You may not want to dirty your hands with this, brother," Liam said to Finn. "There's bound to be some bad stuff going down. We might need a lawyer when all is said and done."

"You're my brother, in more ways than one," Finn answered. "I'm not leaving you out there. *Bí cúramach.*"

"I'm always careful." Liam laughed as he donned his helmet and started his Harley.

Liam rode along 17M, driving into Chester as the cool October evening wore on. Liam made sure to have his knife on him and his gun locked in his saddlebag, knowing they were likely to pat him down when he got to the facility. He made sure to tuck his knife into the hidden compartment he had in his custom-made leather boots, allowing him to carry it undetected and access it when he needed to.

Liam slowed as he entered the industrial park, looking around the deserted and dark buildings. Then, he moved along to Elizabeth Drive, looking for signs that he was being watched. When he reached his destination, he parked next to the lone car remaining in the parking lot.

A glance into the car allowed him to see the familiar backpack Olivia carried throughout their trip.

"At least she was here," he said aloud to himself. "Let's hope she still is."

Liam walked up the stone steps to the door and tugged on the handle. Surprisingly, the door opened, allowing him in. He entered the small lobby there and looked up, seeing an image of himself on the black and white TV hanging above the door. He gave a wave before raising his middle finger. The door in front of him buzzed, and he heard it unlock.

The hallways were lit, allowing Liam to see what lay in front of him as he made his way toward what he hoped would be Olivia. Finally, he reached the swinging doors that led into the warehouse area. He kicked them open forcefully before entering.

On the far side of the warehouse floor stood Benny and Marcos. As he paced toward them, Liam looked around, high and low, for signs of anyone else who might be hiding and waiting to attack.

"Don't worry, my friend," Benny yelled. "It's just Dragón over there and us."

Liam looked right and saw Dragón standing off near a darkened office.

"Where is she, Benny?" Liam yelled as he got closer, his long legs making quick strides to close the distance.

"She's here." Benny smiled. "I'm a man of my word."

"Why doesn't that give me any comfort?" Liam offered as he stopped about six feet short of Benny and Marcos.

"You have what I want?" Benny asked.

Liam reached into his pocket, and he heard a gun cock. He looked over at Dragón and saw him pointing a pistol in his direction while Marcos armed himself with two knives.

"Call off your mutts, Benny," Liam asked. "I'm just reaching for the toy."

Liam slowly pulled the stuffed bear out of his pocket and held it up.

"I didn't realize you needed a stuffed animal to help you sleep at night," Liam said to Benny, waving the bear the entire time.

"Trust me. I will sleep much better once I have it in my hands. So toss it to me," Benny ordered.

"Not until Olivia is standing next to me," Liam countered.

"*Consígala*," Benny yelled to Dragón. The henchman walked to the darkened office and opened the door, pulling Olivia out. He dragged her across the floor and stopped just short of Liam. Liam watched as Dragón placed his arm around Olivia's waist, squeezing her side as he leaned his head close to her. His hand snaked up her body, close to her breast, as he guided her over to Liam. Dragón then pushed her toward Liam and into his arms. He could see that her eyes were glassy.

"What did you do to her?" Liam yelled.

"I just gave her a little something to help her relax." Dragón laughed. "She was so uptight with me."

"If you laid a hand on her, I swear to God I'll fucking gut you," Liam said through gritted teeth.

"Relax, Liam," Benny said, moving forward. "He didn't do anything to her, I promise. Now, if you hadn't shown up, things might have been different. Give me the bear."

Liam handed the bear over to Benny, who greedily grabbed it and lifted the T-shirt off so he could get the drive out.

"Olivia," Liam said softly, brushing the hair from her eyes. He watched as she blinked a few times at him without saying anything before a small smile crossed her lips.

"You said my name," she whispered.

"You're gonna be okay," Liam promised, though he was unsure just how much he believed it himself. He watched as Benny took the USB drive, hoping he would plug it into the computer.

"There must be a better place to stash your porn," Liam said as Benny grabbed a laptop.

"Funny." Benny laughed. "I have access to all the porn I want," Benny said, pointing to the bedroom set. "I was hoping to make your girlfriend there a star. But, no, Liam, this is much more important than porn."

Benny plugged the drive into the laptop and waited a second before typing in the password. Then, finally, Benny's face smiled when he opened the spreadsheets with all the information he wanted.

"Can you stand up?" Liam whispered into Olivia's ear.

"I... I think so," Olivia rasped, working to clear her head.

"You need to get ready to run again," Liam told her.

"I don't know if I can," she said weakly.

"I'm not sure we'll have much of a choice."

"*Gracias*, friend." Benny clapped when he examined all the files. "I think we're done here."

"Great. We'll see you around," Liam answered as he began to lead Olivia toward the swinging doors.

"Oh, I'm afraid not, Liam," Benny said as he heard two guns cock.

Liam turned around and saw Benny and Dragón both aiming guns this time.

"You got what you wanted," Liam yelled, moving back slowly, hoping to buy time.

"True, I did," Benny agreed. "But I also lost. Beatriz and my daughter are both gone. I'll probably never see them again. That I don't like. I'm afraid you're going to have to leave Olivia here."

"No way in hell that's happening," Liam growled.

"Fighting to the end. That's why I've always liked you, Liam. Even after we killed Brian, you still had the balls to fight us. I give you a lot of credit. But, don't worry, I promise to take good care of her. People will pay good money to watch her or be with her."

Liam glanced over and saw the swinging doors within reach but doubted he could get there before someone got a shot off. He shifted his body to shield Olivia as much as he could behind his when he heard Marcos yell out.

"Benny!"

"What? I'm busy!" Benny yelled back.

"Something weird is going on with the computer."

Benny turned back and sighed.

"He probably touched the mouse pad," Benny said. "Dragón, watch them."

Benny marched back to where Marcos stood. Liam looked on, judging how far away the Caiman stood from him.

"The screensaver just popped on," Marcos said.

"So what? That happens," Benny added. "Christ, you're dumb as a stump."

"It... it looked like the mouse was moving on its own. I swear," Marcos replied, pointing at the screen.

Benny bent down, trying to move the mouse, but he couldn't get it to move.

"Maybe the screen is just frozen," Benny answered, tapping the keyboard still without results. Finally, after angrily tapping the keyboard several times, he hit the spacebar with force. The screen went blank, only to have a picture pop up. It was the Cosantóir logo, and written underneath the words '*Chailleann tú.*'

"What the fuck does that mean?" Marcos said.

Another picture popped up immediately.

It means 'You Lose,' asshole.

The computer screen went black, followed by all the lights in the warehouse shutting off.

"Go!" Liam shouted, pushing Olivia toward and through the swinging doors and into the darkened hallway.

Olivia's body skidded across the linoleum floor before she came to rest against the wall. Her vision remained hazy, but she reached her hand out and felt around her, grasping hair in her fingers and tugging on it.

"Feck, that's my hair," Liam exclaimed as he crawled closer to her. "In here," he told her as he forced open one of the office doors and dragged them both into it, closing the door quietly.

Liam covered Olivia's mouth so she didn't inadvertently make any noise in her current state. Footsteps made their way down the hallway on the floor past the room they were in.

"What's happening?" Olivia whispered in her fog.

"The brothers must have cut the power to the building," Liam surmised. "Now we have to figure a way out of here. Can you move at all?"

"Maybe," Olivia said. She looked over, catching a glimpse of Liam in the moonlight shining through the window on the other side of the room. Olivia put her hand on Liam's face.

"I didn't think you'd find me," she told him.

"If you hadn't left in the first place, I wouldn't have had to," Liam answered.

"I thought it would be best for everyone," she lamented.

"Not for me," Liam replied. "Can we fight about it later?"

Liam crawled over to the window, pushing on it and lifting it to see if it would open.

"What good are these feckin' things?" he grunted.

A gunshot rang into the room, bursting through the glass and causing it to spider. Olivia covered her ears and screamed as Liam ducked into the darkness.

Olivia watched as the door swung open and Dragón entered. Moving across the floor toward where Liam lay on the floor. Dragón smiled as he stood over Liam and aimed the gun at him.

"So long, Irishman," Dragón uttered.

Olivia let out a primal yell as she ran across the floor, gripping one of the pencils tightly in her fist before jumping on Dragón's back and stabbing him in the side of the neck. Blood shot out from his vein, and he immediately fell to his knees, dropping his gun and sending it clattering to the floor. He turned, gasping and clutching at the pencil in his neck. Olivia stood over him, shaking. She looked on as he collapsed from his knees, falling over onto his side and driving the pencil farther into his neck.

Olivia panted, staring at the body in front of her before Liam came over and put his arm on her, causing her to jump.

"It's okay," he said softly to her. Olivia turned and embraced Liam, holding him tightly as she sobbed.

"We need to get out of here," Liam said, looking into Olivia's eyes. "Benny and Marcos are still out there."

Olivia watched as Liam reached down, feeling on the floor for the pistol that fell. Finally, he got it in his hand and handed it to Olivia.

"It's a little bigger than what you used, so there will be more recoil," he whispered. "Use the same technique if you have to. You remember?"

Olivia nodded as she felt the cold metal in her palm.

"What about you?" she asked.

Liam reached down and pulled the knife out of his boot.

"I'll be fine," he told her.

Liam gripped Olivia's hand and led her over to the door. He pried it open enough so they could slip out and make their way farther down the hall. Not long after they started moving, Olivia heard a voice come from behind them.

"Shit," Benny exclaimed. "I don't know what you did to the power or my computer, Liam, but I can guarantee you won't get out of here alive. And, Olivia, I know you can hear me too. You think I was rough on your sister. Just wait until I get a hold of you. You're going to wish you died with Liam. But no matter how much you beg me, I won't let you."

Olivia froze in her tracks until she felt Liam squeeze her hand.

"Don't listen to him," he whispered. "I've got you now, and I'm not letting you out of my sight again."

Liam managed to get them back to the lobby door, but it didn't budge when he pushed on it.

"It must have to be opened remotely," Liam said. "Feel around on the wall. There should be an emergency button to press to open it."

Olivia felt on the wall above her, rubbing her hand across the rough paint. She felt the light switch, trying it several times, but it did nothing. She moved her hand to the left more when she caught a view of a shadow moving toward her rapidly.

"Down!" Liam yelled, causing Olivia to lay flat on the floor as she heard the thud of the knife blade hit the wall just above her head. She looked up to see Liam raising his fist and raining blows down on Marcos.

"Go! Find the button!" Liam yelled to her.

"But..." Olivia began.

"Just do it!" he barked as a punch landed in his midsection, forcing the wind out of him.

Olivia scrambled to her feet, pressing everywhere she could on the wall left and right of the door until she hit upon a button protruding from a panel. She slapped it and heard the lock open. Olivia leaned her shoulder against the door and turned the knob, pushing the door open. She took one last glance at Liam and saw his hand on Marcos's throat as Marcos was struggling to grip a knife. Olivia went into the lobby and then out the front door.

The shock of the cold air on her body brought Olivia back to reality further as she stumbled down the stone steps. First, she looked around outside for signs of anyone who might be near, but she saw nothing. Then, finally, she recognized Marcos' car and went toward it, opening the passenger door and pawing around for the sign of any keys, but she saw none.

"You always did have a fine ass, Olivia," she heard Benny say from behind her as he cocked his gun.

Liam struggled with Marcos' strength as the two rolled on the floor. Each had managed to knock the other's knife onto the floor, and in the darkness and tussle, there was no way for Liam to know just how close or far away any blade might be. Finally, Marcos pulled his fist back, landing a blow just below Liam's left shoulder, directly on the gunshot wound. Liam howled in pain and fell back further, clutching his side. He could feel the blood starting to ooze out of the scar already.

"This would have been so much easier if you had just let me kill her at the airport," Marcos huffed as he reached for Liam's boot to pull him back.

"Or if I had killed you at Brian's funeral," Liam grunted, kicking Marcos flush on the chin as he grabbed for him. Liam could see the blood spurt from Marcos' mouth after the kick.

"Fuck, man, you got my teef again," Marcos lisped out.

Marcos had crawled over to Liam, and Liam heard the scrape of a knife blade on the floor as he moved his leather jacket up against the wall. He reached back and felt the large cleaver blade against his thumb before moving his hand down to grip the handle firmly in his fist.

Liam looked and saw a blade rushing toward his head. He moved to the right, with the edge hitting the wall and taking a chunk of his hair with it.

Marcos leaped forward, pressing his forearm into Liam's throat as he attempted to bring the knife up with his left hand. Liam used all his strength to hold the left arm back with his own right until he firmly got the cleaver in his fist. Then, he pulled the knife from behind him and swung it down directly into Marcos' calf until it reached the bone.

Marcos gasped, and his mouth remained open, unable to make any noises as the pain overtook him. Then, finally, he crumpled to the floor, clutching for the dangling portion of his right leg before he tried to drag himself away.

Liam breathed heavily, watching as Marcos whimpered as he crawled. Finally, Liam managed to get himself to his feet. He staggered against the wall for several feet before he righted himself. He stepped over Marcos before bending down and turning him over. For the first time, Liam knew that Marcos felt fear.

Liam gripped the cleaver in his left hand, flashing it at Marcos. Marcos shook his head violently from left to right before Liam tossed the cleaver farther down the hall, listening to it clang on the linoleum.

Marcos seemed to breathe a sigh of relief and relax until Liam reached over to his left and picked up his own knife.

"If I'm going to kill you, it's with my knife. For Brian." He smiled down at Marcos. Liam watched as Marcos' mouth was filling with the blood caused by his lost teeth. Marcos coughed, spewing blood as Liam shielded himself. He looked down at the mess of a man beneath him.

"You know what? You're not worth it," Liam spat. "Bleed to death, you piece of shite."

Liam turned and walked away, leaving Marcos' prone body on the floor. He returned to the lobby door and pushed it open, stumbling into it and catching the light out in the parking lot. He threw open the front door and stepped onto the steps, spying Benny with a gun pointed at Olivia's back.

"Benny!" Liam shouted, getting his attention. Benny spun around and fired a shot in Liam's direction, with the bullet ricocheting off the steel door.

"Man, why don't you just die already?" Benny said with frustration.

"Yeah, your boys inside tried that," Liam answered, holding his knife. "It didn't work out too well for either of them."

Liam slowly walked down the steps, raising his hands and holding his knife.

"Toss it to the side," Benny ordered, pointing the gun at him. Benny rotated so he could see both Liam and Olivia.

"You all right?" Liam asked as he tossed his knife aside. Olivia nodded at him.

"You realize Cosantóir are all over this place," Liam said as he shuffled closer to Olivia. "You might kill me, but you're not getting out of here with her. I guarantee it."

"You know, everything was going along so smoothly until they got you involved in all this, Liam," Benny said, scratching his head. "You guys just couldn't leave well enough alone and let me take care of my own business."

"Is that the porn business, Benny? Or is it drugs and prostitution? Or money laundering and loan sharking? Or is it just the business where you beat up women and intimidate people? It's hard to keep up with all you do for the community," Liam answered.

"It's what clubs do, man," Benny said proudly.

"No, it's not," Liam shot back. "Not the good ones. Not mine. We protect, not hurt."

"Sweet sentiment," Benny offered. "You can have them write that on your tombstone next to your mother."

Benny aimed his pistol at Liam, and a shot rang out.

Benny looked over at Liam, who stood staring back and then down at his own stomach. He saw the patch of blood on his shirt start spreading and then looked at Olivia. Olivia dropped her gun to the ground as she ran over to where Liam stood just as Benny hit the ground.

Liam grasped Olivia and then moved her aside as he went to Benny's body. He took Benny's gun and put it in his jacket pocket before rolling Benny over. Benny huffed and breathed heavily as he clutched at his side.

"That doesn't look good, Benny," Liam said. "Worse than the one your hired goon gave me. At least mine went clean through. Sadly, you'll probably live, though."

Liam heard the cock of a gun and looked up to see Olivia pointing her pistol at Benny's head.

"He doesn't deserve to live," Olivia said shakily as she moved forward. "After all he has done to everyone... to my family... to me..." Olivia stood over Benny, bringing the gun down closer to his forehead.

"You're right; he doesn't deserve to live," Liam said softly as he approached Olivia. "But it's not up to us, Olivia. Let a judge sort out his fate. You take his life, and you have to live with it for the rest of yours. I don't wish that on you. Besides, he won't just have the cops to deal with. Tom Downing will be seeking him out soon enough."

Benny's eyes shot toward Liam in a panic as he coughed.

"Oh, I forgot to mention that to you, Benny," Liam said. "You see, that little drive of yours, when you opened it, it triggered a virus. As a result, we could mail all your files there directly to good ol' Tom so he could see how much you have stolen from him over the years. It was nice of you to keep such clear records. I can't figure out why you would hide them in the bear, but that's your problem now."

Liam stood next to Olivia, who still held the gun against Benny's temple.

"Liv, give me the gun," he said softly. "It's over now."

Olivia pulled the gun back and handed it to Liam. He quickly removed the cartridge and the bullet from the chamber before pulling out his cell phone and calling Finn.

"We're out," Liam said right away. "Get over here before I call nine-one-one. I want a lawyer next to her the entire time."

Epilogue

D ays went by as the police worked on sorting everything out. Liam directed the police to the bodies of Dragón and Marcos. Marcos had somehow survived until emergency personnel arrived, as did Benny. Both had police escorts to the hospital, where Marcos had part of his leg amputated to save his life.

Liam informed the authorities about everything that had happened, letting Finn do his job in protecting Olivia. He told the police about the bodies in North Carolina and what had occurred and had them seek out all the witnesses in Nags Head and Virginia and South Carolina so stories could corroborate. In the end, no charges were filed against Olivia or Liam, and both agreed to testify at Benny's trial.

Most of the Caimans ended up going to jail as well once local and federal law enforcement got their hands on Benny's information and businesses. Not only had Louis made sure Tom Downing got copies of all of Benny's dealings, but he also decided to send copies off to the Orange County District Attorney's office and to the Times-Herald Record. Once the newspaper reported the information, a massive scandal broke out, with dozens of arrests. The FBI swore out warrants for Downing and his business records, but he had long fled the country before they could get their hands on him.

As rattled as Olivia had been from the experience, once she found herself in Liam's protective arms again, she discovered solace. Olivia stayed with Liam at Hog House for weeks as she healed physically and mentally, and he did the same. By the time Thanksgiving had rolled around, both had tried to return their lives to some semblance of normalcy.

Liam eschewed the traditional Thanksgiving meal at the Hog House. Instead, he made his way to Millie Malone's for his holiday meal. Olivia joined him for dinner instead of having to work the event. Thus, the two enjoyed a quiet dinner to themselves before Finn and Preacher, and their respective partners, joined them at Millie's for after-dinner drinks.

"*Sláinte*!" Preacher offered as they all raised their glasses in a toast. Liam watched as Olivia took a strong sip of her Guinness and put it down on the table.

"That's my girl," he said with a laugh.

"I still like to drink other things, you know," Olivia pointed out.

"Sure." Liam nodded. "Whiskey is okay too."

"Don't let him bully you, Olivia," Siobhan chided.

"No chance." Olivia laughed as she took another sip.

"So, brother," Finn said as he put his arm around Siobhan. "Have you decided what you're going to do for Christmas yet? I think Da wants to have a big shindig at the house this year."

"I don't know," Liam said, scratching his chin.

"Oh, that sounds like fun," Olivia said. "I would love to have a big family Christmas. Let's do that."

"I kind of already made other plans," Liam said as he drank some of his Guinness.

"What plans are those?" Finn asked.

"Yeah? What plans?" Olivia asked, putting her hands on her hips. "You never said anything to me."

"I was hoping to wait for this, but I guess now is as good a time as any," Liam said. He began to reach into the pocket of his leather jacket.

"Oh my God, he's gonna propose," Annabella, Preacher's girlfriend, said excitedly.

Olivia shot Liam a look of shock.

"Please tell me you're not going to propose," she said softly. "I don't think I'm—"

"Will you people relax?" Liam said. He pulled the item out of his pocket and placed a small Winnie the Pooh stuffed bear in front of Olivia.

"Open the back," Liam directed Olivia. "And Jaysus, with you people. It's not a ring."

Olivia put her hand under Winnie the Pooh's shirt and found the Velcro back, putting her finger inside. She pulled the small piece of paper out the back and held it up.

"You gave me a picture of yourself?" she said confusedly. "That's... sweet. Thank you." Olivia smiled.

"You don't get it, do you?" Liam said, frustrated. "I knew this would work better if we were alone. Look at the picture."

Liam took the small square from her hand and held it up in front of her face.

"I don't know what I'm missing."

"What kind of picture is it?" Liam insisted.

Olivia was dumbfounded.

"Is it a mugshot?" Finn laughed. "He's got plenty of those."

"Shut up, little brother," Liam barked.

Liam moved his chair closer to Olivia and pulled her toward him.

"It's a passport photo," he said, looking into her eyes. "I went and got my passport, and... well, I bought us two tickets to Peru so we could go see your family for the holiday. We'll go for two weeks, right through New Year's."

Olivia looked at the picture and then back at Liam. Her eyes clouded over before she reached over and threw her arms around his neck, kissing him deeply.

"Wow, who knew he was so nice?" Finn joked as he raised his glass again.

Olivia broke her kiss with Liam and smiled at him.

"You are amazing," she said to him. "How did I get so lucky?"

"I wonder that, too." He grinned.

Liam brought his face closer to Olivia's, so their foreheads rested against each other.

"Can I say it now?" he said softly.

"You don't have to," she whispered back. "I know it's true, and I do too."

Acknowledgements

As always, there are a lot of people involved in creating my book. I could probably write a whole other one just thanking all the people who assisted me along the way with this.

Thank you to Scarlet Lantern Publishing, who keep giving me the chance of a lifetime to live a dream and help me get my stories out there for people to enjoy.

To my beta readers – you know who you are and all the hard work you do, and I can't thank you enough! You keep going on the straight and narrow, so thank you to Michelle, Chrissy, Leigh Ann, and Liz for all you do.

Much research went into this book about different areas, and I couldn't have done it without all the help I received. Thank you to John Schneider for his insight and assistance, Don Geraghty for his help with all that goes on in Lancaster and Charlotte, and Sean Geraghty for talking me through the ins and outs of cybersecurity. I'll never forget to thank the Hudson Valley Romance Writers of America chapter, either. They are the best cheerleaders and inspirations out there!

A simple thank you to Aoife Scott, who I have never met but whose Irish folk music gets me through many writing sessions, enough so that she became a character in this book.

No book ever comes to fruition without my best friend. Since we were twelve, Michelle has been on my side, and she continues to be the reason I can do what I do. Saying I love you never seems like enough.

I also want to dedicate this book to the memory of Isabel Hewitt. Isabel is someone I had known for many years, always had a smile on her face, and was so welcoming and friendly. Not only that, she became one of my biggest fans when I started writing, and I will miss her smiles and comments. I wish I had the chance to tell you in person how much you meant.

Síocháin.

Also By M. Geraghty

The Cosantóir MC

Small Town, Biker Romances

Finn

Preacher

Liam

Demon

The Home Stand Series

Small Town, Sports Romances

Change Up

Spring Fever

The Sweet Spot

The <u>Celtic Sisters</u> Series

Small Town, Dark Romances
<u>A Calm in the Storm</u>

Standalone Romances

<u>For What It's Worth</u>
A Christmas, Rockstar Romance